"Someone has been in here,"

Boyd said as he flashed the light down the corridor. "And not too long ago."

Gretchen didn't like the sound of that. Consequently, Boyd's next pronouncement was hardly what she wanted to hear.

"I'll check down this way," he said gesturing to the left. "You see what there is in the other direction."

He started off before Gretchen could object. She remembered his insatiable curiosity and could almost see it crackling out of him as he moved down the corridor. She felt some of that adventurous spirit herself. In fact, usually she felt a lot of it. Right now, however, she felt nothing but dread. Suddenly, in a flash as bright as the beam of the electric torch she held in her hand, she was convinced that terrible things were going to happen here. Then, fast on the heels of that sudden awareness came another thought: terrible things *had* happened here in the past....

ABOUT THE AUTHOR

Alice Harron Orr grew up in a small city.
Now she lives in a big one and sometimes
wishes she could go back to streets lined with
maples. She shares her New York City life
with Jonathan, her husband and best friend,
and the grown children she adores. She also
has two cats, "one neurotic, the other
unruly." Alice has been writing seriously
since the eighth grade.

Books by Alice Harron Orr

HARLEQUIN INTRIGUE
56–SABOTAGE

Past Sins
Alice Harron Orr

Harlequin Books

TORONTO • NEW YORK • LONDON
AMSTERDAM • PARIS • SYDNEY • HAMBURG
STOCKHOLM • ATHENS • TOKYO • MILAN

To Jonathan—always my romantic hero

Harlequin Intrigue edition published September 1991

ISBN 0-373-22169-X

PAST SINS

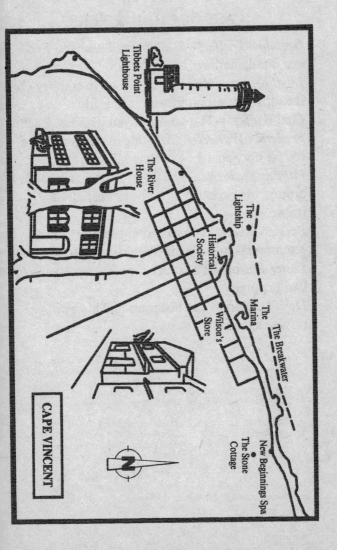

CAPE VINCENT

Tibbets Point
Lighthouse

The River
House

The
Lightship

Historical
Society

The
Marina

Wilson's
Store

The Breakwater

New Beginnings Spa
The Stone
Cottage

N

CAST OF CHARACTERS

Gretchen Wulfert—She returned home to find her family heritage in jeopardy.

Boyd Emory—He came to the north country on the most important mission of his life.

Carl Wulfert—The drama began with his death.

Frederick Wulfert—The ailing man would have the family name preserved at all costs.

Pauline Basinette—The faithful nurse had been around long enough to know *almost* all of the secrets.

Beryll Sackett—The spa administrator's bitter resentments had remained hidden too long.

Lester Wilson—The small-town entrepreneur had big plans.

Herb Dingner—The historian had his own private agenda.

Prologue

Carl Wulfert's pudgy fingers caught the corner of an asphalt shingle and tried to hold on, but there was no chance of that. Instead, the rough surface tore his flesh, and he continued his slide toward the edge of the roof.

Suddenly he remembered, of all things, how adamant he had been when his father suggested that this roof might need better shingles.

"Slate is too expensive. Asphalt will do," Carl had insisted. And, as usual, Frederick had given in. It was pointless to argue with Carl where money was concerned.

A futile wish flashed through Carl's present terror. If only he could undo that day there would be slate on the roof of New Beginnings Revivatorium & Health Spa now, and this cheap asphalt wouldn't be ripping his fingers to shreds. Unfortunately, that conversation had taken place last spring when Carl was more concerned about money than ever. So this afternoon there was only graveled roughness and not a single corner solid enough to stop his downward slide.

It hadn't yet occurred to him to scream. He had been too preoccupied with trying to grab hold somewhere. He had never been much good at gripping onto things.

Baseball had been one of the few kid activities that appealed to him all those years ago when he was young, but he couldn't hang on to the ball because his fingers were short and wide, like the rest of him. Now, that short, heavy bulk was dragging him, faster with every heartbeat, toward disaster.

His chin skidded along, clenched into his fleshy neck as he concentrated every effort on saving himself, though saving himself was hardly likely. From that position he darted one last, pleading glance at the feet and legs, still standing, back where the mansard roof leveled off. Carl couldn't get his chin up high enough to glimpse the face, but he knew who it was and that there would be no help from that quarter.

Carl's descent accelerated as his own feet and legs cleared the roof edge. In the next moment he felt the eaves trough and grabbed for the rim. A wild hope flickered where there had been none and wrenched his mind from its paralysis of shock just long enough to make very clear to him that, even if the trough hadn't been filled with slippery autumn leaves, he couldn't possibly hang on for long, any more than he could hang on to a baseball all those years ago. In that instant Carl also became aware of the high-pitched, keening sound he must have been making all along. Then his scream began, and he was gone.

Chapter One

A gloved hand yanked the drawer past the place where it wanted to stick, then rooted through the contents. There was nothing in this drawer. Nothing in the whole place.

It was hard to believe that Carl Wulfert hadn't been telling the truth about having evidence hidden away here somewhere. He was bargaining for his life at that moment; and there had been the clammy scent of fear about him, so strong you could smell it over the wind on the roof. Carl wouldn't have had the courage to lie when he was so afraid.

Besides, he was just the type to dredge up an embarrassing secret from the past, then hold on to it, even as long as this, until he found some nasty use for it. Of course, bringing out the truth would mean bad talk about the Wulfert family; but maybe that was exactly what Carl wanted. He had resented just about everybody, perhaps even his own high and mighty family.

The drawer slammed shut again, grating along the dried-out splints of the track, but no matter. No one would hear. It was off-season, and there were no patients at the spa, only old Frederick Wulfert up in the top tower apartment, the penthouse suite for the dying head of the clan. No one would notice anything out of order in this drawer, either. Carl had been such a slob that someone could turn this place upside down searching and nobody would be able to guess at anything amiss.

The searching was easy. It was the *finding* that came hard, certainly harder than it had been for Carl—three floors above almost this very spot—to go off the roof in the first place.

GRETCHEN WULFERT LOVED the River House morning room with its white wainscoting and federal blue walls. She could imagine the very first lady of the manor, sitting at this same desk in 1820 or so, keeping her correspondence. According to legend, her husband had adored her so much that he'd built this magnificent house especially for her. Gretchen wondered what it would be like to be loved so totally.

She had never known of such a relationship in her life. Certainly there were none in her family now, and she had definitely never experienced anything like that herself. In truth, she wasn't sure she would feel comfortable having someone so close, invading that private little circle where she had lived her entire life for as far back as she could remember.

Her grandfather was the one exception to that preference for distance in relationships. She had always wanted to be as close to him as she could get, and these past few years she'd nearly achieved that. Strangely enough, however, she hadn't even been here in Cape Vincent, New York, at the time. She'd been flitting around the world, hobnobbing with the glitterati. Except once a week, on Sunday morning, when she would call home and talk to her grandfather and he would respond with an openness no Wulfert had ever been capable of face-to-face. During those precious conversations, she had been transported into a private little circle that also held Frederick Wulfert and was very safe and warm.

Now her grandfather lay in a coma on the third floor of the health spa he had created over fifty years ago, first as a sanitarium for well-off victims of tuberculosis, then more delicately referred to as consumption, and later as a place for all kinds of recuperation and rejuvenation. Important people had traveled there from all over the world, seeking a new lease on the life that her grandfather now held on to so tenuously.

Every afternoon since Gretchen's return here from New York City, she had visited Frederick Wulfert. She would sit for hours staring at his unmoving face. She would talk softly to him of all the things they would do when he was well again, though she knew that, if by some miracle he did survive, he would much prefer to sit in his library and read or write his histories of noble Wulferts and their times. She understood, however, that he was very sick and most likely would reach his life's end right there on the third floor of the place he himself had renamed New Beginnings Spa.

Still, it wasn't her grandfather's illness that had finally brought her home. She had avoided that journey even after he lapsed into unconsciousness. Secretly she had feared that she would return and he would awaken, cool and reserved and distant as he had always been in person. Then her illusion of that warm, safe circle of theirs would be destroyed and she might never be able to get it back again. So she had stayed away but kept in touch by phone with Beryll Sackett, who administered the spa and supervised Frederick's care with utmost efficiency.

Gretchen had actually come back here because of Uncle Carl, and that was the biggest irony of all. Carl Wulfert had been the other reason she stayed away from Cape Vincent. He had driven her away, just as he'd driven her parents before her. No one could stand to be around him long. Her grandfather apparently had no choice, though she often wondered why Frederick didn't simply banish Carl the Odious, son or not.

Gretchen shuddered. She'd forgotten for a moment. Uncle Carl was dead now, and she shouldn't think ill of the dead. Yet in all her memories of the stern little man since her childhood here in this house above the river, she couldn't recall a single virtue to think kindly of him for—except what he'd done for her grandfather these past several weeks since he'd gone into the coma. Beryll Sackett had told Gretchen how Carl had taken personal charge of his father, visiting him several times each day, making sure the details of his treatment were attended to carefully. Whatever Gretchen may have thought about her uncle otherwise, she was very grateful to him for that.

Still, when she thought about him now, all she could remember was unpleasantness. There was one childhood memory in particular that often came to mind when she thought of Uncle Carl. The family had been visiting the estate of one of her grandfather's friends on the north shore of Long Island. Gretchen was about seven or eight then. She'd had a wonderful time wandering by herself through the luxurious gardens, pretending she was a princess and that this was her domain. She hadn't even minded playing alone. She was used to that.

Then it was time to go home, but that was all right because she'd be driving back with her grandparents. Grandma was already sick by then and wouldn't talk much, but Gretchen and Grandpa would have one of those conversations that happened only when he was in the front seat driving, as he loved to do, and she was in the back, bouncing from one window to the other, asking every question she could think of. He would answer, often with a delightful story, until he got tired of talking. Those were very special times for Gretchen.

Unfortunately there was one thing she hadn't counted on about this particular drive. Uncle Carl had decided to come along instead of flying back with her parents as originally planned. She could still remember pressing herself against the door on her side of the car to keep as far away from him as possible, while he insisted on leaning over every few minutes to talk to her, as if he knew how much she didn't like him and enjoyed tormenting her. She would answer briefly and hold her breath until he moved away again. There had been no million questions that day; and, in all the twenty-nine years of her life, there had been no moment when Gretchen had actually liked being around Carl.

Now Uncle Carl was gone, and she couldn't honestly say that she missed him. Still, she felt guilty for thinking that way, and not just because he'd taken such good care of her grandfather. She couldn't help feeling sorry for Carl because of the horrible way he died. She would feel sorry for anyone who was desperate enough to throw himself off a roof.

Gretchen scraped her chair back too hard from the writing desk and rumpled the thin old Chinese rug into faded red and navy ripples. Wide glass-paned French doors looked out across the lawn and down the bank to the beautiful Saint Lawrence River. The water was a dark grayish-green, as it so often was during a northern New York State autumn. An occasional whitecap fringed the nearly flat surface all the way over to the layers of mist that shrouded the Canadian shore. This close to the mouth of mercurial Lake Ontario, the water could froth up quite choppy at times; but this morning all was placid. No stranger would have suspected the fierce power of the current beneath that steady flow.

She had stood on this spot countless times as a little girl when she was still short and wide and barely able to see over the porch railing and down the riverbank. That broadness of body inherited from the German side of the family had made her self-conscious about the way she looked in those days. Then her mother's Swedishness took over, and Gretchen shot up tall and slim as she was now. Still, her cheekbones remained wide beneath green eyes; and, of course, her hair was blond and flaxen straight.

Unfortunately not even the beauty of her cherished Saint Lawrence could salvage her mood right now. Somber thoughts of Uncle Carl had banished the serenity of only a few moments ago. She was suddenly aware of a chilly draft along the floor, and that reminded her of Uncle Carl's frugality. He had kept room temperatures lowered in the interest of saving on fuel, even though there was definitely no lack of family money. Gretchen's trust fund attested to that.

She chafed her hands together impatiently. Another unwelcome topic had arisen to darken her mood. Most people probably wouldn't think of all that money as unwelcome, and maybe she had no right to feel burdened by it. Still, she might not have lived such an aimless life, drifting from one place to the next, if it hadn't been so easy for her to do so.

Perhaps she could stop all of that, come back here and settle down. She might even take over the family interests now that there was no one else to do so. Still, she might not be suited for life here in the north country after New York and Paris and all those other glamorous places. If only her grandfather could advise her instead of lying in his third-floor room without so much as blinking the eyes he might very well never open again.

She stared through the French windows and across the slope. This time all she noticed was the round black scars marring the trunks of the two tall trees that had once spread their branches majestically above the bank. Dutch elm disease had humbled them, like so many of their kind up and down the wide streets of Cape Vincent village.

She was reminded of the amputated limbs of her own family tree. Her grandmother had ended her years in virtual silence. Gretchen's mother hated the north country so much that she vowed she would never return. And Gretchen's father had gone along with his wife, though he missed the river life very much. Now Uncle Carl was dead, and her grandfather lay so still. So many branches gone, and Gretchen could feel the black scar of each one on her heart.

NURSE PAULINE BASINETTE smoothed the case tight around the old man's pillow. Percale it was, fine-textured and sweet-smelling. In the old days things hadn't been so fancy around here. Back when this was just "the san"— short for Wulfert Sanatorium—there had been rough cotton stuff and it had been good enough. That was before the high-muckety-muck patients were all over the place, instead of kept to the cottage down at the back of the property as they had been in the old days after the big war. Now there was a gold-lettered sign out front that said New Beginnings.

Nurse Basinette sniffed her disapproval and elevated her shiny pink nose. New Beginnings, my eye, she thought. We were lucky if the porch had a coat of paint, much less a gold-lettered sign, back in the old days. Now

she had to put up with that highfalutin program administrator, Beryll Sackett, telling her the porch had to be
called a *veranda* and looking down her skinny nose in a
way that was meant to remind Pauline she wasn't really
a nurse, just an LPN, and past retirement age to boot.

Gramps here—she'd been calling him that off and on
for the past few years, now that the two of them were the
old codgers around here—if he was up on his feet and still
running things, he'd make sure she was treated right and
kept on here as long as she wanted to stay. He'd been
generous like that with all the old-timers, at least the local ones, especially in the years when the back cottage
was still open for business. Of course, the staff who actually did the work back there had always been imported
from downstate somewhere. Ordinary, small-town folks
weren't supposed to be good enough for those who had
money enough to lodge back there. Those importeds had
never stayed around long enough for the old man to have
to worry about them. One old-fashioned north country
winter and they'd be gone, scampering back to the city
where they belonged, and good riddance to them.

Sometimes Pauline wondered why Frederick bothered
so much about the locals who had worked for him in the
old days. Maybe it was out of the kindness of his heart,
but she wasn't so sure. He'd never been much of a smiler.
Still, he would walk down Broadway in the village, grin-
ning real wide and grabbing everybody's hand to give it
a good shake. She couldn't quite remember when he
started doing that—years ago it had been. But she
couldn't help wondering what he was really thinking and
why he tried so hard to make everybody like him.

After all, didn't the Wulferts have more money than
anybody else around, not to mention that big house by
the river and all? Why would it make a damn to him what

these farmers and small-town folks thought about him, anyway? She'd asked old Frederick about it, back before he slipped away to where he was now. He wouldn't answer her, of course, just told her to stop pestering him with such foolishness; but she had a sneaking suspicion there was more to it than that.

Everybody in town always *acted* as if they liked him, of course, especially after the money started coming in from the back-cottage types and even more a few years later when he started giving it away for books for the library and gym stuff for the school and any other project anybody could think up around town. Pauline had always suspected that was some kind of tax rip-off and never cost so much that he'd really miss it.

Fat lot of good all of that charity was doing him now, anyway. He'd have been better off to pay more attention to himself. Pauline scowled down at the white face with its wide cheekbones straining at the skin drawn taut over them. Old Frederick here didn't even know his younger son was dead. Took a jump off the high roof and hit the driveway so hard you couldn't see his squinty little eyes anymore. Still, squinty eyes or no, Pauline was one of the few around here who could manage some pity for the man. She remembered when he was a boy, and even with all his family's money, those hadn't been easy times for him.

She wondered how Frederick would feel if he did know Carl was dead. She'd never seen any sign of what she'd call love between those two. But then she'd never seen much sign of what she'd call love between any of the Wulferts. One thing she was sure of, though. The old codger would want to know his Miss Fashion Magazine granddaughter was here. Brought herself all the way up from the big city to flounce her expensive clothes and her expensive car up and down Broadway.

Pauline put a stop to that thought before it could go any farther. There was no need to be so mean about young Gretchen. After all, some people had to live in the city, whether or not Pauline thought it was sensible.

Besides, there was no question that Gretchen Wulfert loved her grandfather. Didn't she show up every afternoon, like clockwork, to sit by the bed here and hold this old man's hand, even though he didn't know her from a hole in the wall? Pauline doubted the girl did that because she was counting the heartbeats he had left till he got around to dying and leaving her a pile of money, as some folks in town might whisper.

Just yesterday Pauline had peeked through the crack in the door when the girl was in here. Pauline had seen for herself how the girl took the old man's hand and sat there patting it so gently. She might be as cool as February other times, but her eyes had been shining then, as if she could barely keep herself from sobbing outright. Pauline had seen that and she wouldn't hesitate to tell it to anybody who asked her, and maybe she'd tell some who didn't ask her, too.

Nurse Basinette tucked the top sheet into a perfect hospital fold across Frederick Wulfert's sunken chest. There was softness in her gaze down at him. After all, the state he was in, he'd hardly be able to tell she'd let up on pestering him for a minute; but, in her heart of hearts, Pauline Basinette wished he could know exactly that.

BOYD EMORY ADJUSTED the focus of his field glasses to compensate for the silt and spray on the windscreen. He stood with his boots wide apart to counter the roll of the lightship against its moorings to the breakwater. His Air

Force surplus parka was well insulated, but he was still aware of the sharp chill of the wind that sailed down the river and pierced the crevices around the cabin's corroding door. He hadn't bothered with a fire in the wood stove this afternoon.

Boyd paid little attention to the cold as he concentrated on the side door of the big house across the stretch of water from the breakwater to the shore. They called it River House. He'd seen that on a sign next to the long driveway when he drove past. He hadn't been able to see the house from the road, but he'd been staring at the place long enough to memorize every detail from this vantage point. He'd also studied the floor plans at the local historical society. Ordinarily his interest would have been purely professional, noting the architectural details that were his business. However, his reasons for watching River House for hours on end had nothing to do with business. They were very personal.

No one had noticed him here. He was certain of that. The lightship had been anchored in this same spot for as long as most people around here could remember. He'd found that out by asking casual questions at the grocery store. They would most likely barely register seeing the lightship even when looking straight at it. They would definitely not be examining it carefully enough to make out a shadowy figure beyond the murky windscreen.

He scanned the glasses upward. He did that periodically to rest his eyes from squinting at a single point. The house was impressive, even to someone who'd seen elegant houses all around the world as Boyd had. It was built of fieldstone, a material readily available to early builders in this glacial river valley and most likely to withstand the rages of fire, which were the chief danger to houses like this in those old times.

This house had been designed with the weather in mind, as well. The long wall that fronted the river was shielded by a wide porch. The pitched roof was angled to block not only the wind, but also the north country winter snow that swirled across the ice from Canada. The windows in that wall were tall and narrow, another concession to the elements. The one impractical feature was the wide French doors at the center of the porch. The floor plans had indicated that those doors opened out from what was called the morning room.

His research into the Wulfert family had revealed that the ancestor who built this fortress house had a single impractical feature of his own. He was desperately in love with his French wife. It wasn't too much of a leap to guess that the wide, vulnerable French doors and morning room had been for her. Boyd tried not to dwell on personal details like that. The last thing he wanted was for any of the residents of that house—past or present— to become too human to him.

He lowered the field glasses for a moment and could just make out some movement at the side door. He clapped the eyepieces back to his face, and there she was. He adjusted the focus as finely as he could get it. Luckily the tree branches had been blown bare by the stiff river wind. Away from the shore, in the countryside, the landscape still blazed with autumn red and gold, but not here. Even so he couldn't see her as clearly as he would have liked.

He'd never seen her in person. So far there had been only these field glass views. Each time he'd caught her in his sights these past few days he'd found himself straining a little harder to make out the details. He'd even wondered if she could really be as beautiful as she seemed, or was that just the softening effect of distance and magnification?

He couldn't actually see the wisps of white-blond hair whipping away from her face in the wind or the tinge of pink against ivory that the chill would bring to her cheeks, but he could imagine them there. She never wore anything close-fitting or revealing, even as she settled in and her dress relaxed from the tailored crispness she'd arrived in. Still, he could almost see the trim, supple body under her sweater and slacks and bulky jacket.

She was a beauty, all right. According to his research, she was a real darling of the international set and had been for several years now. Boyd had run into more than his share of those types on his architectural restoration projects. They were often the owners of the ancient manses it was his business to preserve. Boyd found women like that intriguing, but then he was curious by nature. Still, he kept his distance. He'd never had much interest in superficial relationships; and, as far as he could see, shallowness was the specialty of the international set, especially the women.

A number had tried to lure him into casual involvements, but he had resisted. They were attractive, of course, in the way that women are who have a lot of time and money to spend on keeping themselves up. In fact, all that time and money and not enough to do with it were the reasons they plied their seductive ways among men like him. Most of them were as bored as they were rich and in search of a fling to alleviate that boredom for a while, but that kind of thing simply wasn't for Boyd. When he had a relationship with a woman, he wanted some depth to it.

However, the current circumstances would have to be an exception to his rule. A relationship with Gretchen

Wulfert could be just the ticket to the information he'd come here to uncover; and, if she turned out to be one of those bored, available women, all the better. He didn't want to work too hard or take too much time getting to her. He wanted to get his evidence and get out as quickly as possible.

He watched her walk along the side of the house to the driveway. He knew what he must do next. After days of watching her leave the house about this time and go to the grocery store, he could safely assume she was doing the same today. Today he would be there, too.

He waited until the flash of her red sports car had moved out of sight among the trees that lined the long driveway from the stone manse to the road. Then he hurried out of the cabin to the small outboard he'd tied in the shadow of the lightship. He was eager to get this next step of his plan under way. He didn't dwell on the fact that he was also rather eager to see Gretchen Wulfert up close.

"HI, THERE," Gretchen greeted the plump storekeeper a bit too brightly.

For as far back as she could remember she had tried to forge some real and personal connections with the people of her hometown; but, for the most part, she hadn't succeeded. After all her time away in boarding schools and summer camps, then the university and traveling around, this failure to connect wasn't hard to understand and probably couldn't be helped. Still, she hadn't seen Mr. Wilson since she'd gotten back to the Cape. His wife had been tending the store when Gretchen came in, so she couldn't resist yet another try at friendliness.

"What a difference this extra space makes," she exclaimed more brightly than ever, surveying the expanded storefront with as much enthusiasm as she could muster.

"We broke through into the other building," Wilson said, favoring Gretchen with a smile that at least matched her own in wattage. "How nice of you to notice."

Gretchen was tempted to glance over her shoulder in case he might be speaking to someone else.

"It's so good to see you back here on the Cape," he went on cheerfully before dropping his voice into a more solemn register. Then he added, "We just wish the occasion was a happier one."

That must be why he's so friendly to me, she thought. They think I'm in mourning for Uncle Carl.

She tried to look appropriately subdued. "Yes, I wish that, too."

She'd thought she would enjoy having a congenial chat like this with one of the townspeople, instead of the clipped replies she usually got from them. Nonetheless, she felt rather awkward basking in the warmth of Mr. Wilson's unexpected friendliness and couldn't help wondering how sincere he really was. That thought made her feel more awkward than ever. So she nodded and took her retreat into the rows of canned goods.

Despite the renovations of which Mr. Wilson was so proud, the aisles looked about the same to Gretchen as they always had, except that now they ran from front to back instead of from side to side, and were wider apart. She plunked the handle of a plastic shopping basket over her arm and headed across the nearest aisle. She could remember when she was a very little girl and would shop with her grandmother in this same store. Grandma was still well and happy then and very much in charge of the River House kitchen, especially the marketing. Gretchen had resolved to grow up to be exactly like her. Repeating this ritual now made Gretchen wonder if that resolution would ever come true.

Meanwhile, she had been strolling along, scanning the shelves without much comprehension. Suddenly thoughts of her grandmother connected with several dark-brown-and-silver cans of Hershey's cocoa. Gretchen picked one up and turned it over in her hand. She hadn't seen a can of cocoa in years. Did they still sell it in the city? All she had ever noticed there was the instant kind. This old-fashioned variety was probably out of vogue because there might actually be some work involved. *There* was a point in favor of small-town life—doing things the non-instant way.

In fact, she was sure she could find her grandmother's from-scratch chocolate cake recipe in one of those old cookbooks back at River House. Gretchen wasn't a bad cook herself. Did that particular recipe call for cocoa or unsweetened chocolate squares? Gretchen knitted her brows, straining to remember those childhood after-noons in the kitchen, sitting on a wooden chair with her feet dangling because her legs were still too short for her toes to reach the floor. Grandma never let the cook help with the cakes. She baked them herself, especially her famous chocolate. She would stir the batter in an earth-enware bowl with a big wooden spoon.

Gretchen could almost smell the chocolate now, but was it from the stirring batter or squares melting on the stove? She was staring at the cocoa label, as if the answer might be printed there, when a deep voice drawled out just to the left of her shoulder and the sleeve of a blue-gray parka reached into her field of vision to point at the can.

"I haven't seen cocoa like that since I was in junior high school," he said.

"I was just thinking almost the same thing," Gretchen said, looking around at him.

He was tall and broad, and she could tell that the padded parka wasn't the only reason for that broadness. Impressive shoulders were most likely residing under there.

"What are you going to make from this stuff?" he drawled. "Brownies?"

Gretchen dropped the can into her basket. "I'm going to bake a cake."

He was smiling down at her. "I wouldn't have pegged you for the cake-baking type. In fact, you don't even look like you're from around here. Neither am I."

She continued down the aisle, and he walked with her.

"Actually, I was born here," she said.

"I bet you haven't lived here lately."

"I've been away a while, but now I'm back," she said, more resolutely than she had expected to.

"For good, or for a visit?"

He moved ahead into her path and turned, facing her. She could see the natural curiosity in his gaze, and that somehow made his question less inappropriately prying than it might otherwise have sounded to her. Besides, she was attempting to make connections with people.

"I'm not sure how long I'll be here," she said.

"I see" was all he said in reply as he fell into step beside her once more.

Apparently she had acquired a shopping companion. But did she really want one? He was a handsome man, and Gretchen liked handsome men as much as the next woman. Still, she was hardly accustomed to having strangers attach themselves to her, nor did she generally encourage that sort of thing. This was, of course, a small town, and people were supposed to be more open in small towns, though that hadn't always been her experience here in Cape Vincent. Besides, he'd said he wasn't from here. Nonetheless, she didn't feel she should be rude, so she let him tag along while she picked out her purchases and took them through the checkout line, where the young girl behind the counter gave him a look of approval. Gretchen had no doubt whatsoever of the sincerity of that particular expression.

"By the way," she said, primarily to be polite after he had carried her groceries to the car and opened the door for her to get in, "there's something I'm curious about. Why didn't you ask me if I was going to make cocoa from that can? It seems to me that would have been your first assumption."

She'd meant it as an innocuous exit line to cover the time it would take to slip into the car and make her getaway. A slow grin spread over his tanned features, all the way up to the shock of hair that fell appealingly across his forehead.

"Oh, I knew it wouldn't be cocoa," he said, leaning against the car door to shut it after she'd taken her seat. His arms rested on the open window edge, and his face was so near hers she could smell the scent of fresh river wind in his hair. "You city folks always use the instant stuff for that."

Gretchen felt a jolt of recognition. That was exactly what she'd been thinking back in the store. She wasn't sure she liked having him so close to her wavelength. That was another thing about city folks, as he called them, they're used to being isolated even in a crowd. Maybe she'd have to change that if she was going to make a happy adjustment to small-town life, *but* she definitely didn't have to do it right this minute or for this man.

She shifted the car into gear and made her exit, but not before he caught her in one last gaze that sent the message, loud and clear, that he would be seeing her again— very soon.

Chapter Two

Very few people came to the funeral the next day, and none of them were crying, so Gretchen didn't feel out of place. She'd worn her dark suit and high black boots, though slacks and thermal underwear would have been more appropriate on such a cold day. As always when she was in Cape Vincent, Gretchen was conscious of what her grandfather called her duty to the dignity of the family name. It seemed a little late for that after what Uncle Carl had done, but she'd worn the dark suit, anyway, and covered it with a long coat to keep out the wind.

The Wulfert plot was in the oldest part of the cemetery on River Road. The trees were ancient there and big around the trunk, with branches that spread out to shower autumn leaves across the graves. There had been such a branch over the spot where they buried her grandmother when Gretchen was a little girl. The branch was gone now, but she could still picture herself standing under it at the funeral. She remembered her grandmother's passing so well because of what had happened afterward.

They had never been a demonstrative family; but once Grandmother was gone, River House grew chillier by the day, and not because of the weather. Then there was the night Gretchen would never forget. She had been crouching on the rug behind her closed bedroom door, listening to her parents through the crack at the bottom. Her mother had said they had to leave Cape Vincent or she would go away on her own. Gretchen could still feel her tummy as tight as steel bands as she'd prayed they wouldn't take her away from Grandpa and her beloved river.

The final decision had been that her mother and father would go and Gretchen would stay, to be raised and schooled as a Wulfert should be, under her grandfather's supervision. She had preferred that to being taken away, but what she had really wanted was her family together living happily ever after as in the fairy tales.

Unfortunately the Wulferts had been anything but together from then on. And today was no exception. Her grandfather was on the third floor of New Beginnings, unconscious, as he had been for some weeks now. Her parents had refused to come, not even bothering to make an excuse. Her mother had simply said she couldn't be hypocrite enough to pretend any grief over the death of her worst enemy. Gretchen had been surprised by that statement. To describe a person as your worst enemy suggested some specific, very intense conflict in the past; but she knew better than to question her mother about it.

Gretchen had tried more than once to find out why her mother was so adamant about never returning to Cape Vincent. Those inquiries had always ended with her mother suggesting that, if Gretchen wanted her family reunited so badly, she should move back to the "old homestead" herself. Gretchen had had no real response to that at the time, so the subject was always dropped. Still, she couldn't help wondering what had happened to cause a rift so deep that it outlasted even Carl Wulfert's death.

Gretchen also wondered if her father might feel differently from her mother about coming back home. He had loved the river as much as his father and daughter did. Gretchen half expected him to show up here unannounced one day. That would certainly be in character for him. The thing she remembered best about him was how he would slip out of places, like a phantom, before you knew he was even thinking about leaving. Then he'd suddenly be back again, just as unexpectedly. Gretchen hadn't known him very well, except to be a bit awed by his handsomeness and charm. Still, she had always suspected he carried on a secret life during those times when he slipped quietly away.

She was thinking about that possibility when she felt someone touch her on the arm for a moment, then pull quickly away. Gretchen turned to find a very nervous woman standing beside her.

"I'm Beryll Sackett," she said, speaking rapidly. "We've talked on the phone. Perhaps you remember me. I work at New Beginnings. I'm the administrator there. We've never met. Not in person, I mean. I thought I should introduce myself and offer my...condolences." Her pale eyes darted to the still-open grave and then away again as if it were an embarrassment to her.

"Of course, I remember you." Gretchen took Miss Sackett's hand to shake it and could feel the chill even through Beryll's thick knit gloves. "I don't know what I would have done without you since my grandfather got sick. You've made me feel more in touch with him."

"And there was no reason you should have come up to visit him yourself. He wouldn't have known you were here," Miss Sackett said quickly, excusing the apology Gretchen hadn't made, but suddenly felt she should have.

"There were circumstances that could have made it awkward for everybody if I'd been here."

"Yes, I understand about awkward circumstances." Again Miss Sackett's glance strayed to Carl's grave. "They had a way of happening when *he* was around."

Here was another person who apparently didn't feel much sadness over Uncle Carl's passing. Gretchen wondered how many more there might be.

"Miss Wulfert?"

The touch was on her arm again, then gone. Beryll reminded Gretchen of a small animal making brief human contact, then fleeing, terrified.

"Well, I just wanted to introduce myself," Beryll was saying. "I have to get back to New Beginnings. There's so much paperwork to do now that..." She didn't look at the grave this time, though she seemed very aware of its presence, and uncomfortably so. "Mr. Wulfert handled the books and all, you see."

"I'm sure he did." Gretchen couldn't imagine Uncle Carl letting anybody else take charge of the money. "I'll be at the spa to see my grandfather as soon as I'm finished here."

"I'd like to talk to you then if I could. I have something to ask you that is of the utmost importance." Miss Sackett gripped her coat collar even more tightly and shivered.

"You're cold. You should get inside," Gretchen said as she instinctively reached out to comfort the vulnerable creature.

Miss Sackett backed away quickly, the gesture of comfort seeming to make her more agitated than ever.

"I'm always cold. That's why I don't usually stay north this long after the summer season. That and my mother."

"I remember now. You work at another spa in Florida during the winter. Then you come back up here in the late spring."

"Yes, I do," she said, beginning to tap her toes against the chill, as if Florida was where she'd like to be this very minute. "But I have to get back to New Beginnings now."

Gretchen wondered why Beryll had extended her stay in the north country, and might have asked her that in warmer surroundings. "I'll be there soon," she said instead.

The second those words were out of Gretchen's mouth, Miss Sackett was off, scurrying toward the line of cars at the roadside, her coat clutched around her and her head down. Gretchen followed slowly, since the brief ceremony was over and the others were leaving, as well. She would have liked to ask Beryll about Grandpa and the spa. Gretchen had no doubt that Miss Sackett had everything in order, of course. Before his illness Grandpa had mentioned several times in his letters and phone talks that Beryll was an extremely efficient organizer. The straight line of Beryll's retreating back seemed to attest to that efficiency.

Then another voice speaking in a cemetery hush captured Gretchen's attention. "Poor Beryll wasn't exactly what you'd call comfortable around Carl when he was alive. I don't expect she'd feel much different now that he's dead."

Gretchen was both pleased and surprised to find Lester Wilson, the storekeeper from the village, standing beside her.

"Do you know Beryll well?" she asked.

"She and my wife, Evelyn, get together and swap local gossip every now and then, if you know what I mean," he said with the slight flatness of a nasal north country twang.

Gretchen knew exactly what he meant. The Wulferts were no strangers to village tongue-wagging. She had long suspected it was such idle hashing over of their personal business that had driven her parents away.

"Thank you for coming, Mr. Wilson," Gretchen said, meaning it. So few of the other townspeople had.

"I've always had great respect for your family. The contributions of the Wulferts to this community have been very generous, especially those of your grandfather," he said, flashing her a wide smile. "And, please, call me Lester."

"Tell me, Lester," Gretchen said, hesitating only a second before using his first name, though she had never been invited to do so before. "Was my Uncle Carl equally generous?"

There was a bit of perverseness in that question, but Lester's speech about the Wulfert family sounded rehearsed. She was curious to know if he had also prepared a respectful statement concerning her much-maligned uncle.

"Well, Carl was a...uh...businessman," Lester stammered, confirming her suspicion that he had not liked her uncle any more than anyone else around here seemed to.

"Lester, you're looking pretty red in the face there," remarked another north country twang, even more pronounced than Wilson's. "That's what you get from working so hard to pry your foot out of your mouth."

The lanky man who'd joined them had a face that Gretchen remembered but couldn't connect with a name.

"My foot is square on the ground where it ought to be, Herb," Lester said with some indignation. "In case you don't remember him, Gretchen, this is Herb Dingner, our local historian and smart aleck."

"That's our Les, always the gentleman, making formal introductions and all," Herb said. "He keeps us country folk minding our manners on solemn occasions such as this."

"Yes, it is a solemn occasion," Lester agreed a bit too emphatically.

"Sure it is, Les. We all know how much you loved Carl."

Lester's chubby cheeks turned an even deeper shade of red, and he looked as if he might break into a sweat despite the near-frosty weather. Next to lean, leathery Herb, Lester was round and soft.

"I admit Carl and I weren't the best of friends," Lester spluttered. "That doesn't mean I shouldn't come and pay my respects to the family."

"Didn't I just get finished saying that Lester here was the perfect one to set an example for us country types?" Herb said with a gap-toothed grin. "As a matter of fact, he's one of our leading citizens. Has he had a chance to tell you about his business activities?"

"I wouldn't talk about anything like that right now." Lester's gaze slipped back toward the grave, just as Beryll Sackett's had done.

"Sorry, I forgot. Respect for the dear departed."

There was no mistaking the *lack of* respect in Herb's tone. Gretchen had wondered how many people there were in Cape Vincent who didn't care for her Uncle Carl, and she was beginning to find out. Now she wondered *why* they had disliked him so much.

"That's right, Herb," Lester said. "A cemetery is no place to speak of business."

"But I'm sure Miss Wulfert would love to hear about what all you've been doing around here," Herb insisted.

"Herb is right," Gretchen said, hoping to take the edge out of this exchange. It was beginning to make her uneasy. "I'd love to hear what you've been doing."

"Well, I don't just own the grocery store like you probably remember," Lester began reluctantly.

Herb cut in. "Old Lester here's bought up half the village. You might call him our local entrepreneur."

"That's right. I've made a real investment in this community," Lester said, sounding more indignant by the second. "I've got plans for those buildings and other properties, too. Plans that'll put Cape Vincent on the map."

Lester glanced at Gretchen when making that last pronouncement, as if gauging her reaction. She wondered why. He'd never seemed to care what she thought before. Maybe he wanted to let her know that important things didn't just happen to city people.

"That sounds exciting, Lester," she said, remembering not to call him Mr. Wilson.

"Your uncle thought it was pretty exciting, too," Herb remarked with obvious sarcasm. His next statement was more serious in tone. "Lester here just better make sure these projects of his don't get *too* exciting. He starts messing up those structures on Broadway, and he'll have me to answer to."

"As I said, Herb's our local historian," Lester said. "That's how he got started calling things *structures* instead of *buildings* like everybody else does."

"You know how it is in small towns, Miss Wulfert," Herb said. "Everybody gets a role to play. Les here is our wheeler-dealer, and I like to poke around in dusty old places. I guess you might say it's just another case of natural-born north country nosiness, except I stick my nose into the past instead of the present. That tends to put Les and me on opposite sides of things. He wants to develop Cape Vincent, and I want to preserve it.''

"You want to dig it up is closer to the truth," Lester grumbled.

"The past has got secrets to tell, and sometimes you have to dig for secrets."

"We all know what kind of secrets you're looking for, Herb," Lester said.

"And we all know why you're buying up every old building in sight," Herb snapped back. Then he glanced sheepishly at Gretchen, as if he had just remembered she was there. "Don't pay us any mind, Miss Wulfert. Les and I are at each other like this all the time, but deep down we're the best of friends."

Gretchen wasn't sure she believed him, but she nodded, anyway.

Herb nodded back. "Well, I'd best be on my way now. Speaking of history, River House and New Beginnings Spa, have a long one, too. My father used to work at the spa back in the forties, right up till he died. I remember when I was a kid, listening to him tell stories about that place. They say the cottage on the back end of the property is haunted, you know."

"And my guess is you'd like to be the one haunting it," Lester quipped.

"At least I'm not fool enough to think they'd let me buy it," Herb retorted. Some of the good nature had gone out of his tone. "As I said, it's time for me to be on my way, Miss Wulfert."

"Thank you for coming," Gretchen said with relief as he touched his cap to tip it slightly, nodded again and turned to walk away.

She'd had enough local color for the moment and was suddenly feeling a bit weary. Unfortunately Lester wasn't quite ready to make *his* exit yet. He leaned closer to Gretchen and spoke in a near whisper. "There's something we should talk about soon. A deal that your Uncle Carl and I had been discussing."

"Come on, Lester," Herb called from a few yards off. "You should have figured out by now that you aren't going to talk a Wulfert out of Wulfert land."

Lester squirmed visibly at that and flushed a sudden and pronounced scarlet. He mumbled something about sympathy for the Wulfert family before hurrying after Herb. She could tell that the two of them were squabbling as they walked toward their cars. Gretchen wondered if they were arguing about having blown each other's cover as respectful mourners. She smiled ruefully. Considering how they obviously felt about her uncle, she should have suspected right off that Les and Herb had ulterior motives for showing up today.

However, if Herb was right and Lester really did have aspirations to buy Wulfert land, she couldn't imagine a Wulfert selling. Her grandfather had made it clear, on countless occasions, that the Wulfert estate was to be kept intact. He had even insisted they all make a solemn pledge to that effect, as solemnly as they pledged to protect the Wulfert name at all costs.

"They're quite a pair, aren't they?" a deep voice said close to her ear as a broad, bronzed hand extended to shake hers. "Hello again. Remember me? We met yesterday at Wilson's store. I'm Boyd Emory."

She hadn't noticed him waiting by the limousine, but now she recalled her last thought as she'd left him yesterday—that she would be seeing him again very soon. She hadn't expected that second meeting to be here, of all places, or at this, of all times.

He was more handsome than ever, with the chilly breeze whipping up a healthy glow beneath his tan. However, such thoughts were about as appropriate for a grave side as Herb and Lester's squabbling had been, so Gretchen stopped them.

"I remember you, Mr. Emory," she replied.

His hand remained extended, and she had no choice but to take it. Otherwise she would appear rude in front of the few mourners who were still straggling back toward their cars. His fingers were cool to the touch. Then he closed them over hers, and their palms met. The warmth there was sudden and hard to ignore, but Gretchen tried.

"Did you know my Uncle Carl?" she asked.

"I met him once and liked him. I thought I should pay my respects."

"You liked him?" Gretchen eased her hand away.

She'd encountered so few people in the north country who had anything positive to say about her uncle that Mr. Emory's statement made her instantly suspicious. Her natural intuition about the predatory male was causing her to doubt that Boyd Emory's appearance had anything to do with her uncle. She still remembered the presumptuous look in his eyes when they parted yesterday. Most likely his being here was an excuse to see her again; and a funeral was a most inappropriate place for that, in her opinion.

"You're right," he said, looking suddenly sheepish. "I didn't come here because of your uncle. Actually, I hardly knew him."

"I already guessed that," Gretchen said.

"You've got skepticism written all over you, and I admit you should have. The truth is I wanted to make an appointment to talk with you later."

"About what?" Gretchen asked. She had a feeling that by "appointment" he probably meant "date," and she was growing increasingly impatient with him about that.

"I'd rather not talk about it here," he said, as if she might once again have guessed his thoughts.

"Go ahead," Gretchen said, wanting to get this conversation over with. "Ask me whatever you wish."

"Well, if you insist," he said with obvious reluctance. "I wanted to ask you about a job."

"I beg your pardon?"

"I understand you need a handyman at the spa."

Gretchen turned abruptly away from him and toward the limousine. She couldn't help being embarrassed at having so totally misread his reason for coming here today. She didn't like the feeling or him for causing it.

"I know this isn't exactly the place for job hunting," he went on. "That's why I wanted to get together with you later on instead, but I wasn't sure when you'd be at the spa. I came here to find that out."

Gretchen could hear in his voice that he was as embarrassed as she was. "Are you looking for a permanent position?" she asked, suddenly remembering the code of genteel politeness her grandfather had tried so hard to drum into her.

"I'm not really sure. I was just traveling through."

"I see," she answered, pulling on the black leather gloves she'd taken from her coat pocket.

Gretchen knew all about handsome men who "just traveled through" resort towns like Cape Vincent. She had been warned against them since she was a girl, and she had seen them in action all over the world, usually where the sun was brightest and the bankrolls were biggest—especially the women's bankrolls.

Still, he didn't strike her as one of those jet set pretty boy types. There had always been something weak and jaded about them, and Boyd Emory didn't appear to be either. The way he stood, planted like a sturdy tree, made her think that he had never experienced a weak moment in his life. Maybe he had another story, after all. The fact remained, however, that he was a grown man, obviously capable of better things, bumming around a river town asking for odd jobs. He couldn't have *too* much going for him in the personal strength and maturity department. She suppressed the urge to give him a lecture on getting himself together and pursuing a more responsible lifestyle.

"Miss Sackett is our administrator," Gretchen said. "She would be the person to talk to about a job there. She was here a moment ago but has gone back to the spa."

"She must be the one I saw you with earlier. I think I would rather be interviewed by you."

Gretchen stared up at him. His smile might be charmingly offhand, but there was no mistaking that he was flirting this time. Her coolness dropped temperature to a decided chill.

"As I said, Mr. Emory, you have come to the wrong person. Ms. Sackett does all of our interviewing, and I wouldn't presume to trespass into her territory."

Suddenly his hand was on her arm. She looked down at it, as if she couldn't believe he'd had the nerve to put it there. Actually, the pressure of his grasp was pleasantly firm. Nonetheless, she placed her leather-gloved hand on his bare one and lifted it away. To her surprise and consternation he captured her hand this time.

"Would you do me a great service and tell Miss Sackett I'll be coming in?"

He asked that with a suggestion of pleading in his voice that was very winsome and, Gretchen was certain, equally false. Still, she wasn't entirely immune.

"I suppose I can do that much," she said, pulling her hand from his. "And I wish you the best of luck with that inquiry."

He held her one more moment, with his bright blue gaze this time. "I can't tell you how much your best wishes mean to me."

Gretchen didn't answer. There was something so intimate in his tone that it would have been inappropriate to respond. Besides, for just an instant, her voice seemed to be caught in her throat for some reason, so she simply nodded and walked away.

BOYD WATCHED as she walked toward the limo where the chauffeur was holding the door open for her. She hadn't tossed her head to let Boyd know he was dismissed, but she might as well have and he could guess why. He had overstepped the bounds of accepted behavior for a handyman, and she was putting him in his place.

She was a cool one all right. Maybe not one of those lady-of-the-manor types, after all, at least not in the readily available sense. That could make his job more complicated. Still, there was nothing Boyd liked better than a challenge. He would look at the crumbling facade of a building that had been declared beyond hope by any number of experts, but that wouldn't faze Boyd.

He'd take it on. Gretchen, on the other hand, was a facade he *intended* to crumble. And, frankly, he couldn't wait to get started.

GRETCHEN HAD the driver take her directly to the spa. She stared out at the shoreline as they drove along River Road. A lot had happened at the cemetery, and she needed to sort it all out. She wished she could order the limo to take her to the marina dock so that she could sit at the very end of the pier and watch the river flow past. She'd done some of her best thinking there when she was growing up in Cape Vincent. Now, however, she was supposedly a responsible adult; and hanging out on the pier in her funeral outfit would obviously not be acceptable behavior, especially for a Wulfert.

After all, she was a leading citizen of the community now. She could tell that by the way people like Beryll and Lester and Herb went out of their way to be attentive because they had favors to ask of her, just as the people of the town had always flocked to her grandfather when some local project needed funds. As for Mr. Emory, he was no different from the others. He wanted something from her. Remembering the frankly approving look he gave her back at the cemetery, she wondered if his goal might be more than just a job and, though there were definitely more important concerns than Boyd Emory for her to be attending to, he kept popping back into her head all the way to New Beginnings.

The tall white Victorian house stood at the top of a long driveway with a one-story addition stretching behind to house the therapeutic pool and gym. Gretchen hurried up the steps to the wide porch and through the front door into the main foyer. She was passing under the massive crystal chandelier when she was waylaid by Beryll Sackett.

"There's something I must talk with you about," Beryll said, plucking at Gretchen's coat sleeve just as she had in the cemetery.

"Of course, Miss Sackett, but first there's something I must talk to *you* about." Gretchen told herself she might as well get her promise to Emory out of the way before it slipped her mind. "A man named Boyd Emory may be coming here to look for a job as handyman. Go ahead and hire him. I'm sure he's more than qualified."

He was certain to be good at manual labor with those broad shoulders and that muscular build of his. Gretchen felt a twinge but wrote it off as disgust with herself for thinking of him in such terms.

Beryll said nothing for a moment. When she did speak, she sounded more cool and collected than usual. "We are in need of a general maintenance person, and if you're personally recommending this man, I wouldn't think of disagreeing."

The chill in Beryll's response made Gretchen's faux pas all too clear and banished Boyd Emory from her thoughts. Beryll had been running things here for a long time, and doing a fine job of it, according to all reports. Gretchen had been in town only a few days, and she was already giving orders.

"Of course, all hiring decisions are completely yours, Beryll," she said, using the administrator's first name for the first time and hoping it would ease things between them. "You may not think him qualified for the position at all."

"I would prefer that you tell me your definite wishes, Miss Wulfert. I wouldn't want to do the wrong thing."

Gretchen could see that she wasn't going to undo her mistake with Beryl as easily as she had hoped. "All right, then," she said. "I've only just met him and I know nothing of his history. But I have no objection to hiring him, though I think you might want to keep an eye on him if you do. I don't think he's truly cut out for this kind of work. I'm afraid that's as definite as I can be."

"Whatever you say, Miss Wulfert."

"Thank you."

Gretchen would have preferred a less frosty resolution to this first involvement with the operations of the family business, but right now she was anxious to see her grandfather. Unfortunately, before she could move on, Beryl darted into her path once more.

"I have to talk with you about my mother," she said.

Her efficient demeanor had suddenly dissolved into agitation, and the transformation was a bit disconcerting.

"Your mother?"

"She's in a nursing home in Florida. That's all right during the winter months when I'm down there near her. But in the summer, when I'm up here, I worry about her. I'd like to bring her to stay here at New Beginnings, just for the summers. I know it's a lot to ask, but..."

She was speaking so fast that Gretchen felt compelled to interrupt and reassure her. "Of course your mother can come here."

"But the rates are so high that I'd need to have some kind of discount. I was negotiating that with your uncle, and he was making up his mind about it. Then...he died. Now I don't know what's going to happen."

Gretchen put her hand on Beryl's arm and felt the muscles tense at her touch. "Don't worry, Beryl. I'm sure we can work something out."

"Do you really mean it? I would be so grateful."

"I mean it. My grandfather has told me what a good job you do here. We owe you this in return."

"Thank you so much, Miss Wulfert. I don't know what to say..."

"You don't have to say anything."

Gretchen smiled and patted Beryll's arm once more, then continued toward the staircase before she could be waylaid by either another deluge of gratitude from Beryll, the nervous Nellie, *or* an onslaught of chilly efficiency from Beryll, the fastidious administrator. In future encounters, Gretchen would have to be careful to be certain which Miss Sackett she was dealing with.

WHEN GRETCHEN ARRIVED two days ago, she had expected that her grandfather wouldn't look his normal self; but each time she saw him it still came as a shock. She eased the door shut very softly behind her, though she knew no sound was likely to awaken him. She tiptoed to the bed, feeling, as she had during her other visits, so overwhelmingly guilty that she could have easily sagged to the floor from the weight of it. She knew now that she shouldn't have let anything keep her away from here after he first became ill.

Frederick Wulfert's pallor was nearly the color of the pillow beneath his head. One arm lay outside the covers, and the sight of it stabbed Gretchen's heart. The arm narrowed from elbow to shoulder instead of widening as it would in a healthy person, and was bent so that she could see the fragility of the bones under the near-transparent skin. She wished she could straighten that arm and let the flesh fall slack, the way it did on so many people his age. Then she wouldn't have to look at those birdlike bones. Instead, she picked up the edge of the sheet and covered his arm, very gently, as if it might shatter from the slightest touch.

She was so concentrated on her sadness for her grandfather that she hadn't yet noticed there was another person in the room.

Chapter Three

"He's not hurting any, in case you're wondering."

Gretchen recognized Nurse Pauline Basinette immediately. She had been working at the spa for as long as Gretchen could remember, and it seemed as if she had always been as old as she was now.

"Hello, Pauline," Gretchen said with as much smile as she could muster. "I haven't seen you the other afternoons I've been here."

"I was around. I thought you'd want to have your private time with him." She nodded toward the bed.

"Thank you for that, but I have been wanting to talk with you about my grandfather's progress."

"No progress to talk about. He's been like that ever since it happened. Doesn't get better. Doesn't get worse."

If Pauline Basinette had any special feeling for her patient, Gretchen couldn't see it. There was only that impermeable north country facade. She wondered if this was the best person to be taking care of her grandfather. As she watched Pauline's arthritic fingers struggle with the clamp on the IV bag, Gretchen also wondered if the nurse might be too old for this duty as well as too lacking in emotion.

"What's in there?" Gretchen asked, pointing at the bag suspended from the pole attached to her grandfather's bed.

"Glucose mostly," Pauline said, squinting at the drip to make certain it was right. "There's some other nutrients, too, and antibiotics to prevent infections. The usual stuff."

The nonscientific sound of that explanation didn't make Gretchen any more secure about having Pauline as Frederick's primary caretaker. "You were taking care of him before he went into the coma, weren't you?"

"He wouldn't have anybody else," Pauline said with noticeable pride. "No matter what that Sackett woman had to say about it. I know she was talking behind my back, even though she's too much of a scared rabbit to say anything to my face."

"Beryll did have misgivings," Gretchen said carefully, remembering her phone conversation with Miss Sackett on the subject. "She had some questions about overall efficiency, but I agreed with my uncle that my grandfather's wishes should be respected."

"Sackett would've hired some private-duty stranger from Watertown," Pauline snorted. "He wouldn't have liked that a bit, your grandfather wouldn't."

"That's what Uncle Carl said."

"And he was right." Pauline rubbed her nose, probably the reason it was the only shiny part of her otherwise powdery and wrinkled face. "I'm honest enough to admit that uncle of yours wasn't always on my side, but this time he knew I was the best one for the job."

"I hear he spent a lot of time with my grandfather these past few weeks." Gretchen smoothed the bed sheet as Pauline hobbled around to the other side.

"I wasn't as surprised about that as most folks around here," Pauline said, pulling the covers taut and plumping Frederick's pillow around his face. "I always suspected Carl Wulfert had more heart than he let on, and I turned out to be right, at least when it came to his father. He'd be in here every day like clockwork. He'd sit and watch your grandfather like he was waiting for him to wake up and talk to him, but of course he didn't. He never did talk to Carl much. My guess is that was Carl's biggest problem."

Gretchen sighed, then turned and walked to the window. The gray sky hadn't brightened any. "Do you think that's why my Uncle Carl was—the way he was?" she asked, still staring through the glass, addressing her question as much to the universe as to Pauline.

"You mean, why he was such a mean cuss?" Pauline followed Gretchen to the window and eased herself down into the white rocker that was probably her usual seat while watching Gretchen's grandfather. "He wasn't always that way, you know. He started out a pretty good kid, as a matter of fact. As I see it, he just got tired of trying to impress his father and forever turning up a day late and a dollar short. Made him mad at the world, I'd say. Of course, the world didn't care much. They were too busy flocking around his brother, your father, to notice that Carl was even there. After a while he gave up doing nice things to get attention and started doing nasty ones, and once he'd turned that way he never turned back." Pauline smoothed her white uniform across her lap in a gesture that said she had pronounced the final truth on the subject.

"Do you remember when he changed?" Gretchen asked.

"Sure I do. I'm not getting soft in the head in my old age like some around here think." Pauline snorted again and heaved her ample bosom. "They were in their teens. Carl was about seventeen and your father about fifteen, I'd say. I remember it clear. I remember *everything* clear."

Gretchen was sure she did. Pauline was the one person left who had witnessed those years in the Wulfert family at close range and stayed in Cape Vincent to tell the tale, as she might put it.

So the bitterness had crept into River House long before Grandmother Wulfert's death. Gretchen sighed again and gazed out at the gray afternoon, wondering if perhaps that bitterness had been with the family so long that it could never be expunged.

"Do you think all of that unhappiness was the reason Uncle Carl committed suicide?" she asked, turning back to the wrinkled, powdery nurse for her answer.

Pauline stared directly into Gretchen's eyes without wavering. "You're taking for granted that's what he did."

"What do you mean? What else would he have done?"

"I don't like folks that answer a question with a question, but that's what I'm going to do right now," Pauline said, giving the arm of the rocker a solid rap to emphasize the firmness in her voice. "First, let me tell you this. When Carl Wulfert was mad about something, he hurt other people, not himself. I never saw that to fail in all the years since he was a boy in high school. Now *you* tell *me*. Does a man like that take a flying leap off a roof under his own steam, or is he most likely to make himself the kind of enemies that would give him a little nudge?"

GRETCHEN LEFT her grandfather's room in a daze, but she knew exactly where she was going. She headed straight for the narrow stairway that led through the storage attic, then up some more stairs to the roof. There had been an iron bolt on the roof door when she was a child, mostly to keep her from wandering out. That bolt was gone now. The door to the roof opened easily, then caught in a wind gust forceful enough to pull it out of her hand and slap it against the wall outside.

Dry leaves skittered across the asphalt shingles and lodged around the chimneys or drifted off the edge to flutter downward. She felt the impact of the wind full in her face as she stepped onto the roof. The gusts were strong at this height, and nearly swept her breath away as she moved toward the side where Uncle Carl had fallen. His body had been found in the east driveway that traveled around the main house to the therapy center addition, then back through the woodlot to the old Stone Cottage that had been the original structure on the property.

The pitch of the roof was nearly level here, sloping slightly to a peak that would ease the melting and sliding off of snow from heavy north country storms. This main house had been built after the Civil War on the site where a previous building had burned to the ground. The architecture was a mix of the styles that were popular in the mid- to late-nineteenth century: Victorian for the tall, narrow body of the house; Italian at the square corner tower, with her grandfather's room on its top floor; Roman Revival in the arched windows and entryways.

In keeping with that hodgepodge of styles, the roof was a French mansard—Second Empire, to be exact. That meant there was a lower slope from this level to the vertical drop-off of the building wall. That slope was concave and difficult for Gretchen to traverse in her narrow skirt and boots, but she was determined to get to the edge of the roof. She sat down at the top of the lower slope and began easing herself downward.

The rough surface of the shingles scratched the fine leather of her boots, but she kept going, only stopping once to pull her gloves from her coat pocket and put them on so that her hands wouldn't be scraped, as well. She took her coat off also and tossed it back up onto the level section of the roof. Her progress was easier after that, though she had to hitch her skirt up to make it.

Then she was at the edge of the roof. She lifted herself cautiously to her knees and steadied her balance before looking over the side. The place where Uncle Carl had landed was gruesomely evident even from this height. There had been no rain since then, so the dark stain was still visible against the pale gravel surface of the driveway. Gretchen forced back the wave of nausea that threatened to overcome her.

The stain was a few yards to her right. She edged herself in that direction. The going was more difficult sideways than it had been coming down. The asphalt caught at the wool gabardine of her suit. By the time she reached her destination, her stockings had been torn, there was a rip in her side seam and the back of her skirt was a mass of pulls and ravelings.

She leaned out once more to check the location. She was directly over the dark spot now. This must be where Carl had jumped, or . . . The horror of Pauline's suggestion made Gretchen suddenly dizzy. At just that moment a powerful wind gust struck her. It lifted the beret from her head and sent it flying. She reached out automatically before realizing where she was.

For a terrifying moment she teetered at the edge. She grabbed the rim of the roof to steady herself and threw her weight forward to counteract her perilous sway to the side. Then she was safe, but her heart was pounding and she was trembling so hard that she didn't dare move until she had regained some composure. She breathed deeply to calm herself, and that was when she saw it.

A few inches from where she still gripped the edge, there was an irregularity in the width of the eaves trough that bordered the curb of the roof. It had been pulled noticeably wider at that point, as if someone had grabbed hold there and bent it outward with his weight. Gretchen's nausea and dizziness threatened to return, but she fought them off. She looked more closely at the bend in the trough. She was almost certain she could make out the impression of two hands that had held on for all they were worth.

She could hardly believe what she was seeing. A man falling forward off the roof would have to do a 180-degree turn in midair to be in the correct position to grab this eaves trough and hang on tight enough and long enough to leave these impressions in the corrugated metal. The terrible possibility that Pauline had suggested was more than just a possibility now. It seemed the most likely scenario of all.

"I KNOW WHAT you're suggesting, and it isn't possible," Beryll Sackett said for the half-dozenth time since Gretchen had routed her out of her office and insisted she climb the three flights of stairs to the attic. "Your Uncle Carl committed suicide. That may be difficult to accept, but I'm sure he had his reasons. He wasn't a contented man."

"What *am* I suggesting?" Gretchen asked, since she had actually given Beryll no definite reason for wanting to take her to the roof.

"I wouldn't presume that I know what you're thinking," Beryll said, apparently remembering to be more her unassuming self for the moment. "But it occurs to me you're suggesting that there was something—peculiar—about his death when there wasn't. He simply jumped off the roof. I'm sure of it."

"If what you say is true," Gretchen said, "then you have nothing to fear from what I want to show you."

"What makes you think I'm fearful?" Beryll asked, but she was obviously more nervous than efficient in this situation. "I simply have a lot of work to do on the accounts and think this is a waste of time. Your uncle killed himself, and he left a note behind to prove it."

"That note was typed and unsigned. Anyone could have written it."

The note in question had been only one line long. "I'm sick of my life and everybody in it," it had said. And Gretchen had to admit that sounded like Carl—nasty-tempered to the very end. Still, there was the bend in the eaves trough to be explained.

"Please. Come with me," Gretchen pleaded. She took Beryll's arm and tugged her toward the short flight of steps that led up to the roof door, but Beryll pulled away.

"I can't," she said, growing unmistakably more breathless and shaken by the second.

Gretchen studied her for a moment. Beryll's already thin face was pinched tight, making her look almost skeletal in the shadowy attic light. By contrast her pale eyes were wide open with terror.

"You *are* afraid. Why don't you want to know the truth? Do you know something about Uncle Carl's death that the rest of us don't?"

"No. No. Nothing like that," Beryll denied, but she'd become more unnerved than ever at the suggestion.

"Then come up to the roof with me now."

"I can't," Beryll cried, her voice high and shrill. "You're right. I'm afraid."

"Afraid of what?"

"High places," she sobbed. "I can't go out on the roof. It's too high up."

"I'll be with you. I won't let you fall," Gretchen said, trying to be soothing, though she was feeling quite agitated herself.

She took Beryll's arm again, gently this time, but Beryll snatched it away. The woman lurched backward, stumbling against an old trunk and nearly toppling over it. She righted herself and dashed for the door that led downstairs.

"I'm not going up on the roof with you," she screamed. She was gripping the doorknob so tightly that the sinews in her spindly arm were drawn as taut as the pinched muscles of her face. "Carl Wulfert is dead and good riddance to him. He was a horrible man, and the world is better off without him. People in this town are better off without him, and that includes your grandfather. We don't need you setting things in an uproar. We had enough of that from your uncle when he was alive. So why don't you just leave us all alone and let us be happy he's dead?"

Beryll had shrieked that in a high-pitched, piercing voice. When she had finished, her face was dead white and her lips were quivering. She yanked the door open and ran down the stairs, trailing strangled sobs.

Gretchen stared after her. No matter how unnerved Beryll might be, it was surprising that her all-business side allowed such an outburst. She must have hated Carl a great deal, indeed. Gretchen sat down on the trunk Beryll had nearly fallen over. The very adamancy of Beryll's denial made Gretchen doubt the truth of it. "Me thinks the lady protests too much," she remembered vaguely from a long-ago English class in one of the fancy private schools her grandfather had picked out for her.

Beryll's extreme reaction and her automatic assumption that Gretchen suspected there was something "peculiar" about Uncle Carl's death had made her more suspicious than ever about everything, and that suspicion now suddenly included Beryll's alleged fear of heights. Gretchen hadn't yet said anything about the roof when Beryll started working herself into a state. Besides, what proof was there that she really was acrophobic? She was a smart woman, no matter how nervous she might be. Maybe her supposed phobia was actually a clever way of creating doubt that she could have been out on the roof with Carl that day. She obviously hated him. She'd shouted it all over this attic just moments ago. Could that hatred have driven her to do something desperate? And why exactly did she feel so strongly about him?

Gretchen sighed and stood up. Too many questions. Too few answers, and she was no detective. These were questions for the professionals to be asking, and that was precisely what she needed now—a professional. Her grandfather would, without doubt, disapprove, but she was going to the police.

That resolve had carried her down the stairs to the third floor on her way to the telephone when she noticed a door that had been ajar slide silently closed. It was Gretchen's guess that if she opened that door quickly, she would find Pauline listening on the other side. Nurse Basinette had been known for her curiosity for as long as Gretchen could remember.

Gretchen didn't open the door. She hurried down the next flight of stairs instead, more eager than ever for a professional opinion.

THE SHERIFF WAS A SHORT, stocky man but more agile than Gretchen would have expected, given his build. He sidestepped at a crouch along the edge of the roof instead of getting down on all fours as she had done. He also made no secret of his displeasure at being called upon to do so. He'd been skeptical from the moment he arrived at New Beginnings in response to her call.

"What can I do for you?" he had asked.

She'd told him her suspicions.

"Where'd you get that idea?" was his incredulous reply.

"It was a logical deduction," she'd answered.

She could hear how vague that answer sounded, while he was so obviously taking in every detail of her raveled skirt and torn stockings and just as obviously thinking he had been dragged out here on the whim of a foolish and flighty woman. He didn't appear to have changed that attitude as he crouched now to get a closer look at the bend in the trough that Gretchen had pointed out to him.

"Uh-huh. I see it," he said matter-of-factly.

He had helped her down to the dormer on the lower slope of the mansard not far from that spot, but dissuaded her from following farther. He moved cautiously along the roof border to the corner, then around that corner to the rear side of the house, examining the eaves trough as he went. He stopped a few yards from the corner of the roof to crouch lower for a moment before straightening again and making his way back to Gretchen.

"There's another bend in the trough over there, very similar to the one you showed me," he said. "See that branch?" They were at treetop level, but some of the older trees had thick branches even up this high. "The wind can whip those around pretty good when it gets blowing hard. A branch probably smashed against that trough and bent it." He gestured toward the rear of the house. "No telling how long ago that was. Most likely that's what happened over here, too."

"But there's no tree on this side."

"Look down, right there on the other side of the driveway."

With the dormer to hang on to Gretchen could lean out far enough to see where he was pointing. There was a wide tree stump just across the driveway from the tell-tale stain. The stump had been cut close to the ground and painted black.

"Dutch elm disease got it, I'd imagine," the sheriff said. "And judging from the size of that stump, I'd say she was a real tall tree once. Would have had branches plenty long enough to reach over to this roof, and plenty big enough to knock a dent in that trough. My guess is that's what happened here, Miss Wulfert."

"It's just that there were so many people who didn't like my uncle, and he wasn't the type who would kill himself."

"If there's one thing I've learned on this job, it's that you never can tell what type of person anybody is until they've been pushed hard enough for it to come out," the sheriff said with an indulgent smile. "As for folks not liking your uncle, if everybody somebody didn't like around here got murdered, we'd be hip-deep in corpses."

"In this case I have reason to believe there are a number of people who wanted things from my uncle, and he wasn't exactly what you would call a giving person. I wonder if one of those people might have been angry enough to kill him."

"I knew Carl. Like you say, he wasn't a generous man, and I don't doubt he made enemies. Still, this doesn't strike me as north country type killing. Folks up here get out of control, they're most likely to grab a shotgun and do their business with that. But I think the truth here is probably a lot simpler. Your uncle didn't have any friends, if you'll forgive me saying that, miss. I'd guess that with his father so bad off, Carl may just have been too lonely to go on."

Gretchen searched for an argument to that home-grown wisdom but couldn't find one. She had wanted an alternate explanation, and here it was. Carl Wulfert had put a solitary and pathetic end to his solitary and pathetic life. Only a flighty, foolish person would question further, or perhaps somebody as cantankerous and naturally suspicious as Pauline Basinette. Gretchen hadn't even mentioned the old nurse to the sheriff. Gretchen knew how it would sound to base an argument on the word of a local busybody and sometime crank.

She hadn't brought up Beryll's overadamant denials, either. It struck Gretchen that she hadn't told the sheriff about either woman because this supposed evidence was very flimsy, and she would have been embarrassed to admit she had no stronger reason for jumping to the wild conclusion that her uncle had been murdered.

She breathed a sigh of relief as the sheriff took her arm and helped her back up to the more level slope of the roof.

"Listen here, Miss Wulfert," he said when she was still reluctant to leave the roof altogether. "You're used to the big city where it makes sense to be looking for foul play around every corner. Up here things are usually simpler than that."

Gretchen nodded slowly. Uncle Carl's death appeared to be a simple suicide. Nothing she'd found on this roof proved otherwise. Whatever doubts remained only proved that, no matter how much time she'd spent away from home, she was still a native of the north country where skepticism was bred in the bone.

BOYD HAD WAITED until the day after the funeral to show up at New Beginnings asking for a job. He didn't want to seem disrespectful of the dead, but he couldn't afford to delay any longer. His logical source of information, Frederick Wulfert, was out of commission. The son, Carl, who may have known the truth about what went on here all those years ago, was dead. Gretchen was still around, but Boyd had a feeling she wouldn't know much, other than things she didn't realize she knew.

Thus, Boyd's only recourse was to search this place and see what he could find. Meanwhile, the trail that was already decades old was getting older every day. What if the blond beauty really did know something, or even suspected, and had decided to start covering up for the sake of the good old family name? She could destroy whatever evidence there might be before he had a chance to track it down. He couldn't allow her the time to do that, so he had taken her advice and come to see Beryll Sackett.

He had seen her at the cemetery. She was only a bit less bundled up today indoors. She was dressed in layers of bulky wool, what looked like two sweaters under a jacket and heavy slacks that hung on her scrawny figure. She had stiffened herself into the most officious posture she could manage under all those clothes—back straight, neck and shoulders rigid. He could imagine her knees clamped together under the desk to keep them from knocking audibly.

"You aren't exactly what I expected when Miss Wulfert mentioned you would be coming in, Mr. Emory," Beryll said in a clipped, businesslike tone.

"She mentioned me?"

"Yes, she did."

"I must have made a better impression on her than I realized." Remembering Gretchen's attitude when she took her leave of him at the cemetery, Boyd would have thought she'd dismissed him from her mind immediately, along with her promise to tell Sackett about him.

Beryll picked up a stack of papers and tapped the edges neatly together against her immaculate desk blotter. "I'd say you made quite an impression on her."

"I'm happy to hear that."

"Don't be overly happy, Mr. Emory. It was a mixed impression at best."

"Please, feel free to call me Boyd."

"I prefer last names in a business situation," she said, cutting off his attempt to be less formal.

Boyd was surprised she had the nerve to speak to him like that. She had seemed so much less confident when he observed her yesterday at the cemetery. Of course, she was on her own turf now. Boyd was reminded of a schoolteacher he had once, small and quavering until she got into her classroom, where she was unquestionably in charge. She'd even stood up to Max, and that really took nerve.

"As I was about to say, Mr. Emory, Ms. Wulfert said she didn't object to your being hired, but she obviously had some misgivings about whether you were suited to this kind of work. Now that I meet you, I can see why. There's a great deal of heavy and monotonous labor here at New Beginnings. This job isn't what someone like you might call 'a piece of cake.' ''

Boyd shifted his tall frame in the too-narrow, antique chair. This woman's sudden feistiness was beginning to annoy him. He'd felt the same way about that schoolteacher, as he recalled. "I'm not afraid of hard work," he said with impatience creeping into his tone.

"I'll have to take your word for that for now, but you should bear in mind that I'll be keeping an eye on you. In fact, Ms. Wulfert instructed me to do exactly that."

Boyd felt more uncomfortable than ever in this chair that hadn't been built with a man's dimensions in mind. What had he done to make Gretchen distrust him already? Whatever it was, the result could be most unfortunate. Being under Beryll Sackett's scrutiny would make his search more difficult and riskier, as well. As for Gretchen, he'd have to come up with a way to distract her from her suspicions and do it fast.

"Do I get the job, anyway?" he asked.

"Ordinarily we have our applicants fill out a form or give us a job résumé. Frankly, Mr. Emory, I have a feeling the information you might give me would be—shall we say—less than complete." She favored him with a thin-lipped, chilly smile.

"Why do you think that?"

"When a man like yourself—obviously intelligent, probably educated, most likely well traveled—applies for a handyman's position, one can assume he's either running away from something..." She paused significantly. "Or, if he has your *special* qualifications, one can assume he has other motives."

The sarcastic way she said that and looked him up and down as she did so struck Boyd with a sudden flash of comprehension. She thought he was a gigolo. She probably also thought he was after Gretchen Wulfert and her money. He wouldn't have expected such a uptight lady to be so perceptive. Luckily she had the wrong spin on the bit of truth she had perceived.

"Miss Wulfert said that if I judged you qualified for the position, I should give it to you. I expect you're eminently qualified for carting boxes and bagging trash, whatever your motives." She gave the sheaf of papers one last tap, then set them aside.

"I guess that means I *do* have the job." Boyd stood up, smoothing down the legs of his jeans. "I think we're going to enjoy working together," he added, though he doubted that was true.

"That remains to be seen, Mr. Emory," Beryll said, standing also with her hands clasped in front of her.

Boyd didn't offer to shake one of those hands. She might refuse, and that would be awkward. He anticipated enough future awkwardness in dealing with Beryll Sackett. There was no need to get started on it now. Instead, he bent slightly at the waist in a semblance of a deferential bow that he hoped didn't come across as mocking. He didn't want her as an enemy. That could get in the way of a smooth operation for him here, when what he wanted most was to get the information he needed and get out as rapidly as he could manage it.

Outside Beryll's office he stopped to contemplate the other thing he had learned from this interview, besides what Miss Sackett thought of him. Gretchen Wulfert had recommended him for this job. Whether that recommendation had been wholehearted or not, it still indicated that she hadn't banished him completely from her consciousness. In fact, according to Beryl, he'd made a considerable impression on Miss Wulfert. Maybe he was getting to her, after all. That would certainly make his job easier, but he had better do some more homework before they met again.

An image of her pale blond hair and fair skin interrupted his calculations, and for a moment he wondered whether getting out of here fast was really what he wanted to do.

"It had better be," he muttered to himself in a warning tone as he resolved to police such thoughts straight out of his head from now on.

Chapter Four

The rest of the morning went smoothly for Boyd, especially once he met Pauline Basinette, the aging nurse in charge of Frederick Wulfert. She was as warm to Boyd as Beryll had been cold, and soon they were on a first-name basis.

"How long have you been working here, Pauline?" he asked as he stacked empty cartons in the third-floor pharmacy.

"Close to half a century," she said proudly. Then she added with a coy twinkle in her eye, "But if you're trying to find out how old I am, I'll never tell."

Boyd chuckled and she laughed along. "I never ask a lady to part with her secrets," he said, though that was exactly what he intended to do. "Things must have changed a lot here since you came."

"We were much smaller then. Only used the top floor here for patients, except when we had real contagious ones and they were kept down back in Stone Cottage so they wouldn't infect anybody." She took two sheets and two pillow slips from the pile she'd had Boyd carry from the linen closet and walked out of the pharmacy toward Frederick's room with Boyd following close behind. "Business picked up after the war. We started getting a fussier brand of customers. After that, nothing much was the same."

Boyd's attention perked up. He was glad he was walking behind her so that she wouldn't notice. "What started those fussier folks coming here?" The minute the question was out of his mouth, he knew he should have led up to it more subtly, but it was too late for that now.

She eyed him warily for a moment. "Why would you be wondering about that?"

"Just curious." He hoped his offhand manner would disarm the natural north country suspicion he saw in her face. "People are always telling me I'm too nosy for my own good, but sometimes I think I must have been born that way. I just have to know everything about everything. All you have to do is tell me to get lost if I get carried away."

"I'll bet I can guess what you really want to know about." Pauline's wariness seemed to have disappeared, and she was obviously teasing him now.

"What is it I really want to know about?"

"Not *what*—*who*. You want to know all about Gretchen Wulfert." Pauline looked very satisfied with herself for having figured that out.

Boyd opened the door to Frederick's room for her. "What makes you say that?"

"That fancy-pants administrator hinted there might be more than meets the eye between you and Miss Gretchen."

"Beryll Sackett said that? Are you two in the habit of swapping gossip?"

"Hardly," Pauline snorted as she laid the sheets on the stand next to Frederick's bed. Her voice had lowered to a near-whisper. "You were asking what's changed in my time here. Well, I'll tell you one of those changes I don't care for one bit, and that's having the likes of that Sackett woman breathing down my neck with all her rules and regulations. We ran this place just fine before she came along, and we'll run it just fine after she's gone. I pray that happens soon.''

Pauline cast her glance heavenward for a moment. She'd raised her voice some during that angry speech. Now she caught herself and put a hushing finger to her lips.

''Maybe we shouldn't talk here,'' Boyd said, motioning toward the frail figure in the bed.

''He can't hear us none,'' Pauline said, speaking softly again. ''I just try to keep things peaceful around him.''

''So what can you tell me about Miss Gretchen?'' If he couldn't get Pauline to talk about the past, maybe he could find out something useful about the present. He told himself he had no more personal interest in Gretchen Wulfert than that.

''See? I told you I knew what you really wanted to hear about,'' the nurse said with a grin that wrinkled her round cheeks.

She had removed the blanket and the top sheet from the bed and was rolling Frederick gently onto his side in order to free the other half of the bottom sheet so that she could take it off the bed and substitute a fresh one.

''Let me help you with that.'' Boyd stepped forward to offer assistance.

''No,'' she said abruptly, and put up her hand to stop him. ''No offense meant, but I scarcely ever let anyone take care of Mr. Wulfert. He's my responsibility.''

Boyd stepped back and watched Pauline continue her sheet-changing. It occurred to him that she did seem to be going out of her way to be gentle with the old man, especially considering the fact that he was unconscious and most likely to stay that way. Boyd wondered if that extra-gentle care might indicate some personal attachment between nurse and patient and, if there was such an attachment, how far back it might go.

"Well, are you going to tell me about Gretchen Wulfert or not?" he asked in a lighthearted tone, as if he had nothing more serious in mind than going along with Pauline's teasing.

"How much do you know about her already?"

"Nothing really. We only met a couple of days ago. Then I saw her again yesterday after the funeral."

"I'll bet she wasn't looking all that grief-stricken, either, was she?" Pauline's voice had hardened some, but her attentions to Frederick remained as tender as ever.

"Why do you say that?"

"There was no love lost between her and her uncle. Not on Gretchen's side, anyway."

"Why did she dislike him?"

"He used to bedevil her a lot when she was a little girl, teasing her, bothering her when she didn't care to be bothered, that kind of thing. But, more than that, she hated him for running her mother and father out of Cape Vincent and nearly busting up their marriage to boot, though nobody ever told her about that last part."

"How did he manage to nearly bust up their marriage?"

Boyd was careful to maintain his casual tone. He was worried about pressing too hard for personal details about the Wulfert family. On the other hand, he needed to test the limits of how much Pauline was willing to talk about.

"Gretchen's daddy wasn't the most faithful husband I ever met," Pauline answered, apparently without a qualm. "I expect he needed the attention he got from all those young girls down at the marina. Some of you men are like that.'' She made a disgusted little snort before continuing. ''I doubt he cared much about them. He loved Gretchen's mother. You could tell that. I expect she knew the truth about him, too. Everybody in town did, and she was one smart lady. Still, as long as nobody talked to her face about his carrying on, they got on all right in their own way. Until Carl did what he did, that is.'' Pauline shook her head hard with disapproval, as if she still felt very strongly on the subject.

''What did Carl do?''

''He went straight to Gretchen's mother and spelled it all out, all about Mr. Wulfert's philandering, with names and dates and everything. After that there wasn't likely to be much pretending like there hadn't been some playing around going on.''

''Why do you think Carl did that?''

''Jealousy, pure and simple. I'd bet my silver tooth he was crazy in love with Gretchen's mother from the minute he laid eyes on her. I saw him gawking at her more than once. It was the same old story as always. His brother got whatever he wanted in life, especially where people were concerned, and Carl got the leavings. But that Carl didn't get mad. He got even.''

''What happened after he told Gretchen's mother what had been going on?''

Pauline pulled the fresh sheet and blanket over Frederick's wraith-thin body and smoothed them gently around him before answering. She walked to the white rocker by the window, hobbling as she went, and sat down.

''There was a big blow-up, and that isn't something that happens real often in the Wulfert family. They generally keep the lid on their feelings, but not that time. Old

Frederick here was fit to be tied. Finally Gretchen's
mother put her foot down and said if she and Gretchen's
father didn't move out of this place, she was leaving him.
Before you could turn your head they were gone to Florida, bag and baggage. They've never come back, neither."

"How did Gretchen feel about that?"

"She was off to college by then. Nobody told her the
real reason it happened, just that Carl and her mother
couldn't get along. Still, Gretchen was so mad that she
came straight back here and ran her Uncle Carl up one
side and down the other even worse than her mother had.
Miss Gretchen went so far as to tell him she'd like to kill
him for breaking up her family and that he was the one
who should be getting out, seeing as how nobody wanted
him around, anyway."

"I can't imagine her that angry. She's always so cool."

"Well, she wasn't cool then. Nobody was. Things had
been going bad for the family before that happened, but
there was no saving it after."

Boyd saw her glance toward the bed with what looked
like pity in her eyes before she put on the flat, noncom-
mittal expression he'd observed on so many faces up
here. He understood what it meant. The curtain was
down, the shop was closed, there was nobody home and,
definitely, no more information would be forthcoming.

Pauline had gone back to staring out the window. She
barely nodded as he said goodbye and slipped quietly out
of the room.

GRETCHEN ARRIVED earlier than usual that afternoon for
her visit with her grandfather. She stopped by Beryll
Sackett's office to check on things and was told that Boyd
Emory had, indeed, come in looking for a job as she'd

said he would. In fact, he'd been at work all morning cleaning up the side yard, and now he was up in the attic getting started on organizing things there.

A few minutes later Gretchen was on her way to the attic. Her grandfather would expect her to welcome a new employee on behalf of the family. He had always done things like that himself, and now that he wasn't able to she must take his place. The fact that this particular employee made Gretchen a bit uneasy didn't alter her responsibilities, and there was no time like the present to fulfill them.

Boyd obviously hadn't heard her approach up the carpeted attic stairs, because he didn't turn around when she appeared in the open doorway. He had his back to her and was lifting a heavy trunk to carry it to the far end of the attic where he'd already lined up several others. It was stuffy, and he'd taken off his shirt. He bent to grasp the trunk at either end, and the muscles of his back moved beneath his smooth, tanned skin into a ridge as tense as steel down both sides of his spine. The soft, faded denim of his jeans pulled taut along his thighs. Gretchen reminded herself of how often she'd seen men with exquisite bodies and far less covering them on beaches all over the world. There was no reason she should find this one any more disturbing than the rest.

Meanwhile, Boyd was walking to the other end of the long attic with the trunk. She remembered these trunks well. She had loved to play up here when she was a little girl. She would dress up in old clothes from the ancient clothes press in the corner, pull out yellowed papers from the trunks and pretend she was reading to her dolls. Her grandfather had been horrified when he found her. Apparently those papers she'd been tossing merrily around were pages of the priceless family history that he was so

dedicated to preserving. The attic was off-limits to
Gretchen after that.

She was smiling fondly at that memory as Boyd set the
trunk down on the floor, but what he did next wiped the
smile from her lips. He was unclamping the metal hasps
that held the trunk lid shut. Gretchen took a step inside
the doorway to get a better look at what exactly he was
doing. There could be no mistaking what she saw. He had
lifted the lid of the trunk and was searching, very intently, through the papers inside.

THE MOMENT HE TURNED around and saw her standing
there Boyd knew he had made a crucial error. He looked
guilty as hell, crouched over this trunk and pawing
through it like a kid caught with his fist in the cookie jar.

He looked guilty while she looked perfect—perfect
hair, flawless skin, expensive cashmere touching her body
in just enough places to show it off well without being
obvious. Most perfect of all was the face, with those
green eyes staring straight at him, revealing nothing. He
longed to tousle that perfect hair and wrinkle the cashmere. More than anything, he wanted to see something
other than cool confidence in those eyes.

Suddenly he knew what he had to do to distract her
from his searching of these trunks *and* to break through
her coolness, as well, if only for a moment. He stood up
and walked toward her, staring straight back into her
unyielding eyes. As he lengthened his stride to close the
gap between them, he saw it happen—a flicker of surprise in her calm green gaze.

Then he was near enough to grab her; and he did,
pulling her to him before she could think to escape, and
covering her lips with his before she could speak or cry
out. He breathed deeply, drawing in the scent of her as

his mouth moved on hers, savoring the softness and un-expected warmth he found there. He molded his body to hers, so tight and close that there was no chance she could get away. And, as he did, the soft fabric of her sweater seemed to melt from between them, and he could feel the roundness of her breasts against his chest almost as if it were her smooth, bare skin pressing his.

A jet stream of heat seared his loins, and for an in-stant he would have sworn she was naked in his arms. He could feel her and smell her and taste her as she would be at the moment he was about to make her his own, and that moment was sweet torture. Suddenly he could hardly think, other than to register that he had never experi-enced anything like this before. Then the faculty of rea-son returned and, with it, the awareness that he had to be in control right now and attentive to his purpose.

He had slid his hand across her shoulder to her neck and was holding her head so that she couldn't twist away from him. She had begun to move against him, strug-gling to get free. She was stronger than he would have guessed, and that would have inflamed him more if he let it. Meanwhile, he had his own struggle going on, to keep from forgetting what this kiss was really about. He thrust his tongue between the lips he wouldn't allow to close against him, but no amount of self-control could pre-vent his noticing that the depths of her mouth were ago-nizingly sweet. The groan that rose in his throat was beyond his power to repress.

For only a second or two, so briefly that later he would wonder if he'd imagined it, he sensed rather than heard an answering moan beneath her breast and felt her resis-tance falter for no longer than a second or two. Then she was fighting him again, more fiercely than ever. His physical strength was still far superior to hers. He could have continued to overwhelm her with little effort, but those two seconds of vulnerability, whether real or imagined, had done their work. He couldn't bring himself to force his attentions on her any longer. He released her from his grasp as abruptly as he had dragged her into it and retreated a step backward.

He'd thought she might run away as soon as he let her go, but she stood her ground absolutely rigid in front of him and stared into his face. He could hear her breath coming hard and ragged and more unmistakably outraged by the instant. The green of her eyes had turned so dark that scarcely any color remained. By contrast a spot of bright red fired each cheek, stark against her pallor. But it was her lips that caught and held his attention. They were swollen from his bruising kiss, but softened, as well. He was torn by the urge to reach out and touch them gently. He fought to suppress that instinct as Gretchen took her own step backward.

He saw her right fist clench at her side and even noted it beginning to rise. If he hadn't been so preoccupied by his conflicting emotions, he would have connected the significance of those two actions more quickly than he did and stepped out of range. Instead, he continued to gaze into the dark green of her eyes as her fist arched, exactly on target, propelled by the passion of her rage.

Her blow struck him square on the jaw, and so solidly he felt an explosion of real pain that startled him from his daze. He raised his arm to ward off another assault in case one was forthcoming, but he didn't touch her. She took another step backward but didn't swing again, though he couldn't remember ever having seen the imprint of fury so unmistakably emblazoned upon a face.

She didn't say anything, either, being most likely too angry to manage words at the moment. She spun away from him toward the doorway and stormed through it to disappear rapidly down the stairs. Boyd gaped after her, his head still reeling from the force of her punch. Several seconds passed before he recognized the potential foolishness of what he had just done. He might have distracted her for the moment from asking him what he had been doing in that trunk. In the bargain, however, he could very well have literally kissed himself out of the job he'd so carefully wangled himself into.

On the other hand, what he *had* accomplished was to dispel forever the myth that Gretchen Wulfert was an ice princess to the bone. The mark of her fiery temper still smarted on his cheek, and the body of the woman he had held in his arms was anything but cold and hard, though the memory of it sent a shiver through him. In fact, he continued to feel a tension in his thighs that had only abated slightly since he'd released her from his grasp. He hadn't expected to react so strongly to a single kiss. Now he wondered whose facade had actually been melted in the heat of that embrace—hers or his.

He touched the tender spot where her fist had connected with his jaw, then let his fingers stray to his lips, which were as swollen as he'd observed hers to be. The part of him that was more human than logical couldn't help thinking that the experience might have been worth whatever it had cost.

GRETCHEN FOUND the back stairs from the third floor more by instinct than by conscious movement. She was too shaken to be conscious of much of anything, other than her desire to get somewhere private and collect herself. Her palm still throbbed painfully from the force of the blow she'd delivered in the attic, so much so that she had to use her left hand to open the door of her Uncle

Carl's office when she finally reached it. She slipped inside quietly, feeling a bit like a trespasser to be creeping around this way, and turned the lock behind her.

There was no denying that she was badly shaken or that she knew the reason why.

"Of all the impertinent, arrogant men," she spluttered to the empty office, but she understood that had little to do with the turmoil she was feeling.

She had run into plenty of impertinent, arrogant men in her travels; and not a one of them could have set her ajangle like this. Boyd Emory was different because he had managed to insert himself inside the barricade she kept around her emotions. None of those others, impertinent and arrogant or not, had ever done that. Men had kissed her passionately before; and she had *let* them do it, but not until she had her defenses firmly in place. Emory had taken her by surprise. If she had been ready for him, she would hardly have noticed either his mouth or his arms. She was reasonably certain of that. At least he wouldn't have succeeded in getting so close, which was far too close for her.

How could she have let this happen? Disgusted with herself, she trudged across the room and plopped into the worn leather chair behind her uncle's desk. What she had to do right now was busy herself with other thoughts and activities that would distract her from Boyd Emory once and for all. She looked around her uncle's office. This is what she should be concentrating on—the family business that had been left without leadership now that Carl and Frederick Wulfert were both gone from this chair. She pulled open a drawer, saw the unruly mess of papers inside and pushed it shut again.

She was deluding herself. She hadn't the first idea of how to go about running a health spa and rejuvenation clinic. She'd been content all these years to leave that to Carl, just as everybody else had done. She was completely out of touch with the operation of New Beginnings. She wasn't even sure she felt up to taking on such a big responsibility right now when her self-control was apparently so precarious that she could be knocked off balance by one kiss.

In the meantime, thank heaven for Beryll Sackett. She'd be able to keep things running smoothly around here until Gretchen could get her bearings. That meant she'd better not take a chance of losing Beryll, which brought to mind her anxious request concerning her mother. Gretchen would have to make sure that arrangements were finalized for bringing Mrs. Sackett here in the spring. Beryll had said the paperwork was ready for Carl's signature when he died. Gretchen would be the one to do that signing now, and there was no time like the present to get at it.

Several filing cabinets lined one wall of the office. Gretchen tried the handles. Most were locked, but the ones containing recent patient records and applications weren't. She searched through the folders twice without success. Then it occurred to her that if this was a current case, her uncle might have had the file out to work on it. She went back to the desk and began to search in earnest.

Going through the disorder her uncle had left behind wasn't as easy as flipping through the files had been, but her efforts finally paid off. She found the manila folder she was looking for stuffed into the back of the lap drawer. The application for Beryll's mother, Eva Sackett, to come to New Beginnings was inside. Uncle Carl had apparently spent some time going over it. Gretchen recognized his nervous doodles along one of the margins, but that wasn't what caught her eye and struck her as really curious.

The handwriting was very neat, with the sort of upright, meticulous lettering she would expect of Beryl, but the application was dated last spring. Yesterday Beryl had made it very clear how important this matter was to her. Why hadn't it been acted on months ago? Uncle Carl's stinginess was most likely the answer. He would have hated the thought of letting any patient in here at the discount Beryl was asking for. In fact, Gretchen was surprised that he had even considered the application long and seriously enough to make doodles in the margin. She would have thought a flat-out "No!" more typical of him.

Well, whatever her uncle's reasons for delaying this application so long, Gretchen wouldn't delay it any longer. She signed the form at the bottom and dated it, feeling suddenly better about herself, as if this act of both kindness and sound business judgment redeemed her somewhat from her earlier foolishness in the attic.

AN HOUR OR SO EARLIER, from inside the darkened third-floor pharmacy, someone had watched Gretchen walk past on her way to the attic. The watcher noted that the once-chubby child had grown into a good-looking woman. Of course, her photographs in the society columns had thoroughly documented that beauty for all to see. Frederick Wulfert could have demanded more discretion from his granddaughter, but how could he be expected to know the first thing about discretion? Wasn't he always calling attention to himself with conspicuous charity and that man-of-the-people pose of his? Still, Frederick had his uses.

The watcher didn't try to leave this hiding place after Gretchen passed by. The pharmacy was a secure spot, with visibility in both directions up and down the hallway and a lab table to hide behind in case somebody came. It was relatively easy to get into places and stay as long as necessary without being detected. The secret was slow, quiet movements and never panicking, even when detection seemed unavoidable.

It was also essential to be smart—smarter than all the rest of them, smarter than you ever let anyone guess you to be. Then there was the thrill of crouching in the dark, just like now, watching people who didn't know you were there, listening to what they said, finding out information that could be of use later on.

Of course, these days there were devices to do the listening and watching for you, small metal disks and tiny all-seeing eyes that anybody could buy in any small-town electronics shop. Those devices were much more efficient than in-person surveillance, but not half as much fun. Still, without them it was difficult to catch everything that went on. There were too many gaps in the information.

The watcher was still frowning over those lapses in intelligence when Gretchen came back down from the attic in a big hurry. She was in obvious disarray, her hair disheveled, her sweater wrinkled. Even more intriguing was the expression on her face. From a distance she actually looked frightened. Then, as she hurried past, only inches away from this hiding place, the watcher revised that assessment. She looked terrified. And wasn't her lipstick smeared?

The new handyman was in the attic. What might have happened up there to make her lose her composure? She and this same handyman had been together at the ceme-

tery yesterday. They hadn't talked for long, and she had
left rather abruptly. Was there something going on between those two? Or maybe something beginning to go
on? Was she after the young stud? Or was he after her?
Wasn't that precisely what Frederick Wulfert's failure to
provide a discreet upbringing would lead to?

The watcher pondered those questions as Gretchen
disappeared down the staircase to the second floor. It was
crucial to know exactly what was going on here and how
those circumstances might be used to advantage. Thanks
to the case of small metal disks nearby, after today the
watcher would be in a perfect position to be a listener, as
well.

Chapter Five

By the time Gretchen arrived at her grandfather's room for her regular afternoon visit, she had put the incident in the attic out of her mind and was quite calm. Unfortunately Pauline Basinette's mention of Boyd Emory threatened to undo that.

"That's quite a man you hired yourself," she said while Gretchen was still pulling up a chair to sit by her grandfather's side. "If I was forty years younger, I'd give you a run for your money where he's concerned."

"That would hardly be necessary." Gretchen knew immediately who Pauline was talking about.

"Are you trying to tell me you don't think he's a fine-looking young man, with those shoulders of his and those blue eyes?"

"To tell you the truth I hardly noticed."

"If you're going to tell me the truth, then that's what you should do," the nurse said with a snort.

Pauline was standing next to the chair, looking down at Gretchen, and she could feel the red heat in her cheeks.

"Your grandfather would like him," Pauline said as she shuffled away with her lopsided, arthritic gait.

"What makes you say that? I doubt my grandfather would pay much attention to him at all."

"Then you don't know Frederick Wulfert as well as you think you do." Pauline was preparing a new IV bag from a bottle of premixed solution. "He'd take one look at Boyd Emory and say, 'There's a *real* man for you. They don't make many like that anymore.' Then he'd look over at you and start thinking about what healthy, handsome great-grandchildren you and Mr. Emory could come up with together."

"Whatever are you talking about? My grandfather wouldn't think any such thing. Boyd Emory is a handyman!"

Pauline turned from her preparations to squint hard at Gretchen. The wrinkles around Pauline's eyes were soft and powdery, but her gaze was unrelenting. It pinned Gretchen to her chair with no chance of escape.

"I'll tell you one thing your grandfather *does* think about. He wonders when you're going to get around to giving him those great-grandchildren—with Boyd Emory or anybody else. Mr. Frederick has told me more than once how nothing in this whole wide world could make him happier."

Gretchen looked at her grandfather. His expression hadn't changed, and he didn't appear to have moved a muscle since yesterday and the day before that. He obviously didn't even know she was there. He might never know anything or anyone again. The truth of Pauline's words struck Gretchen like a stinging rebuke for the way she'd lived for the past several years, with little thought of anything but her own restlessness, heeding nobody's priorities but her own. Once again she experienced the nearly overwhelming guilt that had plagued her other visits here. The feeling was even more powerful this time, as if it had been building up for years or decades or maybe even for longer than she'd been alive.

Gretchen burst up from the chair and almost ran to the window. She was determined to rid herself of these oppressive feelings and this topic of conversation, as well. "There will be a new patient next spring. I think she should be given special consideration," Gretchen said, latching onto the first subject she could think of.

"Who might that be?" Pauline asked. Her voice and expression had turned suddenly impassive, as if she regretted having strayed into such personal territory with the young woman who would someday be her employer.

"Beryl Sackett's mother. My uncle may have mentioned her."

"Oh, yes," the nurse said, drawing out the words as she carried the IV bag to the bed. "I heard about Miss Sackett wanting her mother here."

"Don't you approve?"

"It's not my place to say. And, much as I don't like somebody, I wouldn't want for their poor, old parents to suffer because of it."

"Why don't you like Miss Sackett?" Gretchen turned from the window to watch Pauline as she hooked the new IV bag to the pole.

"Let's just say we've got our differences and leave it at that. Still, I wouldn't use her mother against her the way your uncle did."

"How did he do that?"

"By dangling a patient discount in front of her nose like it was a carrot and using it to get what he wanted out of her."

"What do you mean? What did Uncle Carl want from Beryl?"

"I think you'd better ask *her* about that."

Pauline finished clamping the new IV bag into place and removed the old, flattened one. Meanwhile, she'd also clamped her lips into a firm line, signaling very clearly that she intended to say no more.

BERYLL DIDN'T ANSWER when Gretchen knocked on the door to the administrative office, though she thought for a moment that she heard someone moving around inside. Gretchen considered taking a walk around the grounds while she waited for Beryll to return, but there was a possibility that Boyd Emory might be out there doing yard work. Gretchen didn't want to risk running into him again, so she went back to Uncle Carl's office. When she came downstairs again later and finally did get a response at Beryll's office, there was no mistaking the nonwelcoming expression on her face. Their scene in the attic yesterday had obviously not been forgotten. Gretchen wondered if Beryll might have been pretending to be out earlier.

"Did you find Mr. Emory?" Beryll asked, rearranging her features into a more appropriately respectful expression.

Gretchen was amazed at how in control Beryll could be in situations like this one, though she was a nervous wreck in others.

"I found him in the attic where you said he'd be." Then a suddenly remembered suspicion supplanted all thought of Beryll's erratic personality. "By the way, what did you assign Mr. Emory to do up there?"

"I instructed him to create some order by making the trunks more easily reached. I was intending to ask if you would perhaps like to go through them while you're here. One of the local historians is eager to examine the Wulfert family papers. He feels they could be of historical significance. You may know him. His name is Herbert Dingner."

"Yes, I know him," Gretchen answered absently. She was thinking about how she'd caught Boyd going through those trunks in the attic. What had he been after?

"You might want to take some time to determine what you do and don't want Mr. Dingner to see," Beryll was saying.

"What? Oh, yes...I mean, no. My grandfather should do that. The family papers have always been a special interest of his."

Beryll didn't answer. Instead, she breathed a sad sigh and averted her eyes from Gretchen's face to the desk blotter. Gretchen quickly deduced the meaning of Beryll's silence.

"You don't think my grandfather will be able to go through those paper, do you? You don't think he'll ever come out of this coma."

"It's not unheard of that he might," Beryll said cautiously.

"You've had a lot of experience with people my grandfather's age, haven't you?"

"Yes, of course. Geriatrics is my field of expertise."

"Based on that, what do you think the chances are that my grandfather will regain consciousness?"

Beryll looked down at the blotter again for a moment, then answered in measured syllables. "The most likely scenario is that he won't awaken. The usual course of a condition such as his is that the patient fades gradually as his body functions naturally weaken due to his advanced years and sedentary state. And..." She hesitated before continuing. "Even if he should miraculously regain consciousness, there's a strong possibility of mental impairment."

"I don't suppose you're much of a believer in miracles."

"I've seen a few."

"But not many."

"No. Not many."

"I see." Considering the torment she was feeling, Gretchen had spoken those painful words so dispassionately that it might have been someone else saying them.

She'd taken a seat in the antique chair facing the old cherry wood desk. Now she found herself gripping the arms of that chair just above the place where they curved down into carved replicas of animal paws. For an instant she was certain that if she let go, she would fly apart in several directions all over the room. Nonetheless, she willed herself to unclamp her fingers, relieved that they were below desk level and, therefore, out of the line of Beryll's vision. Gretchen's grandfather had taught her long ago that such strong emotions weren't for public display.

"I appreciate your honesty," she said, still so cool that her voice seemed to echo from far off.

"I imagine you do."

That enigmatic response from Beryll and the cold tone she said it in were followed by a moment of awkward silence. Gretchen was grateful for the opportunity to switch gears to a less agonizing topic.

"I've gone over the application you filled out to have your mother come here to New Beginnings." She picked up the file folder she'd set in her lap earlier, then forgotten. "I have some questions about it."

"What kind of questions?" Beryll asked quickly.

"I'm curious about the date you made this application. That was early last spring. Why hasn't it been acted on yet?"

"Your uncle was . . . weighing the decision."

"For nearly six months?"

"He felt there were...factors to consider." Despite the obvious care with which Beryll was choosing her words, there was no mistaking her rising agitation.

"What factors?" Gretchen asked.

"Well...first of all, availability had to be taken into account."

"Beryll, this is a large facility. My grandfather often mentioned that it was never filled to capacity. In fact, he preferred it that way. He never liked having a lot of people underfoot and poking around, as he put it. I'm sure there would have been an empty room available for your mother."

"Your uncle wasn't as sure about that as you claim to be."

Beryll's fingers fussed at the corners of her blotter, tapping them straight first this way then that, though they were already perfectly aligned with the desk edge.

"Was he keeping you waiting because he didn't want to give you a discount?"

"Yes, that was it," Beryll answered, too quickly again, as if she were grabbing at a piece of flotsam in a flood, while her fingers found the neat stack of papers on her blotter and fidgeted with them. "You must be aware of how cautious he was about money."

"That's an understatement."

"Yes. I suppose it is."

"I have reason to believe my uncle was holding something else over your head, as well."

Beryll's fingers froze in midfidget, and for a long moment she sat rigidly still.

"What did my uncle want from you?" Gretchen insisted.

Those words seemed to break through Beryll's paralysis, but not pleasantly so. The muscles around her eyes and mouth twitched into motion as if sprung loose suddenly against her will.

"He told you all about it, didn't he?" Her voice was trembling. "How else could you know? I can almost hear the two of you snickering your dirty little laughs at me. You wouldn't care how he made me feel because you're just like him."

Gretchen ignored what was obviously meant to be a crippling insult. "I do care about your feelings," she said in a soothing tone as she set the file folder on the edge of the desk and got up to go to Beryll and offer her comfort.

"Don't you come near me!" Beryll leaped up, pulling the desk chair in front of her to stave off Gretchen's approach. "I wouldn't let him put his hands on me, and I won't let you touch me, either."

It was Gretchen's turn to freeze in place as the truth she'd been so eager to uncover burst upon her with all the pieces dropping instantly into place. Carl Wulfert had tried to force himself on Beryll. He had threatened her with sexual blackmail, using her extreme concern for her mother against her. Gretchen had seen enough of Beryll's uptightness to be able to imagine how frightening and even repulsive such a predicament must have been for her.

"I think I understand what happened to you," Gretchen began, "and—"

"I don't care whether you understand or not. Just stay away from me."

Beryll had lifted the chair off the floor and gripped it in front of her. Gretchen sensed Beryll's desperation and that she might be unnerved enough to use the chair for a weapon as well as a shield. Gretchen backed off around the corner of the desk.

"Please, believe me, Beryll. I'm not your enemy. Uncle Carl never told me he was threatening you. We barely spoke to each other. Pauline Basinette simply mentioned that—"

"Her!" Beryll slammed the chair down on the floor. "I wouldn't put it past that old witch to try to pin it on me."

"Pin what on you?"

"See what I mean? You *are* just like your uncle. Always lying and manipulating. Pretending you don't know what's going on when everybody in town is talking about how you dragged the sheriff up here yesterday because you think somebody pushed Carl off the roof. Now you and that shrew of a nurse are trying to make it look like *I* did it."

"Beryll, I don't think—"

"Well, I won't stand still for it. Do you hear me?" Beryll was shouting now as she advanced a menacing step toward Gretchen. "If anybody had a reason to want Carl Wulfert dead, it was Pauline Basinette. He'd already told her he was going to have your grandfather declared incompetent, which would nullify the agreement he made Carl sign to keep Pauline working here as long as she wanted to stay. He was going to get rid of her, and this place has been that old woman's life."

Gretchen was the one retreating from Beryll now. It was her words that Gretchen wanted to distance herself from. She had just about decided the sheriff was right and there was no reason to suspect that Uncle Carl hadn't jumped off the roof of his own free will. Yet today she was being assailed with motives for someone else having pushed him. She suddenly realized how much she had preferred the sheriff's version and that what she had to do right now was go off somewhere by herself and sort all of this out.

"We'll talk later," she said, backing toward the door without stopping to retrieve the file folder she had left on the desk. "You'll be calmer then."

Once again Gretchen's words appeared to strike Beryll dumb for a moment, as if she had just remembered who was employer and who was employee and that she had definitely overstepped the bounds of that relationship.

"Yes," she stammered. "We can talk later."

Gretchen slipped through the door and shut it behind her. She was tempted to run immediately up the staircase and lock herself in her uncle's office, but she stopped for a moment to catch her breath instead.

"Are you all right?"

Boyd Emory's voice was already instantly recognizable to her, and so was her reaction. She had been upset before he'd come along; now she was more so. But after what had happened in the attic, she had no intention of letting him know that.

"I'm fine," she said curtly, avoiding his bright blue gaze and straining to give the impression that his presence was of no consequence to her.

"I heard loud voices and thought there might be trouble. Then when I saw you come out of there just now looking so rattled, I thought you might need some help."

"Did you hear or *over*hear those loud voices, Mr. Emory?" she snapped.

"Are you trying to suggest I was eavesdropping?"

"I'm more than suggesting it." She walked past him to the staircase with her head held high and her back straight in her best don't-trifle-with-me posture. At the foot of the staircase she turned. "And when I need your help I'll ask for it. In the meantime, confine your efforts to the tasks Miss Sackett assigns you, which doesn't include snooping through my family's private papers—in the attic or anywhere else.''

Then she was off up the stairs, taking each step firmly and decisively in a manner that she hoped would discourage any response from him. She didn't look back to see if he was watching her, but she could *feel* him doing exactly that.

BOYD HAD THREE STRIKES against him with Gretchen, and he knew it. First, she'd caught him searching the attic, which meant that from now on she'd probably have the staff on alert to make sure he didn't do anything like that again. Second, he'd upset her so much by kissing her that she'd hauled off and belted him. And third, she suspected him of listening at keyholes. That was almost exactly what he'd been doing, of course, but he didn't want her to know it. The worst part was that he hadn't even heard anything. He could tell the voices were loud and angry, at least Beryll's had been; but these old oak doors were too thick for anything more intelligible than that to get through.

As for Gretchen, he would have to figure out some way to improve her opinion of him. For the moment, however, Boyd was thinking about how provocatively her hips had swung beneath her slacks as she marched away from him up the stairs.

WHEN GRETCHEN ENTERED her grandfather's room, Pauline was in the rocker once more. She'd moved it away from the window and toward the foot of the bed, probably so she could see her patient more clearly. It occurred to Gretchen that there was little likelihood her

grandfather would make any movement worth watching
for, but she was glad to see that Nurse Basinette remained attentive, anyway.

"Did you talk to Beryll Sackett?" the old nurse asked.

"What? Oh, yes. I did."

Gretchen had almost forgotten the scene in Beryll's
office. It had been upsetting enough, but not nearly as
much so as encountering Boyd Emory unexpectedly. He
had a way of making Gretchen very annoyed, indeed.

"What did she have to say?" Pauline asked.

"She explained the situation with Carl." Gretchen had
no intention of going any farther than that on the subject of Beryll. She wasn't about to spread gossip if she
could help it. So, before Pauline could question her more,
Gretchen went on. "She also told me something interesting about *your* relationship with him."

"What's that?" Pauline appeared to be as undis-
turbed by the subject as Beryll had been agitated.

"She told me that Uncle Carl was going to have
grandfather declared incompetent and then let you go."

"He'd been making noises like that." A whimsical
smile wrinkled Pauline's powdery face as she looked
Gretchen over for a moment. "You think I may have
bumped him off to keep my job?"

"I didn't say that." Gretchen guessed that Pauline
would also have heard the talk in town about the sheriff's visit to New Beginnings.

"Whether you say it or not, the truth is that Carl was
wasting his time. I'm too close to retirement to care much
if I get fired. I'd still have my pension, and I've got a nice
nest egg set by so I don't need the money. Sure, I like
what I do here, but I'm getting tired of working every
day."

Pauline looked Gretchen over again, then turned her gaze back to her patient. "That's all I've got to say on the subject. You can believe it, or you can believe Sackett. It doesn't make much difference to me either way. I know what's true from what's not."

Gretchen's instincts told her she should probably believe Pauline because the woman did seem to talk such good sense. At this point in a very unsettling day, however, Gretchen wasn't sure she should trust her own judgment on what good sense might be.

GRETCHEN LEFT New Beginnings shortly after her conversation with Pauline and escaped to the relative serenity of River House. Unfortunately being serene wasn't in the cards for her that day. She roamed the rooms and the riverbank, trying to occupy her restless thoughts for the remainder of the afternoon and into the evening. It was then that she began to notice how uncomfortably chilly the house had become. Last night might have been almost as cold, but she hadn't been affected by it. Today's events had obviously left her more vulnerable than usual.

She found a long knit shawl that had probably once been deep purple but had faded with age and laundering to a soft mauve. The washings had also thickened the weave, and Gretchen was grateful for the added warmth as she went from room to room in search of the thermostat. She finally found it in the library, and the source of the problem with the room temperature was immediately obvious. Someone had installed a locked box around the regulating mechanism. Through the Plexiglas Gretchen could see that the dial had been set at a low figure for this time of year. That would be Uncle Carl's handiwork, she was sure. He would rather freeze than spend extra for fuel. That was his nature, but it was definitely not hers.

She had seen a stack of firewood in the rear shed, but she didn't really feel up to the effort of kindling a blaze in one of River House's many gigantic fireplaces. She would do that tomorrow night. For now, her plan was to break into the thermostat and turn it up to a sensible level. All she needed was a hammer, and the logical place to look for one was in the cellar.

She remembered the River House cellar from her childhood, and all of those memories came flooding back the minute she opened the door off the kitchen. The smell of years of root vegetable storage, coal bins and being below the ground on a riverbank rushed up to greet her, bringing the past with it. The root cellar and the coal bins had been gone for a long time now, of course, but Gretchen was certain she could detect the distinctive odor of both. Maybe that was because they held such vivid connections for her.

She was halfway down the stairs and all the way into those memories when that all-too-familiar, decidedly masculine voice assaulted her for the third time today.

"Miss Wulfert, are you here?"

She could tell he was in the morning room. She must have left the French doors unlatched, and he had actually had the nerve to let himself in. She stood quietly on the cellar stairs, contemplating the possibility that if she stayed right here and snapped off the light, Boyd Emory might give up and go away. That was absurd, of course. She wasn't about to cower in the cellar from a man who was trespassing on her own property.

She had climbed back up the stairs and was emerging from the cellar entrance when he came into the kitchen.

"There you are," he said, and held out a bouquet of flowers in glorious autumn colors. "I'm here with a peace offering and an apology. When nobody answered my knock, I walked in. I suppose that means I've offended you again and I'll owe you another peace offering tomorrow."

He actually looked sheepish and that, even more than the ruddy hue that the brisk evening had brought to his cheeks, made him an appealing sight, indeed. The high turtleneck of the navy blue sweater that he was wearing beneath his usual blue-gray parka accentuated the squareness of his jaw and the sculpted lines of his face. Gretchen did her best not to pay much attention to that.

"You really didn't have to bring me flowers, Mr. Emory."

"I managed to make a very bad impression on you today, and that was the last thing I wanted to do. I knew you were upset to find me looking through that trunk in the attic, and I don't blame you for feeling that way. It's just that I've always been fascinated by old things, and I couldn't stop myself from having a look. I'm afraid that my insatiable curiosity is both the worst and the best of my qualities. Anybody who has ever known me can tell you that."

He seemed so open and almost boyishly apologetic that it was hard not to be disarmed by him. He'd placed the flowers carefully on the kitchen counter when Gretchen didn't take them from him. Now he was walking toward her as she stood in the doorway. She had to stop herself from stepping backward to avoid another assaulting kiss. She felt the heat rising in her cheeks at the thought, but apparently Mr. Emory had no such intentions at the moment.

"What were you doing down there?" he asked, peering past her into the cellar.

"I was looking for a hammer to break into the thermostat."

"I can help with that," he said rather eagerly and, before she could protest, he had brushed by her and bounded down the cellar stairs two at a time. "There must be tools around here somewhere."

He had already found the workbench by the time she could hurry down after him. The rack with hammers of all sizes still hung on the wall where she remembered it.

"This should do the trick," he said, selecting a medium-size specimen with a metal, mallet-shaped head. "This certainly is a great old cellar. I'll bet you had some adventures here when you were a kid."

"Yes, as a matter of fact, I did."

He was circling the main basement room, looking around, with her following, when she noticed something interesting about one of the walls—a tall, narrow space where the stonework was less discolored by age than the rest. She was almost certain there had been a highboy cabinet in front of that very spot. She wondered if this newer stonework had been behind that cabinet all along, or if it had been done since her growing-up days. She was about to remark on it to Boyd, but he had already moved off toward the stairs.

"Lead me to the thermostat," he said, brandishing the hammer. "This place feels a little like a meat locker, and I'm just the man who can heat it up for you."

That brought Gretchen up short. But if Boyd meant his remark in the suggestive way she had taken it, there was no sign of that as he bounded back up the cellar stairs to the kitchen. Meanwhile, Gretchen resolved to resist his boyish charm with all her might. She would let him hammer the lock off the thermostat. Then she would firmly but graciously eject him from her house.

A half hour later she had almost succeeded in fulfilling that resolve. They were standing in the shadowy vestibule that led to the outside door nearest the driveway. Gretchen's hand was reaching for the switch to turn on the carriage lamp overhead when Boyd's fingers closed upon hers.

"I don't need any more light," he said in a low, husky voice. "I can see you just fine."

Gretchen withdrew her hand.

"You may have noticed I didn't apologize for what happened in the attic," he went on more softly but still with a husky rasp in his words. "That's because I'm basically an honest man, and there are few things I've ever done that I feel less sorry for than kissing you."

Gretchen didn't know how to answer that, but she didn't have to. Boyd was already opening the door for himself, and in another moment he was gone.

SOMEONE HAD BEEN watching from the undergrowth of the woodlot near River House as Boyd let himself in through the French doors. The watcher had hoped that Boyd would take the girl out somewhere and leave the house empty for a while, but that didn't happen. Boyd left by himself not much more than a half hour after he entered. He was whistling as he went, obviously happier than he had been that afternoon following his encounter with Gretchen Wulfert in the foyer of New Beginnings.

It would be very useful to know what had happened in the past half hour to put Mr. Emory in such a jolly mood. Well, this place was sure to be empty at least part of the day tomorrow. After that, neither River House nor New Beginnings Spa would be able to hide their secrets any longer.

Chapter Six

Gretchen woke up the next morning missing her grandfather more than ever and wishing she could rush to his room at the spa, take his frail shoulders in her hands and shake him back to consciousness. He could tell her what was really going on here, the way he could always show her the pathway through confusion to the truth of things when she was a little girl.

She would give anything for a hint of which way to turn. Should she press to find out more about her Uncle Carl's death? Or should she let it be, the way everyone—Pauline, Beryll, even the sheriff—wanted her to? She probably wouldn't ask her grandfather about the other thing on her mind—the way she found herself thinking about Boyd Emory at unguarded moments when she wasn't keeping charge of her thoughts as conscientiously as usual.

Gretchen searched her memory for some remnant of the many gems of advice her grandfather had given her over the years. The sound of his voice was what she truly longed for; but, short of that, the tenor of his particular manner of thinking would do. Wait a minute! What about his stories? She'd nearly forgotten those and how he'd once hinted that the most important truth he knew was written there. Maybe that truth would help her now.

She knew in her rational mind that it was most likely a foolish notion, but she didn't care. In fact, the most rational thing she could do right now would be to busy her brain with something besides running back and forth over the events of the past few days, getting nowhere. Figuring out where her grandfather might have stashed those stories would keep her preoccupied, for the moment at least; and the library was the logical place to begin her search.

It was very drafty there. Gretchen pulled a blanket from the back of an old leather couch and wrapped it around her shoulders. Through the tall, narrow windows she could see the river, which was restless this morning like her unsettled mood. The surface rippled and billowed into small points of wave constantly in motion. She lifted the window a few inches and breathed in deeply. The breeze carried the scent of last night's woodsmoke from the fireplace chimneys of the village. Gretchen reminded herself to have someone come in today and check the fireplace flues. There would be fires roaring at River House tonight. She could almost see the rosy glow dancing along the library walls and remember how that sight had made her feel so cozy and safe as a child. She wouldn't need Boyd to help her with the thermostat this evening and told herself she felt no regret about that whatsoever.

The bird chatter wasn't as loud as she recalled it from summer visits. Most feathered species had headed south weeks ago. Only the heartier individuals remained and, maybe, some not-too-wise or stranded ones. She wondered which of those two groups she fitted into. Maybe she should follow the lead of the wise migrators and wing her way south to climates that would be warmer in more ways than one. She could visit her parents in Palm Springs....

Gretchen let the thought trail off, out the window and into the breeze. She wasn't going anywhere. She couldn't—not this time. She had made too much of a habit of running out when circumstances became uncomfortable. She'd be on her way before anybody ever suspected she had leaving on her mind. This time she had promised herself she would stick around for a while, maybe a *long* while, until she woke up one morning with the restlessness only a memory. The brutally honest aspect of her nature told her that was a long shot, but she had to try it, anyway.

A gust too strong and cold to be called a breeze pushed through the narrow window opening, and Gretchen shut it quickly. Watching the river and feeling the wind had always given her a sense of being free and alive and wonderfully solitary. She had hoped to recapture that feeling this morning. Instead, she had managed to make the room chillier than ever; and, rather than the pleasant privacy of solitude, she was suddenly aware of being very much alone. She told herself it was the chill rather than the loneliness that prompted her to change her mind about beginning the search for her grandfather's letters here at River House.

WHEN GRETCHEN ARRIVED at New Beginnings, she went in the back door and up the service stairs to the second floor. She let herself into her uncle's office, which had been her grandfather's before Carl had taken over the running of the spa.

She pulled out the top side drawer of the desk and had to apply some extra force when it stuck halfway. The hodgepodge of papers inside obviously had no order to it. Beneath that uppermost layer of chaos, however, was some evidence that her grandfather's things hadn't been cleared out yet. Here the papers were neater and generally in file folders. Many were addressed to Frederick Wulfert. They all related to some facet or other of the operation of New Beginnings. Gretchen would have to read through all of this someday if she had any intention of taking over the spa, but right now she was in search of her grandfather's more creative efforts.

No stories here, or in the middle drawer, either. She was about to open the deeper bottom drawer when she noticed a few faint scratches in the veneer above the lock. It appeared that someone had used a flat-bladed instrument to force the lock. Gretchen could easily imagine disorganized Uncle Carl, having forgotten his key, compelled to break into his own desk. What she couldn't imagine was his being so delicate about it that he left only these inconspicuous marks.

Gretchen's suspicions were aroused once more, just as they had been when she saw the bend in the eaves trough on the roof. But she wasn't going to call the sheriff this time. She'd learned that, when it came to behavior that was even the least bit out of the ordinary, word got out fast around Cape Vincent. She would be absolutely certain of her facts before she sought official help again.

There was also another reason she preferred to keep the jimmied desk lock to herself for the time being. She'd caught Boyd Emory going through a trunk in the attic. He had explained that away as natural curiosity, and she was inclined to believe him. But how far would he carry that curiosity? Would he force a lock? And, if he had, would she want the sheriff investigating him for it? Yesterday her answer to that question might have been in the affirmative. Then, last night, she'd seen another side of Boyd. Her instincts told her that he was a decent man, whatever his life-style. Other instincts told her that he was also an attractive man, in ways she didn't feel up to thinking about right now. Meanwhile, she didn't really want to get him in trouble. She knew how the locals could be about strangers here, as hasty to accuse the outsider as they were to cover up for their own. Besides, these marks could be years old for all she knew.

She continued her search in the filing cabinets against the wall. She was almost at the end of the third drawer before she found anything worth much notice, but it wasn't one of her grandfather's stories. The unmarked file folder contained two clippings from *The Thousand Islands Sun,* the weekly paper that covered events along the Saint Lawrence.

The clippings were from early last spring and dated a week apart. The first article included a photograph of Lester Wilson and a man Gretchen didn't recognize. Lester looked even larger and more doughy than in real life, but it was the place where the picture had been taken that prompted Gretchen to bring the newsprint close to her face for a clearer look at the grainy black-and-white image. She was sure she knew the location but couldn't quite identify it. The printed text did that for her.

Lester was standing in a field near New Beginnings that belonged to the Wulfert estate. The article said he was there to announce the construction of a mini-mall on that very site, which he was supposedly purchasing from Carl Wulfert. How could that be? Gretchen wondered. Uncle Carl wouldn't have sold Wulfert land, not after being raised by his father to believe that was the first among cardinal sins.

The second clipping answered that question, but brought to mind some others. This was primarily an account of Carl denying that he had made a land deal with anybody. He said that Lester had approached him about such a sale and been refused. Carl closed by stating exactly what Gretchen had believed all along—that Wulfert land wasn't for sale under any circumstances.

But if that were the case, how could Lester have been so misinformed? Would he have gone to the newspaper if he wasn't certain of his facts? He might be eager for success, but he was no fool; and only a foolish man would knowingly make a laughingstock of himself in print.

Gretchen grabbed her bag from the desk and shoved the file folder inside. The search for her grandfather's stories could wait. There were too many loose ends around here for her. These clippings were one such loose end that she intended to tie up into a neat bow—the way her grandfather would have done.

"I DON'T BLAME you for wondering how Carl came to fall off that roof," Evelyn Wilson said without looking up from the pork chops she was arranging on a white porcelain tray. "That *is* what you're here to talk to Lester about, isn't it?"

"Not exactly," Gretchen answered.

"Why don't we go into the office and talk privately?" Lester said, glancing nervously at his wife.

"Are you inviting me to this little confab, Lester?" Evelyn slid the meat case door shut and wiped her hands on the butcher's apron she was wearing. "I think I might like to hear what Miss Wulfert has to say."

Before Lester could answer Evelyn had sauntered past him into the office with a frosty smile on her lips. Lester gave Gretchen a resigned look, and she understood immediately his impotence where his wife was concerned.

"Come on in," he said, gesturing toward the doorway behind the meat counter.

Gretchen preceded Lester into the small, cluttered office where Evelyn stood, leaning against a glass-doored bookcase filled with dog-eared ledgers.

"She wants to know where we were at the time of Carl's alleged suicide," Evelyn said. "She's probably going around town taking a survey. And, like I said, I don't blame her, considering the number of people who are damn happy to be shut of her uncle. We should be selling alibis instead of pork chops. I figure we'd do a land-office business."

"I take it you heard that the sheriff was at the spa the other day." Gretchen had decided to meet Evelyn's bluntness straight on with some bluntness of her own.

"You take it right."

Evelyn had probably been pretty once. Now she simply looked faded and sour. Her hair was cut unattractively short, and the tint she had used on it was way too red.

"Do you think my uncle was murdered?"

"She doesn't think any such thing, do you, Evvy?" Lester said hastily.

It was him Evelyn didn't bother looking at this time when she spoke. "I believe that a creep who doesn't care about anything in the world but his own sorry hide isn't likely to splatter that hide all over his driveway."

"Evelyn!"

"That's all right, Lester," Gretchen said, sounding calmer than she felt. "I appreciate hearing an honest opinion."

Lester's round cheeks colored a mottled red in response to the suggestion that he could have been more honest himself.

"So tell her you didn't kill her uncle, Lester. Then she can go back to her big, fancy house and leave us alone."

"Actually, these are what I came to see you about," Gretchen said, pulling the newspaper clippings from her bag and handing them to Lester.

As he examined them, he grew suddenly still, almost calm. When he looked up at her again, his gaze was much steadier than she expected. "What do you want to know?" he asked as he passed the clippings to Evelyn.

"I wondered why you made that first announcement if you didn't have a deal with my uncle."

"We had a deal, all right. He welshed on it."

"He sure did," Evelyn said, thumping the clippings down on top of a pile of grocery special circulars.

"Why would he agree to sell you Wulfert land when my grandfather has always made it very clear that the land isn't to be subdivided?"

"Maybe what Carl wanted was to humiliate me in front of the whole town."

Gretchen could guess how furious Lester must be by the steely way he was able to control that fury. "Why would he want to make you look bad?" she asked.

"Because Carl liked to remind everybody that he was the lord of the land and we were the peasants."

"He's been doing that ever since we were all in high school together," Evelyn chimed in.

"I'll handle this, Evelyn," Lester said.

She looked surprised to have him take charge like that but didn't say more as he picked up the clippings and returned them to Gretchen.

"I guess this means there's no sense approaching you about buying that parcel of land," he said.

"I have no authority to sell family property," Gretchen said.

"And Wulferts don't sell their land, anyway. Isn't that right?"

"That's right," she answered, returning his steady gaze as she put the clippings in her shoulder bag. "I'm sorry if my uncle led you to believe otherwise."

"There are other parcels of land for sale. We'll manage without the Wulfert plot."

Gretchen knew there would be few locations as desirable as the one she was denying Lester, but she nodded, anyway, then said a quick goodbye and left the office. She stopped outside to replace the clippings more neatly in their file folder in case she should need them again.

Need them for what? she asked herself. Evidence? A lot of people seemed to think Uncle Carl was murdered. Did she think so, too?

Gretchen was distracted from the uncomfortable question by the sound of Evelyn's voice back inside the office.

"I told you what Beryl said about her, how she sat there as cool as a cucumber, making sure her grandfather wasn't likely to come out of his coma. Now here she is, making just as sure her precious inheritance is kept all in one piece until the old boy gets around to passing on and she gets it all. She's a cold one. I wouldn't be surprised to find out she did Carl in herself."

"She wasn't even in town when it happened," Lester answered.

"With her money she could have hired somebody. I hear she's pretty chummy with that big guy she's got

working up there at the spa. He blew in a few days before Carl died. Maybe she sent him.''

"Don't talk crazy, Evelyn. Why would she call in the
sheriff to investigate if she was the one who had something to hide?''

"Those Wulferts have always thought they were
smarter than everybody else around here. Maybe she's
trying some foxy move that will make somebody else look
guilty if it should come out that Carl really didn't jump
off that roof on his own. Maybe you're the guilty party
she's got in mind.''

A woman with a shopping basket over her arm had
stopped near the meat counter to stare at Gretchen with
disapproval. She suddenly realized how obvious it must
be that she was eavesdropping. She would have liked to
hear Lester's response to his wife's theories about Carl's
death, but it wouldn't be a good idea to have them find
out she was listening in. The woman with the basket
looked as if she was about to speak up and let them know
just that. Gretchen put on what she hoped was a confident smile, meant to indicate that she had every right in
the world to be hanging around by this doorway, then
hoisted her bag more firmly onto her shoulder and
walked out of the store.

GRETCHEN HAD LEFT the heat on high all day at River
House, and by evening most of the damp and drafts had
been warmed out of the walls and floors. Thus, room
temperature wasn't the reason for the chill she felt down
her spine when she remembered what she had overheard
outside Lester Wilson's office that afternoon. Whatever
Evelyn had heard from Beryll, the rest of Cape Vincent
had, without doubt, been told, as well. Gossip spread far

and fast in a small town, especially when the subject was greed and murder.

Like Evelyn, most of them would believe that the only thing Gretchen cared about was inheriting her grandfather's money. Beryll must have gotten that impression from Gretchen's coolness yesterday when she was asking about her grandfather's condition. How could Beryll have known that it took every bit of Gretchen's willpower to remain calm on the outside while sorrow tore her apart on the inside? How could anybody understand why she covered up that way, unless they were a Wulfert and that was what they had been raised to do?

That wasn't the only thing bothering Gretchen about her visit to Wilson's store. The thought of her uncle deliberately making a fool of a village shopkeeper for no apparent purpose other than his own perverse amusement sent the chills tremoring through her more frigidly than ever. She told herself that a fire in the library hearth would help. At least building it would give her something more pleasant to think about. Mostly she didn't want to think the coldest thought of all—that Evelyn and Pauline could be right and Uncle Carl killing himself was too far out of character to be believed, leaving the more likely scenario that one of his enemies had done it for him.

Gretchen threw on the sheepskin jacket that had become part of her daily uniform since her arrival in the north country and pulled the curly fleece collar around her face before hurrying outside. The woodshed was at the edge of the riverbank off to the left from the house. She was sure to find plenty of split logs there, all stacked and ready to be brought inside for the fire. There hadn't been any rain since she'd arrived, so the wood should be dry enough to burn.

Gretchen had always liked being outdoors at night, especially when there was a frosty snap to the breeze and a bright moon over the river, like tonight. When she was a little girl, growing up here in River House, she would often slip outside on nights like this when she was supposed to be upstairs asleep in her miniature poster bed. She would stand on the riverbank and smell the clean scent of the wind, loving the way it numbed her nostrils and seemed to sweep the breath from her body for an instant, until she could adjust to breathing in such, crisp, thin air. She would listen to the night sounds and feel as if she had been allowed into a very private place where humans weren't usually permitted.

Unfortunately Gretchen wasn't experiencing such pleasant feelings now. Instead, as she moved out of the lee of the house and along the riverbank toward the woodshed, all she could feel was apprehension and the beginnings of what she hesitated to call fear. She told herself it was the unsettling events of the day that had her nerves on edge. Even so, when she stepped out of the shadow cast by the long facade of River House, she could have sworn that the night animals, the frost-stiffened grasses and the wind had all stopped stark still for a moment, as if hushed in anticipation of what would happen next—what would happen *to her.*

Her first impulse was to run back to the house, but she didn't let herself do that. She had heard about having the "night spooks," though she had never actually felt them before. She was determined to dismiss that feeling for the figment of a troubled imagination, but when a twig snapped loudly in the underbrush of the woodlot that bordered the River House lawn, she couldn't help spinning around and straining to see into the shadows. She couldn't make out anything unusual among the blurred nighttime shapes but, despite telling herself that she was acting like a jumpy female, she persisted in *sensing* someone there.

The sound of a car approaching along the road beyond the trees distracted her only temporarily from her intense examination of the shadowed underbrush. Then the car turned into the driveway that led to River House, and she glanced up for a moment in that direction. Her gaze was on its way back to the woods as the headlight beams swept through the trees. In that brief moment of illumination she was almost certain she had seen something move—a form crouching along the ground but too large to be any of the animals indigenous to this shore region.

Gretchen didn't think of herself as a coward. In fact, she had been known to choose the nervy, even foolhardy approach to potentially dangerous situations on more than one occasion. However, she had no intention of being foolhardy now. She turned and ran toward the house. She looked back over her shoulder just once, half expecting that crouched form to emerge from the trees and follow her, but the moonlight made it clear there was no one on the riverbank for as far as she could see.

Still, her pounding heart was certain she was being pursued, and that certainty made her run all the faster. She was so elated when her feet hit the solid surface of the fieldstone path leading to the River House driveway that she actually uttered a short, nervous laugh as she kept on running—smack into the outstretched arms of the man running toward her.

What Gretchen uttered then was a scream.

"Don't be afraid. It's me. Boyd."

He clasped her in his arms for a brief moment until she could struggle free.

"That was you in the woods," she gasped. "Get your hands off of me!"

She twisted away from him. She intended to make a dash for the house, but he grabbed her wrists and held her so that she couldn't escape.

"I wasn't in the woods," he said. His dark hair had fallen into his eyes during the struggle, making him look almost as boyishly innocent as he was claiming to be. "I just drove up. Didn't you hear my car?"

He was too strong for her to break free from, but she kept struggling, anyway. It took a moment for the logic of his words to get through to her. Then she quieted down some, though her heart was still pounding and she could barely catch her breath.

"What are you doing here?" she managed to blurt out, simply because it was the first thing that came to mind.

"Something happened at the spa that I thought you should know about, but we'll get to that later." He let go of her wrists and put his hands on her shoulders gently, as if to steady her. "Right now I want to know what you were running away from. Did you say there was somebody in the woods?"

His gentleness and the reassuring tone of his voice had begun to calm her. "I thought I saw something," she said, gesturing back toward the woodlot. "Over there."

"You stay here. I'm going to check it out."

He was off down the fieldstone path before she could call out for him not to leave her alone. Then, as she forced herself back under control, she was glad she hadn't said that. She didn't want Boyd Emory or anybody else to see her as a panic-stricken ninny who needed to be rescued from things that crept around in the night. Still, the thought of those things made her cringe.

Gretchen straightened the collar of the sheepskin jacket and raked her fingers through the tangles of her hair to make herself at least appear settled down and in charge of her emotions. She was walking back down the path toward the riverbank when Boyd returned.

''Whatever was out there is gone now,'' he said.

Gretchen kept from sighing audibly with relief, but she couldn't keep herself from feeling very glad that Boyd Emory was here with her now.

Chapter Seven

Boyd had struggled through some hard times in his life. He was still very young when his parents died, and he had missed them terribly. Max had taken him in right after that; but, even so, there was a long, lonely period of adjustment that lasted into Boyd's teens. That was when he met Jessica. They became close friends during high school and went on to the same college together. The loneliness of Boyd's life made him value that closeness above all else. He truly believed it was enough to build a life on, so the two of them married while they were barely more than kids.

He told Jessica that the work he planned to do would require a life of travel; and, at the time, she thought that sounded exciting. Then they were out of college and he got started in the international building business, being transferred from country to country and job site to job site. All Jessica could talk about in those days was settling down. He had believed they could live a traveling life and have a family, too—maybe not the kind of family seen on television sitcoms, but a family nonetheless. He had wanted that close-knit, loving center for their existence more than anything. Unfortunately Jessica hadn't wanted it on the same terms as he did. After she left him, there had been another long, lonely period of adjustment. Last month Max had died; and, with him gone, Boyd was truly alone. He had been struggling with that reality ever since.

He was here because his last promise to Max had been to find the evidence needed to expose the terrible crime committed in Cape Vincent going on fifty years ago. Most of all, however, Boyd was here because he knew in his gut that Max hadn't committed suicide, no matter what his note said. Boyd suspected that Carl Wulfert hadn't killed himself, either. If his suspicions were correct, he was after no mere murderer but one who had very likely been in league with one of the most insidious murderers of all time. Max's murderer would stop at nothing to protect his secrets.

Still, the struggle that troubled him most right now was the one he could feel himself getting into over Gretchen Wulfert. When she rushed up that path and into his arms less than a hour ago, he had felt the kind of stirrings he had always hoped for but never experienced with Jessica. She had been a friend at the best of their times together, a safe haven at others. But he had never longed for her in the way he would long for a part of his soul. He sensed the beginnings of that kind of longing with Gretchen, and that was the last thing he could afford to have happen here.

He had been much better off when he thought of her as little more than a challenge to be conquered. Now he not only found himself drawn to her and wanting her, he had seen her vulnerability, as well. She had become far too human to him. The perfect creature of the impervious facade had been easy to objectify and calculate about. This flesh-and-blood woman, with her own passions and her own terrors, was fast turning into someone he would rather hold in his arms than manipulate.

Boyd crunched another piece of crumpled newspaper in among the kindling at the bottom of the library fireplace grate and struck a match to it. The moment of anticipation that followed, as he wondered whether or not the flame would catch and travel successfully to the logs above, reminded him of how he had felt when he first arrived here tonight and wondered whether or not Gretchen would let him in. He couldn't remember experiencing such trepidation about a woman in a very long time. He was experiencing it again now as he waited for her to return from upstairs.

Actually she had been gone too long if all she really had to do was find a sweater. Even if she had stopped to powder her already-perfect nose, she should have been back down here by now. It occurred to him that maybe she was trying to avoid him. Outside earlier there had been a moment of definite awkwardness when she had realized she was in his arms and backed quickly out of them again. Even so, she had been upstairs a long time.

He listened for a moment to the silence of the huge old house. Something told him there might be trouble in that silence if he could only hear it. What if Gretchen really had seen something lurking in the woods and that person had slipped into the house somehow?

Boyd threw down the pages of newspaper he'd been holding and hurried to the main foyer where he took the steps of the grand staircase two at a time. He didn't know which direction Gretchen's room was from the landing. He went to the right first. Ordinarily he might have stopped to admire the quality of the several dark-hued portraits that lined the hallway and to examine professionally the gilt of their frames for spots that needed restoration. Right now all he could think about was the silence, weighing heavier upon him by the second. He called out more to shatter that silence than because he expected an answer.

"Gretchen, are you up here?"

The hollow echo of his voice down the long hallway was the only reply.

He turned and rushed back the other way, trying door handles and peering into empty rooms as he went. Then he saw a shaft of light from a doorway that was several past the staircase. The corridor was illuminated by wall sconces, so the shaft was only visible from this distance, casting a slightly brighter reflection on the carpet than the others. Consequently he hadn't noticed it when he had glanced quickly to the left at the top of the staircase before heading in the opposite direction.

He dashed toward the patch of light to the open doorway. Gretchen was standing very still inside the room, obviously listening intently, just as he had done downstairs in the library. Despite that listening pose, however, she didn't appear to have heard his approach. Her attention was concentrated on the space of wall between the white marble fireplace mantel and a narrow door that most likely led to a closet.

"Shh," she whispered with her finger to her lips. Obviously she had heard him, after all.

"What is it?" he couldn't help but ask.

"I heard something," she said, still whispering. "There. In the wall."

She pointed to the spot on the wall where she had been staring. Boyd examined it closely and strained to hear the sounds she was talking about. Then, after a long moment, there was still only silence. He shifted his attention to Gretchen, who continued to stare at the wall as if she hoped to bore through it to see what was on the other side. It occurred to him that she could still be experiencing the aftermath of her earlier scare outside. In fact, she might, understandably, be flinching away from shadows and jumping at the slightest sound for some time yet.

"I don't hear anything," he said gently.

"I'm not imagining things," she said, as if she might have been listening so hard she'd overheard his thoughts. "There was something moving in that wall."

The earnest conviction in her voice propelled Boyd to the closet door. He opened it and was assailed by the odor of plastic garment bags and things stored away for years. However, the closet itself didn't extend back to the point on the wall where Gretchen had supposedly heard her noises.

"There's nothing in here," he said.

"I know you think I'm imagining things," she repeated, at his side now. "And I have to admit that what I saw in the woods before could have been a deer, and the sounds I heard just now could be field mice driven inside by the cold, nesting in the walls. But I *did* see movement in the woods. If I built it into something fearful, it's probably because I've been here alone for several nights now. A big place like this can get spooky after a while." She managed a small smile that looked only slightly forced.

Boyd considered mentioning the additional unsettling effects of the rumors he'd heard in town about Gretchen calling the sheriff to the spa because she suspected foul play there, but decided against it.

"Ms. Sackett is skittish about the spa, too," he said. "She thinks there may have been a prowler on the premises. Of course, that's probably because she found a paper clip out of place on that very orderly desk of hers. Anyway, that's what brought me here tonight.''

"Disordered paper clips?" Gretchen asked as she walked over to the bed to retrieve the blue sweater she must have tossed there earlier.

Boyd was watching the way she moved and aware that he shouldn't be doing so. Keep to the plan, he reminded himself.

"Ms. Sackett has asked me to move into the spa for security reasons. I thought you might have some objections.''

"What objections?" Gretchen asked, sounding suddenly as if she didn't have a care in the world, about security at the spa or anything else.

She certainly could turn it off fast, Boyd thought. A moment ago she was breaking her neck to pick up a mouse step in the walls. Before that she was running for her life from somebody in the woods. Now she was as cool as a cucumber.

"If Beryll thinks that having you around is good for security, then so be it. She strikes me as a woman who knows what she's doing.''

And you strike me as a woman who's acting a lot more nonchalant than she feels, Boyd thought.

"And is there something *you* think I could be good for around here?" he asked, following her out of the bedroom and down the hall. "Raking leaves? Blanketing shrubs for the winter? Plugging window leaks where the cold creeps in?"

"Actually, there is something," she said. "You can help me look through the library bookcases for some stories my grandfather wrote and may have left there.''

Boyd suspected that Gretchen had come up with that idea because, however cool she might be acting now about her earlier moments of fear, she wanted to keep him around for a while until she was more comfortable with being alone in this massive house full of shifting shadows and skittering noises behind the walls. Boyd also suspected that he was happier than he should be to oblige.

"LOOK AT THIS!" Boyd exclaimed, pulling an unusual-looking package from the library bookcase.

"That's an old diary," Gretchen said.

She couldn't help admiring the way he seemed to take delight in new discoveries, as if he found everything intensely interesting and could hardly wait to explore it further. In fact, she not only admired that quality in him, she responded to it with what she would have to call affection. Maybe he was more than a ne'er-do-well, after all. Perhaps what she had previously seen as irresponsible, immature behavior was really a spirit of adventure and curiosity in action.

"That diary belonged to the first mistress of River House," she said. "Her husband was the Wulfert who built this place. He'd been one of Napoleon's German officers. There were a number of those, you know. After Napoleon's exile, many of his followers emigrated from France. My ancestor came here."

"To Cape Vincent? Why not some place in the mainstream of things?"

"I imagine they wanted to keep a low profile, especially since they had plans to bring Napoleon himself here eventually. But they could never get him off Saint Helena."

"Really?"

She smiled up at Boyd, enjoying his enthusiasm for the local folktales she had come to take for granted. "You can read some of it if you'd like."

Boyd unwound the plastic wrapping, and they sat down together on the old leather cushions she had left in front of the crackling hearth. Firelight illuminated the worn brown cover of the journal that was over a century old. The smooth, brittle pages were covered with faded, spidery handwriting and smelled of dust with a hint of mildew. Boyd turned the pages as carefully as her grandfather would have done.

"Have you read this?" he asked.

"My grandmother used to read to me from it when I was a little girl and tell me all about those early days here, but I haven't really thought about it much since then."

"You should," Boyd said. "They say that knowing who came before can give a person a real sense of who he is now."

Something clouded his eyes just then, and he looked away.

"Read some of it to me," Gretchen said, suddenly eager not to lose the mood of the moment.

He began leafing through the pages, picking out passages here and there. His earlier ardor for the discovery seemed to have cooled some, but Gretchen had become too absorbed in the reading to let that bother her as she laughed freely at the quirky personality of the journalist coming through in her writing. Gretchen remembered her grandmother telling stories about how much General Wulfert adored his wife. Gretchen was beginning to understand why.

"Listen to this," she said as she scanned ahead along a page. " 'I went down to the riverbank today. How they would cluck and coo in the village should they discover I was sitting in the sun with skirts pulled past my ankles. Thanks to my beloved Frederick, I traverse there by my secret way and none shall ever know.' My grandfather was named after her husband.''

''Keep on reading.'' Boyd's interest had obviously perked up again. He was squinting over her shoulder at faded script. ''What's this farther down here about a 'secret place'?''

Gretchen scanned where he was pointing. ''She says something about having a 'secret place' that seems to relate to the 'secret way' she mentioned earlier. That place is where she says she keeps this diary.''

''What do you suppose she's talking about?''

Gretchen stared into the fire for a moment, remembering. ''My grandmother told me about the French émigrés from that period being very cautious and secretive. They had been through the Revolution back in France when the peasants broke into the homes of aristocrats and stole all of their valuables. My grandmother used to laugh about how some of those émigrés had probably been at the head of the looting mob back home, but by the time they got here *they* were the aristocrats and didn't want the peasants robbing *them,* so they kept everything hidden away.''

''They could have had passageways built into the house,'' Boyd murmured, poring over the rest of the page, then moving on to the next. ''That must be what she's talking about here when she refers to a secret place.''

''That's right!'' Gretchen perused the page along with him. ''Where do you think it could be?''

They both looked up from the diary at the same instant and stared into each other's eyes. Gretchen could almost hear the same thought crackling simultaneously between them, like the sudden snap of a piece of tree bark in the fire.

"The cellar," she said in an excited whisper as she remembered the area of less-aged brickwork on the wall down there. That patch was roughly the shape of a doorway, and now she was almost certain what the door led to.

IF GRETCHEN HAD BEEN solely in charge of this expedition, they would have scrounged up picks and shovels, raced immediately to the basement and begun hacking away at the wall. Boyd, however, counseled a more organized approach. He suggested a trip to the historical society to examine the original floor plans of River House for the most likely location of a hidden corridor. Otherwise, he reasoned, a good deal of hard work could be wasted. Gretchen did get her way in one respect. They weren't going to wait until morning for their visit; they were going right now.

"I assume you have a key to this place," Boyd said as Gretchen pulled her red sports car to an abrupt stop in front of the one-story, square-stone building near the ferry dock.

"We don't need a key. We can let ourselves in," she said as she pushed open the door and slid out of the low-slung car.

"Are you telling me we're going to break in?"

Gretchen cast him a reproving look in the light from the wagon lamps that flanked the entrance. "First of all, Mr. Emory, you were the one who insisted on coming here. And, secondly, I would have expected more love of adventure from such a free spirit. Besides, my grandfather is a major financial supporter of the historical soci-

ety. I doubt they'll put me in the penitentiary for making
an unscheduled visit.''

"But will they be as understanding toward me?" Boyd
asked as she tried the front door handle, found it locked
and moved on to the windows.

"I will make very clear that this was entirely my idea."
She tried the windows along the front of the building
until the one farthest from the doorway slid upward.
"People here may be a cautious lot, but they still don't
always lock all of their windows."

Boyd helped boost her through the window opening,
then followed her inside. "I hope you know what you're
doing."

"Trust me."

Nonetheless, he glanced back through the window as
if expecting someone to hop out of the bushes and catch
them in the act. After all, the red sports car had hardly
made a quiet approach.

"It doesn't look like the place is really closed, anyway. There's somebody else here," Gretchen said.

She was pointing at a light from the lower-floor stairway, and there were sounds of movement below, as well.
Boyd tried to grab Gretchen's arm and stop her, but she
was already off down the stairs.

"Herb," she said in a surprised tone when she saw who
was working at the wide-plank table on the lower level,
which was part storage room, part study space. "You
really are a local history buff to be down here this late in
the evening."

"It isn't anywhere near late yet," he said, rather de-
fensively as he began rolling up the yellowed papers he'd
been poring over when she entered. "What are *you* doing here?"

"I'm researching secret passages in the old houses around Cape Vincent, especially River House. Maybe you'd know something about that."

"You've been talking to Lester Wilson lately, haven't you?"

Boyd had come down the stairs behind her, ducking to keep from cracking his head on the low clearance at the bottom. Gretchen glanced over at him, wondering if he found Herb's assumption as curious as she did. But, if Boyd considered anything here out of the ordinary, he was showing no sign of it.

"Actually, I did see Lester this afternoon," she said to Herb.

"I knew it! The only thing bigger around her than Lester's belly is Lester's mouth. I can hear him now, carrying on about me and those old tunnels."

Herb was obviously agitated, tapping the table with a pencil he had pulled from behind his ear. Of course, Lester hadn't said a word to her about Herb or the passageways, but it was apparent from Herb's reaction that such tunnels did exist and he knew something about them. Gretchen was determined to find out what, and a crafty approach might work best.

"I did gather that you know more about those tunnels than anybody else around," she semifibbed.

"And I don't guess he meant that as a compliment." Herb grabbed the pile of rolled-up documents from the table and stuffed them into the open drawer of a long cabinet against the wall.

"Well, you know how Lester can be," Gretchen said coyly.

Herb snatched his notes from the table and shoved them into the pocket of his dust-smudged down jacket. "I'm interested in those old tunnels because they've got to do with history. I've never found anything in a one of them that would bring me a plug nickel if I tried to sell it, which I haven't, by the way. I'm not on any treasure hunt, no matter what Lester Lard-Bottom and all the other nosey parkers in town have to say about it.''

Gretchen would have tried goading him into further revelations, specifically about River House, but Herb had already pushed past Boyd and was pounding up the stairs. A moment later she heard the outside door slam behind him.

"You certainly handled that well," Boyd said as he joined her at the table. "I'll bet that a professional interrogator couldn't have maneuvered that old boy better than you just did. From the vehemence of Herb's denials, I would guess he heard those same stories your grandmother told you about the French émigrés stashing their valuables in secret hiding places.''

Gretchen went over to the long wall cabinet and yanked hard on the drawer Herb had shoved closed. It jerked reluctantly open with a groan. "Look at what's right on top of the things Herb was looking at.''

The label on the roll indicated that it was one of the floor plans of River House. Boyd helped her open it carefully on the table. This wasn't the actual original drawing. That would have been too brittle to roll up this way. Still, it was an old copy and fragile. Boyd leaned over the drawing to study it.

"Do you know what to look for?" Gretchen asked.

"Of course," he said in a preoccupied tone while he pored over the lines of the drawing as if memorizing them.

"How do you know so much about such things?" she asked, suddenly curious about more than just the design of River House.

He glanced up at her. She could see that her question had startled him for some reason.

"Restoration architecture is a hobby of mine," he said.

"Another example of that insatiable curiosity you told me about?"

"You might call it that."

"So does this floor plan tell you anything about tunnels at River House?"

"Some of the walls are thick enough to allow for that," he said, returning his attention to the table. "But there are no passageways actually marked off here. I didn't expect there would be. I only wanted to check where a tunnel would be most likely, and a cellar entrance is a definite possibility."

"I thought so." Gretchen rerolled the plans hastily but carefully. "Let's get back there. We've got some work to do."

"I was afraid you'd say that," Boyd groaned.

BOYD DIDN'T ARGUE with her assumption that he would pitch in to demolish the brickwork in the cellar. He had only pretended to be disgruntled about tackling the job. He had his own reasons for wanting to uncover whatever secrets River House might have in store. He would have preferred to investigate on his own. Yet, earlier that evening, when Gretchen Wulfert told him to trust her, he had realized that he did. Whatever the rest of the Wulferts might have been guilty of, he was certain she knew nothing about it and wouldn't have gone along with a cover-up if she had known. His gut told him that was true; and, even more than he trusted Gretchen, he trusted his gut.

Unfortunately that didn't alleviate his uneasiness on another question: how long before he would have to tell her what he was really after here in Cape Vincent? That was a moment he both longed for—because he wanted to be honest with her—and dreaded.

"I think this section is almost ready to give way." Gretchen's words broke through Boyd's thoughts.

They had found a drill in the workshop area of the River House cellar, and he had been using it to blast away the mortar around a section of brick near the center of the doorway-shaped space. Gretchen had cleared away the rubble as he drilled. Now the section was nearly dislodged. Boyd set the drill down and picked up a sledgehammer. Gretchen stepped back and shielded her eyes from flying debris as he made his swing.

The head of the sledge hit the target straight on, jolting the last, stubborn pockets of mortar free from the surrounding brick and sending the approximately three-foot-square piece of wall toppling into the opening behind it.

The rush of chill, dank air that met Boyd from the other side made him hesitate for an instant, suddenly reminded of scary movies in his early teens, about creatures from the crypt and the like. More than once, only the prospect of mockery by his peers had kept him from running straight out of the theater. But he hadn't run then, and he wouldn't run now.

He dropped the sledge and grabbed the flashlight Gretchen had been holding for him as she pressed forward to see. He could almost hear her heart pounding as wildly as his own as he trained the light into the blackness of the unknown.

Chapter Eight

The surrounding bricks gave way without much protest to open a hole big enough for crawling through. Gretchen was glad she had thrown on a pair of jeans and an old turtleneck sweater before their jaunt to the historical society. She wished she had on a jacket, as well. The warmth of the furnace in the basement hadn't penetrated into this tunnel, but that wasn't what chilled her most. She had the impression of things hanging from the ceiling—damp, unpleasant things. She shot the beam of her flashlight upward and swept her hand across the passageway in front of her face, then cringed when her fingers touched fragile strands of the cobwebs that glinted in the light.

"Let me walk ahead of you," Boyd said, who couldn't have missed the look of revulsion on her face even in the sporadic illumination of their flashlights.

He had preceded her through the opening they had made in the basement wall, then pulled her through after him. He stepped in front of her now to clear away the dusty cobwebs from their path.

"No one has come through this way in a long time," he said.

Gretchen was beginning to wish she hadn't come this way, either. She could feel a definite case of the creeps coming on as Boyd arced the beam of his light over the tunnel ceiling and then down its length ahead of them.

The walls were constructed of the same heavy gray fieldstone as the rest of the house, and the floor was packed earth. There was nothing particularly formidable about that. In fact, once Boyd had banished the cobwebs, Gretchen wouldn't have minded it at all if it hadn't been for the thought that this was an old, forgotten place, intentionally entombed and not meant to be opened up again.

Boyd had started moving down the tunnel, and Gretchen hurried to catch up. She tried not to be too furtive in the way she darted her flashlight this way and that. She didn't want Boyd to know that the less rational side of her was half expecting the light to pick out the dull gleam of skeletal remains at any moment.

The tunnel ended abruptly at a door with a massive handle of tarnished brass. Gretchen grabbed hold along with Boyd when she saw him struggling to pull the door open. Obviously no one had come through this way in a long time. They both grunted from exertion as the thick, ponderous door grudgingly budged, only a crack at first, then a hard-won inch at a time until there was an opening wide enough to slip through.

"Look at this," Boyd said, training his light on the other side of the door, which had been cleverly disguised with a fieldstone surface that matched the surrounding walls. "With this door shut you wouldn't know that passage to the basement was there. Unless, of course, you were the one who put it in."

"Or if you had a map," Gretchen said.

"I doubt they would have put these passages on a map," Boyd commented rather absently as he flashed the light up and down the new corridor they had just entered. "Not if they wanted to keep them a secret, anyway. I can tell you one thing for sure, though. This passageway has seen more traffic than the one from the basement."

"What makes you say that?"

"See?" Boyd directed her attention to the path of his light sweeping across the opening. "The cobwebs have been cleared away except for some strands left hanging from the ceiling. Someone has been in here, and not too long ago, either."

Gretchen didn't like the sound of that. Consequently Boyd's next pronouncement was hardly what she wanted to hear.

"I'll check down this way," he said, gesturing to the left. "You see what there is in the other direction."

He had already started off before Gretchen could object. She remembered his insatiable curiosity and could almost see it crackling out of him as he moved away down the corridor, eagerly exploring with the darting beam of his light. She felt some of that adventurous spirit herself. In fact, usually she felt a lot of it. Right now, however, she was experiencing dread, as well. Suddenly, in a flash as bright as the beam of the electric torch she held in her hand, she was convinced that terrible things were going to happen here. Then fast on the heels of *that* sudden awareness came another. Terrible things *had* happened here in the past.

"Are you all right?"

The hollow sound of Boyd's voice echoing along the tunnel made her jump.

"Of course, I'm all right," she lied. "I was just getting my bearings."

"Do you want me to come with you?"

"Don't be silly," she snapped.

There was that good old Wulfert pluck leaping to the fore, exactly as she would expect it to do. Longtime conditioning had a tendency to kick into gear at moments like this. Still, she had a sudden urge to run after Boyd and leap into his arms instead. Naturally she didn't succumb.

She could tell he was watching as she turned to start down the corridor in the other direction.

"Okay. If you say so," he said finally, and walked off the way he had originally been headed.

She wished she had the nerve—for that was what it would take for a Wulfert to betray wavering courage—to call him back. The next thought she had almost compelled her to do just that, but for another reason. Being reminded of the family reputation for courage had brought it to mind.

She had tried most of her life to keep away from her Uncle Carl. Still, she had known him well. The legendary Wulfert fortitude—or, at least, the family obsession with the *appearance* of such fortitude—had taken the form of bravado in Uncle Carl. The last thing he would have wanted was to be seen as a coward. Many people considered suicide an act of cowardice, the fear of facing life's consequences. Carl would have agreed with that judgment. Here was yet another reason to suspect that he hadn't taken his own life.

She was tempted to run after Boyd and insist that he set his curiosity aside long enough to let her unburden her suspicions to him. She was ready to do exactly that when she remembered something her grandfather had said to her many times as she was growing up. "Never forget who you are and what you represent," he would tell her. Chasing after Boyd and forcing him to listen to her fears wouldn't measure up to the standards her grandfather was talking about.

Gretchen took a resolute grip on her flashlight and continued along the corridor to the right. It occurred to her that before long she might decide it was time to ignore her grandfather's admonition and confide in Boyd. She had to get somebody else's opinion of the startling thoughts she was having about her uncle's death. Otherwise the pressure of withholding such a frightening secret could be too much to bear.

Shaken by that realization, Gretchen reached out to touch the corridor wall and steady herself. The stone surface was cold and clammy, as well as somewhat slimy from years of dampness. The sensation of touching that surface would have been enough to stop Gretchen's heart for a chilling instant even if the wall hadn't moved under her fingers.

She screamed and pulled that hand away as her flashlight slipped out of the other and clattered to the ground, clicking off as it landed to leave her in darkness blacker than any she had ever experienced. Out of that deep dark came the crystal-clear awareness that she was on the verge of panic. She was letting a musty passageway and some scary suspicions get the better of her, and she had to snap out of that state of mind immediately. She had been about to scream again but clamped her lips shut in what she was sure would look like a very grim grin were there any light to see it by.

She crouched where she had heard the flashlight clatter to the ground. She felt carefully, hand over hand, along the packed earth of the passageway floor until her fingers touched the cool metal cylinder and found the button to restore its beam of welcome brightness. Then she turned the beam on the opposite wall, where she had felt that shocking motion just seconds ago.

By the time Boyd came running up, she was staring into a square opening about the size of a wall safe. Unfortunately it appeared that someone else had already found this particular hideaway. There was a brass box inside, obviously an antique, and just as obviously empty. The lid was open, but from the look of the smudged fingerprints on the brass surface, the trespasser was *not* of antique vintage. He had been here very recently, indeed.

BOYD'S EXPLORATION of the tunnel had taken him to the riverbank. That was most likely how Gretchen's foremother got to the sun without anyone suspecting she was doing something as scandalous as warming her shoulders and ankles. At that entrance to the tunnel Boyd had found the overgrowth newly thinned, as if to allow access to someone in the fairly recent past. He had been speculating on who that someone might be when he heard Gretchen scream and plunged his way back here.

After checking out the empty wall cache, they continued on along the tunnel in the direction Gretchen had been searching. It led to the back of her bedroom closet. Boyd found the latch that opened the door, and together they tugged until years of resistance gave way. They ducked through the clothes hanging inside and emerged into her bedroom, where Boyd told her all about his discoveries at the riverbank.

Nothing seemed to surprise her at this point, after learning she had grown up in a house honeycombed with secret passageways and cubbyholes for stashing heaven knows what.

"Maybe you really did hear more than field mice in these walls earlier tonight," Boyd was saying.

Gretchen stared at him. Had that been just this evening? She felt as if at least a day or two must have passed since then.

"Gretchen, are you all right?"

The way Boyd said her name, in a voice that was suddenly caring, began to rouse her from the limbo state she had been in—for how long?—since the wall had moved under her fingers and she'd dropped the flashlight. Whatever doubts she might still have about him, she could tell his concern was sincere. She also couldn't help noticing that having him concerned about her felt good.

She shook herself, not so much to dismiss that feeling as to get rid of the remaining cobwebs clouding her mind as a result of so many bewildering experiences happening so fast. Meanwhile, the thought of cobwebs made her cringe as she remembered their slippery threads touching her to cling then evaporate, like something disturbingly otherworldly.

"You're not all right, are you?" Boyd said.

His voice had turned even more gentle; and, after she cringed, he had begun stroking her arm. She was a bit surprised at how alert that gesture made her feel. For the first time she noticed how dingy they both looked. Boyd had wisps of cobweb in his dark hair and smudges on his face. They had soiled and dusty patches on their clothes, and their hands were quite dirty. Just then an image from earlier in the evening popped into her head.

"I know who was in that passageway earlier tonight," she exclaimed.

Boyd drew back his comforting hand. "Tell me."

"Remember how Herb Dingner looked when we saw him at the historical society?"

"What do you mean by how he looked?"

"He looked like we do right now. Dirty, disheveled. As though he had just made his way through a dusty old tunnel." She was suddenly excited, the way a fox probably felt when first scenting a rabbit. "And those floor plans he was looking at were for River House."

"That's true. They were," Boyd said slowly. For a moment Gretchen thought he was going to say more, but he didn't.

"I know how to find out for sure if it was Herb," she said.

"How would we do that?"

"We set a trap, then see if he goes for the bait," she answered enigmatically.

She was enjoying the secret investigation element of all this, though a corner of her mind kept wondering what, if anything, it had to do with Uncle Carl's death and reminding her that something so sinister should hardly be enjoyable.

She opened a drawer in her bedside table and pulled out the phone directory. It was less than an inch thick and still covered the entire north country, including Watertown, the only honest-to-goodness city up here, which was located approximately twenty-five miles to the south. Herb Dingner was among the couple of pages that constituted the population of Cape Vincent. His address was recorded as Tibbetts Point. Gretchen punched the buttons for his number on her bedside phone and waited while the raspy, rural-sounding ring buzzed in her ear until Herb answered.

"I'm sorry to bother you again, Herb, especially so late," she said. "But we've made a discovery here at River House that I thought you, as a local history buff, would find fascinating, and I couldn't wait till morning to tell you about it.''

"What kind of discovery is that?''

Gretchen could tell that Herb was working hard to sound casual and only partially succeeding. She smiled at Boyd to indicate that her bait was enticing Herb just as she had planned.

"We found an old drawing of the original house plan. It shows that there are two tunnels here at least.''

"Two?'' Herb retorted too quickly. He had taken the bait all the way now.

"The main shaft comes up from the river to the house. Then we found a branch off that tunnel about halfway up from the riverbank. We had to pry open a hidden door to get through.'' She deliberately didn't tell him about the opening from the basement.

"I see,'' Herb said cautiously. "Have you had a chance to look for those tunnels yet?''

"We were going to wait until morning to do that. We have to go out to New Beginnings right now and take care of a problem there, so we won't be able to get to the tunnels tonight. I'll be sure to let you know what we find when we do. In fact, I'll probably be calling you about that tomorrow afternoon.''

"I would appreciate that,'' Herb said.

"Then you can come over and take a look for yourself, if we actually find anything, that is.''

"Sure, sure. I'd like that.''

"I thought you would.'' Gretchen winked at Boyd to indicate that the trap had been sprung, with Herb securely inside. "Till then, Herb,'' she said, and hung up the phone. "Now,'' she said, to Boyd this time and with more than a little glee in her voice, "the *real* cloak-and-dagger act begins.''

BOYD HAD HIDDEN the cars down a wagon track in the woods. Luckily the ground was nearly frozen, or his heavy pickup truck might have been mired in mud. There was no such problem with Gretchen's little red sports car, which fitted in easily between two trees. Neither vehicle was likely to be noticed from the road, and Boyd suspected that Herb would be in too much of a hurry to take time for a thorough search of the area, anyway. He would want to get in and out of River House as fast as he could manage. He should be here soon, if he was actually coming. Like Gretchen, Boyd was certain he would be.

Boyd turned out to be right, and even sooner than he would have thought. He was just getting back to the house when he heard a car approaching along the highway from the direction of Tibbetts Point. The sound of the engine slowed, then stopped some distance from the driveway on to River House property. Boyd hurried through the back door and locked it behind him.

Gretchen had left on only the outside lights. The glow of those lights through the kitchen and dining room windows was enough to guide him to the staircase, where he felt his way to the top, then turned left toward Gretchen's room. She would be in the closet waiting. He was to join her there.

Before Max's death had sent Boyd to Cape Vincent on this quest for evidence of a forty-five-year-old horror, he would have considered Gretchen's scheme too crazy to be taken seriously. Ordinarily he wasn't the kind of man who crept down corridors in the dark or lured the unsuspecting mark out into the night for the purpose of catching him in a guilty act. That was too much like a scene from a bad melodrama for Boyd.

He was, after all, a sensible person; and, on the face of it, what he was doing right now seemed ridiculous. Boyd, however, had already been involved in what Gretchen referred to as the cloak-and-dagger act for longer than even she would have guessed. His trip to the north country, and the weeks before it, as well, had been exactly that—covert operations. By now he had begun to doubt where the parameters of sensible activity actually lay.

He slipped into the closet and shut the door behind him to black out even the shadowy light from the bedroom windows. Earlier he and Gretchen had hastily removed the clothes from this relatively small compartment and stacked them on her bed so that there would be room inside for both of them to crouch and wait. They had also left the door ajar from closet to tunnel, just wide enough to peek through but not wide enough to be noticeable from the tunnel side.

"I'm back," he whispered, realizing how obvious that statement must sound, but feeling the need to say something, anyway.

Gretchen snapped her flashlight on for a moment, illuminating his face as she shone the beam around the narrow space. The eerie, bluish light made her pale skin appear translucent, her pale hair like a halo of white gold. Boyd was suddenly aware of how physically close they were in here.

"I haven't heard anything yet," she said, snapping the light back off.

"I think I heard his car stop on the highway. He's probably on his way through the woods on foot."

"What if he stumbles across the cars?"

"They're on the other side of the property. He'd need a lot of dumb luck to find those cars on the path I figure he'll be taking. Besides, I doubt he suspects you were telling him anything but the truth on the phone, and that means he won't be looking for hidden cars. He's too busy thinking about hidden tunnels.''

"Yes, you're probably right about that." Gretchen sighed, and Boyd wished he could see her face again. "Let's hope the dumb luck is on our side tonight." He could almost feel her staring at him in the dark. "You must think all of this is pretty dumb itself. When I stop and think about what we're doing here, I can't imagine why you've gone along with me so far."

She had come too close to Boyd's own thoughts for comfort. He couldn't tell her the truth, of course—that he'd been going along with somebody else's crazy-sounding agenda for quite some time now. He would have loved to make a clean breast of it with her, about Max and forty-five years ago and everything. Instead, he had to divert her attention from anything close to that, *and* from wondering why anyone *would* go along with this strange business as far as he had. He remembered very well the tack he had taken when he wanted to distract her from her suspicions the other day in the attic. He couldn't help noticing that he was even more willing to venture in a similar direction now.

"Actually, I have gone along with all of this, as you put it, because I hoped it would give me the chance to get closer to you," he said. "That wish seems to have come true."

Their bent legs brushed one another in the dark. She didn't exactly flinch at the touch, but she did pull carefully away. The scent of her filled that cramped closet and was disturbingly sweet. Once more he wished he could see her face and was tempted to snap on his own light for just an instant.

Then he heard something.

The sound came from down the incline of the tunnel where it led to the river's edge entrance. The cracking of near-frozen vines and branches was too loud to have been caused by the wind. A few seconds later Boyd thought he felt a draft of cold air such as might have been caused by a parting of the curtain of undergrowth that covered the tunnel opening.

Maybe what he felt was only a chill shivering through his own blood as he waited in a dark closet off an even darker tunnel for a possibly desperate man to approach. There was no way of knowing how badly Herb Dingner wanted whatever he was after, or how far he would go to get it. Maybe this obsession had already driven him to kill Carl Wulfert. Herb Dingner might appear to be harmless enough on the surface, but this wouldn't be the first time such a harmless facade disguised a dangerous man.

That thought brought out an instinct in Boyd he never knew he had. He reached out for Gretchen and tugged at her arm to pull her behind him. He had never really considered himself to be a protective male. He certainly hadn't reacted that way to Jessica. In fact, in that situation he had sometimes felt he had to protect himself against her. On the contrary, the current circumstances made him feel very protective indeed.

"I hear him, too," Gretchen whispered, only allowing him to nudge her partway into the shadow of his shoulder.

The sounds of movement in the tunnel were louder now. The arc of a flashlight bounced eerily in and out of view through the crack in the door between the closet and the tunnel. Then Boyd began to hear a brushing sound. He listened intently but couldn't tell what it was. He inched closer to the opening, pushing the door farther ajar ever so slowly and carefully. At the first, small scraping sound of the door beginning to resist, he stopped pushing and listened again. The brushing continued and seemed closer now.

The door was open just wide enough at this point for Boyd to peer out and down the tunnel corridor. When he did, he saw immediately what was causing the brushing sound. Herb Dingner was out there all right. He was sweeping his gloved hand over the wall of the tunnel, obviously in search of some mechanism that would open a portal into the other passageway Gretchen had told him about. Boyd had closed that doorway and pressed dirt into the cracks, which were already barely visible. There was no handle on this side to give away the location. It was possible that the door could only be opened from the tunnel that led up from the basement, but Boyd wasn't completely certain about that.

He held his breath as Herb's sweeping motions neared the door. Boyd and Gretchen had talked out their strategy before he went to move the cars. They would keep Dingner headed in this direction, toward the opening with the empty brass box. They didn't want him to detour down the other tunnel. Boyd said a small prayer that Herb wouldn't find a way to open that hidden doorway, after all.

Boyd was suddenly aware that Gretchen must be just as tense as he was. She seemed to be holding her breath, as well, or at least breathing very shallowly. The hush in the closet was so complete that he might have suspected she had crept back into the bedroom were it not for the hand she had placed on his shoulder as she peered past him through the door opening.

Her body was leaning against his back in a manner that was more familiar than she probably realized, the apprehension of the moment having most likely driven such considerations from her mind. It felt good to have her leaning against him this way. Boyd could smell her scent so distinctly now that he was able to detect a hint of gentle spice added to the sweetness, making it still more disturbing. He had to force himself to concentrate on Herb Dingner's approach.

He was past the passageway entrance area now, and it didn't appear that he had noticed anything out of the ordinary there. The fieldstone wall face had remained solid and unmoving, after all, as Herb's searching hands brushed on toward the hidden niche and the empty brass box. Boyd and Gretchen had closed that up, as well. This time Herb apparently knew exactly how to reopen it, as if he had explored these walls before and found the same release mechanism that Gretchen had touched by accident. Boyd watched as Herb deliberately pushed one particular stone, which then swung slowly outward to reveal the niche.

Herb shined his flashlight into the opening and was intent on examining the compartment and the brass box, possibly to determine whether or not anything had been disturbed since his previous visit. While he was thus preoccupied, Boyd and Gretchen made their move.

Boyd shoved against the door with all of his weight. Gretchen joined in that effort, and the door eased open with less resistance than he had expected. In seconds they were flanking Herb and flashing their lights in his astonished face.

"Okay, Dingner," Boyd said in a voice that was calculated to intimidate. "We've caught you. Now you had better tell us what you did with the contents of that box."

FORTUNATELY FOR KRAFT he needed very little sleep to keep going. He could survive for long periods on noth-

ing but brief catnaps grabbed here and there. Even then
he dozed so lightly that the slightest sound from his
headset would waken him. This was yet another of the
many talents that had distinguished him from the rest all
those decades ago when he last used the name that meant
"strong one" in German and which he loved so well.

He had parked the van behind a cottage a few lots away
from River House in the direction of Tibbetts Point. The
devices he had planted inside the mansion were so sensi-
tive that they picked up the tiniest sounds, and his state-
of-the-art equipment had no trouble receiving those sig-
nals even at this distance.

"A craftsman is only as good as his tools," Kraft
murmured to himself, chuckling aloud with a satisfied
grin.

Still, there had been periods of silence from River
House this evening. The voice-activated microphones
tracked the Wulfert girl and Emory from the library to
her bedroom upstairs, and then tracked them back again.
Kraft had heard them discover the old journal and read
from it. He had chosen to stay where he was while they
made their little sojourn to the historical society. He had
no listening devices planted there, of course; and there
was too much risk that he would be noticed in the quiet
village this late at night. He wished he had bugged their
cars, as well, and probably would tomorrow.

Meanwhile, he had counted on them returning to River
House and discussing whatever they had discovered on
their trek into town. Kraft was elated when they did return before an hour had passed. He heard them discuss
going down into the basement and something about a
secret passageway there. Kraft hadn't bugged the basement, either, but he still remained calm and confident.
His experience with such situations had taught him that

eventually people would talk where he could hear them. Then all he had to do was put together the pieces of what they said and fill in the gaps with clever guesses. He had always been good at that, and he doubted he had lost his touch.

Consequently he let himself doze comfortably while the two of them did whatever they had to do in the basement. Kraft was then fully awake again when he heard them speaking once more—in Gretchen Wulfert's bedroom this time. After that it didn't take much second-guessing at all to figure out that they had found a hidden passage—a couple of them, in fact—linking the bedroom to both the basement and the river. Kraft made a mental note that, when it was safe to do so, he would check out those passages himself. Maybe that was where poor old Carl had hidden his evidence.

But . . . what if that evidence had been in the brass box they talked about finding empty?

The thought hit Kraft with startling force. If Gretchen and Emory's conclusions were right about who had pilfered the contents of the box, and Kraft suspected they were, Herb Dingner had found that evidence.

When Dingner drove past Kraft's hiding place and parked not far away to sneak through the woods to River house, Kraft was tempted to waylay the meddling fool and find out exactly how much he did know. Kraft had always been most talented at extracting such information, another skill he was certain he hadn't lost the knack of. That, of course, would have been an unwise and impulsive move. Kraft wasn't the kind of man who succumbed to impulse.

"Do not panic," he reminded himself, as if panic were something he could actually be capable of.

A better opportunity for getting to Dingner would most likely arise, and the odds were slim that Kraft would have to jeopardize his cover to take advantage of it. He simply had to remain calm the way he always did and let the situation develop until said opportunity presented itself. Kraft knew he could do that. His reputation for having ice water in his veins wasn't undeserved.

Still, he didn't doze this time during the long period of silence from his headset that followed Herb Dingner's disappearance over the embankment above the river not far from River House. And, when Kraft finally did hear Emory and the girl emerge from her bedroom once more, apparently dragging Dingner with them, Kraft cupped the earphones with his gloved hands and listened hard so that he wouldn't miss a word.

Chapter Nine

"Don't you think you're making too big a deal out of a few old stories?" Herb asked after Boyd had pushed him into the front seat of the pickup with Gretchen on the other side to keep Herb from getting out the opposite door. "I read them, and they aren't worth all of this trouble." He had regained some of his customary cockiness but still spoke cautiously.

"They're worth a lot of trouble to me if they're the stories my grandfather wrote," Gretchen said as Boyd turned the ignition key and shifted the grinding gears into reverse.

"I'm sure Herb was counting on just that, Gretchen," Boyd growled, backing up the truck in a rather abrupt three-way turn to face the driveway. "He hoped you'd want those stories so much you'd pay to get them. Isn't that what you were after, Herb?"

Herb didn't answer. Gretchen had felt him flinch at Boyd's threatening tone. Now Herb stared straight ahead through the windshield, where the headlights cut a bouncing swath in the darkness as they bumped over the uneven track toward the highway. Uncle Carl was always too stingy to repair the pavement, which was rutted and cracked from the freezing and thawing of many harsh north country winters. She usually drove along its considerable length very slowly to avoid being jostled around like this.

She might have suggested that Boyd slow down, but she had seen his anger in action back at the house and thought better of asking him to do anything right now. She had tried to calm him down when he dragged Herb out of the tunnel and backed him against her bedroom wall. From the dark look in Boyd's eyes she was certain he had been about to beat Herb severely. She could tell Herb thought so, too, as he crumpled into visible fear while being lifted clear off the ground against the wall.

Gretchen had suggested then that Boyd take it easy, but he didn't seem to hear her. Instead, he kept on firing questions at Herb about what had been in the brass box and what he had done with it. At first Herb claimed he didn't know what Boyd was talking about. That was when Boyd rapped him hard into the wall. The darkness in his eyes loomed darker still, and there could be no mistaking the seriousness of his rage. After that Herb told them everything he knew and didn't require further encouragement to do so.

It had occurred to Gretchen at the time that Boyd was taking this situation very personally. He acted as if it was his territory that Herb had invaded and his property that Herb had stolen. The obvious explanation was that Boyd was worried about her, and his protective instincts had aroused this angry reaction. She had been flattered by this possibility. But now, as she glanced over at the set of Boyd's usually congenial profile into hard, almost cruel lines, she wondered if there might be more to it than that.

He had continued badgering Herb about what was in the brass box besides Frederick Wulfert's stories, though Gretchen would have sworn Herb was too frightened by then to tell him anything but the entire truth. Still, Boyd kept the pressure on, as if he was after something else that had been in the box. Boyd had even made Herb tell them what the stories were about.

"Monsters. They were all about monsters," Herb shouted back in a trembling voice.

"What kind of monsters?" Boyd insisted.

"All different kinds, right here at the Cape."

"What happens in the stories?"

"I don't know what happens." Herb was obviously desperate and fumbling for an answer by that time. "The monsters kill people and then take off out of here before anybody can stop them."

"What happens then?"

"They turn up all over the world killing people and causing trouble there, too. Then the story ends. That's all I know."

Boyd stopped questioning Herb then, almost as if Herb's vague answer had told Boyd what he wanted to know. At the time Gretchen had been too busy wondering why her grandfather would write horror stories to pay much attention to Boyd's reaction. Remembering it now, she realized just how peculiar the scene had been.

They turned right onto the highway heading toward Tibbetts Point. Herb had said he lived out there near the lighthouse, and Gretchen remembered a small house and her grandfather mentioning Herb. That had been during one of their jaunts out there to watch the light sweep across the treacherous waters where the Saint Lawrence met Lake Ontario, the most easterly of the Great Lakes. The memory sent an ache to Gretchen's heart, and she wished her grandfather were here right now. She was sure he would be able to keep Boyd from being carried away by his temper.

The road changed suddenly, narrowing to a lane and a half of cracked, patched asphalt. They had passed the town line. Beyond that the village didn't have to make repairs, especially since so few people lived out here and many of those were summer folk. The river was very close to the road on the right-hand side of the truck. Gretchen lowered the window a little to let in some air and maybe ease the tension. She could hear the water moving even over the rumble of the truck engine. Ordinarily she found that sound soothing. But hardly anything about tonight was ordinary, so the rushing of the river only reminded her of how deep it was out there and how dangerous the current.

Back on shore occasional driveway lanterns cast pools of yellow light to the left along the landfall side of the road. The houses beyond those yellow pools were dark, some because it was off-season and the vacation residents had boarded up and left with only the automatic timer remaining to turn the yard lights on at night. The houses of the year-round residents were also dark. The north country wasn't a vacation spot for them. They had to be up in the morning and off to work. It was nearly midnight now, too late for them to be awake. Only the wind never slept this close to the Point, blowing the bare branches at the upper reaches of the headlight beams and waving through the underbrush and stalks of wild grass at the side of the road.

Gretchen could feel the tension grow even more taut in the truck cab as they approached the Point. She welcomed the blast of cold river air through the open space at the top of the window and didn't shut it again until she saw the boulders that marked the parking area at the bottom of the hillock leading to the lighthouse. The truck jolted to a stop, and she had her door open before the engine died. She was so intent upon getting away from Boyd's anger and Herb's fear and into the liberating freshness of the river wind that she wasn't paying attention to much else. Herb was out of the truck and past her before she noticed he had moved.

"Stop him!" Boyd shouted against the wind as he bounded out of the other door.

Gretchen started after Herb who had vaulted the white rail fence that bordered the lighthouse grounds. Even in her jeans she wasn't quite up to vaulting after him and had to climb over. Boyd leaped the fence and passed her without so much as a glance in her direction. He was off up the slope after Herb, who was obviously a strong runner and had a substantial lead. Gretchen saw him run into the shadow of the lighthouse tower. She headed for the wire fence that bordered the riverbank and was the most direct route to that shadowed area.

There was no place for Herb to run past the lighthouse. If he came back down the slope, he would have to pass either Boyd, who was headed uphill, or Gretchen along the fence.

She was in the midst of thinking that it was lucky she had on boots that were good for running when she glanced ahead, toward the tower, and saw Herb emerge from the dark shadows into not-so-dark ones on the river-edge side of the light tower. She thought she might have heard him cry out, but the wind was so powerful up here she couldn't be sure. Its howling and buffeting could have accounted for the sound. What happened next took only an instant and was so obscured by moving shadows that, later on, she couldn't be sure about that, either.

Herb appeared to turn around with his back to the river. She thought she saw him raise his arms, as if to ward off an attack. She could see Boyd off to the left, just

reaching the top of the slope. The light tower was between Boyd and Herb. He wouldn't be able to see Boyd
coming. So who was he warding off? Gretchen slowed
down a little and strained to see, but the shadows at the
base of the lighthouse near Herb were too restless from
the reflection of wind-tossed branches for her to make
out anything clearly there. She did think she saw one
shadow move more abruptly than the rest. But, later,
when questioned about it, she couldn't swear she had
seen anything at all.

Then her attention was drawn to Herb. She started
running faster even before she saw him teeter on the
ledge. Something had told her that was going to happen
and she must run her very hardest to grab him before he
toppled over. Something also told her she couldn't possibly get there in time, but she surged ahead, anyway. She
wasn't exactly the athletic type, and she had never known
she could run so fast. Her momentum was so strong that
she didn't stop when she saw Herb fall, his arms flailing
wildly, off the ledge toward the rocky bank below. She
ran on, charging up the bank, only peripherally aware
that her throat was emitting a high, shrill scream into the
wind.

GRETCHEN LOOKED as if she had lost her best friend. No,
that wasn't it. She looked as if she had *killed* her best
friend.

Of course, Herb Dingner had been hardly more than
an acquaintance. Still, Boyd had seen that guilt in her
eyes the one time she looked up at him as the sheriff and
the men of the Cape Vincent Volunteer Fire Brigade
swept the shoreline with their long flashlights. She hadn't
looked at Boyd again directly, and he sensed that was
because she didn't want to include him in the accusation

she was inflicting on herself. Yet there had been a voice in that one glance, and it said, "If we hadn't been chasing him, he wouldn't have fallen."

Now she kept her eyes averted in obvious shame and sadness. He felt those things himself but not because of Herb Dingner. Boyd's shame was motivated by yet another internal voice. It belonged to Max, and it was saying, "This is a good and decent woman." Boyd knew that to be true with every well-honed instinct in him. Yet he was here in Cape Vincent to destroy her life. He wasn't sure he could live with that any more than she would be able to live with the image of Herb Dingner going off that ledge into the rocky waters below.

"Why couldn't I have been the one to see that?" Boyd asked the wind as the knot of frustration tightened in his chest. "Why couldn't I be the one to have that picture burned into my brain for the rest of my life?" His eyes stung, and there was moisture in them. He didn't try to tell himself that the stiff wind had put it there.

The sheriff was toiling back up the rocks. His expression was grim beneath the dark knitted watch cap he had pulled down over his ears against the chill of the riverside. His hip-height waders shone wet to above the knees in the glow of the truck and car headlights that were trained on the scene. Boyd went over to lend him a hand up the ledge, but the sheriff ignored the gesture.

"Did you find anything?" Boyd shouted over the wind.

The sheriff rolled the cuff of the watch cap up from his ears and indicated he hadn't heard. Boyd repeated the question.

"Nothing" was the sheriff's answer as he shook his head. The hollows of shadow cast on his face by the stark headlamp light made him look weary to the bone. "I didn't expect to find anything. The current swept him away. He'll turn up in a day or two somewhere along the shore.''

The wind made conversation a strain, and the sheriff obviously had questions to ask. He herded Boyd and Gretchen into the police car for that purpose. Before starting his questions, the sheriff jacked up the heater full blast. He had peeled off his waders before getting into the car. Now he chafed his legs with his hands to start the circulation moving again.

"You must be nearly frozen," Gretchen said in a voice that was strangely flat, as if the wind had howled all the feeling out of it.

''The river is pretty cold this time of year, and I was standing in it for a while,'' the sheriff said.

He had stopped chafing his long legs and was looking intently at Gretchen. Boyd did the same. He saw the masklike immobility of the face that was becoming more and more dear to him despite himself. She was staring straight ahead, but her eyes could have belonged to a blind person. They didn't blink or shift or follow the motion of things that passed in front of them. Her facial features were similarly frozen. Whatever life there was in her might be moving underneath that mask, but the outer shell of her had been struck lifeless by the impact of what had happened earlier. Gretchen was in shock.

Boyd started to tell the sheriff that, but he motioned for silence. Boyd understood then that the sheriff also recognized the nature of Gretchen's present state of mind and intended to take advantage of it to get information. Boyd would have liked to prevent that, but couldn't risk making it worse for Gretchen by doing so. He couldn't suggest that she shouldn't be questioned until she had a lawyer present. She wasn't being charged with anything, even though she was acting so guilty that such charges seemed inevitable. Boyd decided he would keep his mouth shut, for the moment at least.

"Tell me exactly what you saw, Miss Wulfert," the sheriff said less gently than Boyd would have wanted.

Gretchen didn't answer right away, but she did turn her head, first toward Boyd, then toward the sheriff, as if she had heard a voice speaking to her but couldn't tell where it had come from. The sheriff repeated his question, even less gently than before.

"I saw Herb fall," Gretchen answered at last, sounding more like a recording than a human being.

"Can you be more specific? I'd like to hear the details," the sheriff said, and Boyd hoped he heard some softening there.

"He ran up past the lighthouse. Then he turned around all of a sudden with his back to the water. Then he threw his hands up in front of his face. Then I think I may have seen someone push him over the ledge." She hesitated, and it was the turn of the two men to stare. "But I'm not sure of that last part," she added.

"You're not sure whether you saw someone push Herb?" the sheriff asked.

"That's right," she said.

"What makes you think there *might* have been someone up there with Herb at all?"

"I thought I saw movement in the shadow of the lighthouse."

"It must have been pretty dark up there at the time."

"Yes, it was."

"And you were back down the slope near the fence, and running."

"Yes, I was."

"I see."

Boyd had listened without intervening to the exchange between Gretchen, speaking in her expressionless tone, and the sheriff, in his increasingly skeptical one. It was clear that he didn't believe Gretchen had seen anything. Boyd had considered mentioning her earlier scare in the woods near River House, but decided against it. With no one to corroborate Gretchen's story of an intruder crouching in the undergrowth, she would appear to be more the victim of an overactive imagination than ever. *And* there was the gossip Boyd had heard about Gretchen calling the sheriff to New Beginnings to check out the site of Carl Wulfert's supposed suicide. All of which added up to not much chance the sheriff was likely to believe anything Gretchen said.

The more significant question for Boyd right now was: did he believe her?

AFTER BOYD TOOK Gretchen back to River House, he had wanted to stay but understood that what she needed was to be alone. Besides, he had his own agenda, which had been shunted out of priority position somehow, especially during the past several hours of this very long night. He wished he could feel more guilty about that than he actually did. After all, Max had always come through for him. Max had been there when Boyd's parents died and other times past counting. Max had been father, brother, uncle, friend—despite the fact that they weren't even blood relations. Now he was gone, and the last time Boyd saw him alive, Max had asked something of him. In all of their words together Max had never done that. Boyd was always the one doing the asking, and Max, the coming through. That was the way it was between kids and parent figures. Now payback time had finally arrived, and Boyd couldn't let Max down.

Boyd shook himself to banish any thought of sleep however tired he might be. He had work left to do to-night—for Max. Boyd drove to the marina and took his small motorboat across to the lightship moored against the breakwater. He resumed his post behind the field glasses and waited. The light was still on in Gretchen's window. He could imagine her, trying as diligently to go to sleep as he was trying to stay awake while, behind her closed eyelids, Herb Dingner went over that ledge again and again.

Boyd shook himself once more, this time to banish Gretchen from his thoughts. She was the reason he kept veering off track and forgetting why he had come to this town in the first place. He had to stop that and get back on course. He suspected he would have more trouble do-ing that than he would have staying awake.

Her light winked out at last, and Boyd eased himself down the lightship's rope ladder to the motorboat for the next leg of his quest. He cut straight across the shore, then down-throttled the motor to make it quieter as he moved more slowly toward River House, keeping paral-lel to the shore and just far enough out so that the pro-peller blades wouldn't hit the bottom. When he reached the River House waterfront, he cut the motor altogether and rowed.

All the way from the lightship he'd had an eerie feel-ing about these being the same waters that had swept Herb Dingner to his death. In fact, he most likely had been carried directly past this spot. Boyd dipped his oars gingerly, as if he might possibly hit a floating corpse with one of his strokes. He knew that thought was less than rational, but he kept on rowing with great care, anyway, which made progress even more tedious against the strong current. When he finally did reach his goal, he secured the boat by its bowline to a low-hanging tree and hauled himself out onto the shore.

He dreaded what he had to do next. He had been in some strange and unsettling situations since Max had first sent him off in search of the long-buried truth, but the events of this evening had made Boyd truly skittish for the first time. Nonetheless, those same events had revealed a possible source of hidden evidence. Despite the whisper of dread prickling the skin at the back of his neck, he had to explore this lead.

He shot a glance over his shoulder, though his common sense told him nothing was there but the dark river lapping against his own boat as it bobbed up and down where he had left it. A freighter was approaching from downriver. He could just make out her black-hulled silhouette against the slightly lightening sky. Her prow plied the channel along the Canadian shore to avoid the treacherous shoals for which this river was known and feared. The bridge was up front and the smokestack astern, with lights strung along the rails between, giving her the appearance at this distance of a fancy cruise liner rather than the beast of burden that she was.

The freighter was too far away, and the waning night was still too dark for anyone on board to see Boyd on the shore. Still, he waited until the vessel rumbled past. He didn't really think he could be spotted here. He simply didn't relish the prospect of going back into those dank, dark tunnels alone.

THIS NIGHT OF LISTENING and watching had provided Kraft with just enough action to set his blood moving hot and fast the way he loved to feel it. It occurred to him that he should involve himself in more such operations. They would keep him from slipping into the senility that had claimed younger but less vigorous men—not that such a phenomenon was likely in his case. Even so, he wouldn't leave so much of the fun to hirelings in the future, especially since he was so good at this kind of thing.

He had remained in his van listening while Emory and the Wulfert girl had interrogated that historian fellow in her bedroom on the second floor of River House. Kraft had been most fascinated by Dingner's description of Frederick Wulfert's stories. He had understood immediately what the old fool had meant by writing about monsters. The man hadn't the nerve to tell the whole truth and make a direct confession to assuage his guilt, so the weakling had made up symbolic guessing games instead. How typical of a coward like him.

Kraft doubted there was anyone around here smart enough to figure out what Frederick had been getting at, but precautions were in order all the same. Dingner had said he'd hidden the stories well, "in a place no one could find in a million years." Kraft's instincts—fine-tuned by experience to separate truth from lies in an interrogation situation—had told him Dingner had been telling the truth. The rest was simply a matter of waiting for opportunity to present itself, as it inevitably did.

He had heard Dingner tell them where he lived. Kraft's van was already near the road. He had driven to the Point ahead of them and had the vehicle well hidden back down the road and himself in the shrubbery well before they'd arrived. The instant Dingner had begun to run, Kraft had known he had him. A running man, especially a panicked one, made a vulnerable target. It was child's play for Kraft to track his prey to the lighthouse ledge and then to do what had to be done.

Kraft had slipped away in the shadows and was off quietly, back toward the village, while the girl and her friend were still scrambling around attempting to save a sleazy, insignificant man who was already long gone downstream.

Kraft had returned to his hiding place near River House and stashed the van well out of sight from the road by the time the sheriff's car had shrieked past. Once again Kraft had assumed that Gretchen and Emory would be back here eventually. Kraft had even allowed himself a refreshing nap until he'd heard the pickup return and drop her off. Kraft had then decided to follow Emory, since he hadn't gone inside the house and there would thus be no more conversation tonight at River House to eavesdrop upon. Also Kraft was growing more and more suspicious of Emory. He could be another meddler who would have to be dealt with.

Sure enough Mr. Emory's behavior tonight had proven very curious, indeed. He had boated out to a rusting hulk near the town breakwater and disappeared into the cabin. Kraft had been patient as usual in waiting to see what his subject would do next. Eventually Kraft's binoculars revealed Emory in his motor launch once more and headed back across the river, but not to the marina this time. Kraft needed hardly an instant's thought to guess where the meddler was headed.

Kraft turned the van back toward River House, but didn't wait inside this time. Instead, he crept into the woods near the old mansion and up to the shore. Many decades of survivalist expeditions had hardened Kraft against cold and damp and other physical discomforts. Consequently he had acquired the endurance needed to crouch by the frigid river on such a windy night. He suspected he had been born with his extraordinary night vision.

He had no trouble spotting Emory's rowing approach, at a pace that was surprisingly slow for someone with such husky arms and broad shoulders. Kraft would have been pleased to think that indicated the brawny oaf to be a muscle-bound weakling, but the possibility seemed unlikely. Thus, Kraft took along a bit of insurance, in the form of a cudgel that some hoodlum types liked to call a sap, as he ventured forth to follow Boyd into the river-edge passageway.

UPSTAIRS IN RIVER HOUSE Gretchen's fitful sleep had been invaded by snatches of what her grandmother used to tell her were "fever dreams," because a person woke from them hot and sweaty with a head full of what felt like angry champagne fizz. Gretchen had been drifting in and out of that disconcerting state for what seemed like days but must have been only a couple of hours when she found herself awake again. Something had jolted her into consciousness. And, though she was still bleary and out of focus, she was almost certain she had been roused from sleep by something she'd heard.

Gradually the details of the past evening came back to her—among them, the memory of standing in this same room listening to sounds in the walls, where she had since learned there was a tunnel that led from the riverbank. She eased herself quietly out of bed and pulled on her robe. She didn't turn on the light but felt her way to the wall near the closet door. She didn't have to listen intently this time. What she heard was loud and clear—a clatter and then scuffling noises accompanied by grunting sounds.

She made her way as quickly as was possible in the near-darkness back to her bedside and grabbed the flashlight she had left there earlier. She used the beam to guide her to the closet but kept it trained on the floor directly in front of her so that the light would be less likely to flash ahead very far and be seen.

She stopped at the rear of the closet to listen just inside the closed entrance to the hidden passage. She did so for several moments but could no longer hear anything from the other side of the wall. It occurred to her that she should have a weapon. She grabbed a wooden hanger that had been left behind in the closet when she and Boyd removed the clothes. This thing would hardly be much protection against anything particularly formidable. It certainly wasn't preventing her heart from hammering loudly in her ears. Still, she had to find out what it was she had heard.

She pushed against the passageway door. It moved more easily than it had earlier, but she still wished she had Boyd's strength assisting her. One flash of her light across the opening told her why such assistance could hardly have been possible at the moment.

Boyd was on his back, sprawled across the passageway, obviously unconscious—or worse.

Chapter Ten

Boyd could hardly believe he had let himself be jumped from behind like that. At first he thought it was Gretchen. She could have heard someone coming up the tunnel from the river and attacked, not realizing it was him. Then he grabbed hold of a handful of slippery material that felt a lot like his own Air Force parka. The bulk of the person inside that jacket was considerably more substantial than Gretchen.

At that point Boyd began struggling in earnest. He had held back while he thought he might be grappling with Gretchen. When that proved untrue, he pulled out the stops and fought with all his might. He doubled his fist and swung as hard as he could, considering that he was still in a scrambling clutch with his assailant in the pitch-dark. Boyd's blow connected, and the response was a decidedly masculine grunt of pain. With that blow Boyd had hoped he might reverse the tide of the contest, which had been running against him because of his less than total effort in the beginning. Unfortunately, by the time he started battling seriously, it was too late for a comeback.

Boyd couldn't remember if he actually felt the punch that knocked him out. All he could remember was the throbbing ache he woke up with. Now he pressed his eyelids closed to shut out the gleam of Gretchen's flashlight, which felt as if it were blazing straight through his battered head. She was talking to him, but he didn't answer. He was too preoccupied with piecing together what had happened from the time he'd entered the tunnel at the riverside.

Gretchen helped him to his feet while his head reeled. He nearly toppled both of them as she did her best to hold him up and they staggered out of the tunnel. Whoever hit him had done a good job of it. When Boyd reached up to touch the sore spot on his head, he felt sticky wetness that could only have been blood. From the concern in Gretchen's eyes Boyd could surmise that he must look a mess. He would have liked to quip something like, "Wait till you see the other guy," but Boyd was fairly certain he hadn't managed to inflict much damage in that direction.

"What happened?"

Gretchen had already asked that question several times. Now she was asking it again, and Boyd's head had cleared enough for him to know he must answer. She was still looking concerned about him, even though he must look less ghastly than he had before now that she was washing his wound. Nonetheless, he could assume that curiosity and then suspicion would soon take the place of her solicitousness if he didn't come up with an explanation and make it a good one. After all, what could he possibly have been doing in that tunnel in the middle of the night when he had just dropped her off here at River House?

He considered telling her the entire truth, and that thought brought with it a rush of blissful relief. He cared for her, and he knew it. Yet there was this deceit between them, a wall he longed to break down. He looked up at her, and a wave of tenderness washed over him. On the crest of that wave he reached up and touched her cheek, so soft the feel of her skin made him ache, especially when she took that hand in hers and gazed straight into his eyes.

"Tell me," she said, not forcefully, though he heard it as a request not to be ignored.

Boyd gazed back at her, poised for that moment on the brink of the truth. He turned away only with the greatest reluctance. The reality of the situation was that he couldn't indulge himself with confession no matter how liberating that would be. He had made a resolution to keep his priorities straight, and first among those priorities was finding the evidence Max had wanted so desperately. Telling Gretchen the truth could create the biggest obstacle Boyd had yet encountered to that quest.

As far as she knew, Herb Dingner had been the culprit here, and now he was dead. Letting her know that there was another villain in the picture, and more at stake than some stories by her grandfather, would only encourage her to get even more involved in whatever was going on here. Boyd didn't want that. So he had to come up with an explanation for what he had been doing in that tunnel and how he managed to get bopped on the head while doing it.

Make it just outlandish enough, he told himself. That way she'd believe it was true because nobody would concoct such a story and think they could get away with it.

"Bats," he said, trying not to sound as if he had picked that word, both literally and figuratively, out of the air. "I thought there were bats in the tunnel, and I guess I panicked."

"Why would you think that? There weren't any bats in the tunnel earlier."

Boyd considered panicking for real at this point, because what she said was true. Maybe his story was *too* outlandish. Maybe he had strayed into the utterly implausible.

"I'm not sure now whether there was anything in the tunnel or not. I think I may have been a bit disoriented from lack of sleep, but I could have sworn I saw bats swirling around my head. I can't stand rodents, so I started waving them away. I dropped my light. Then I must have been flailing around so erratically that I banged into the wall. That's the only explanation I can think of."

That last statement was certainly true. Boyd shook his head to show how befuddled he was, then wished he hadn't. It felt as if he might have some loose parts in there, and they all had sharp edges.

"What were you doing in the tunnel in the first place?" Gretchen asked.

Boyd's prediction had come true. Concerned as Gretchen might be about the burgeoning bump on his head, there was an edge of suspicion in her voice.

"I kept wondering if we missed something earlier, maybe something Herb didn't tell us. I knew I was probably being paranoid, but I couldn't get it out of my mind. I didn't want to worry you about it unless I came up with something definite. So I decided to check the tunnels one more time on my own."

"How did you get in there? Did you go through from the basement?"

That was a harder one to answer. It would sound pretty farfetched to tell her he had gone to all the trouble of taking out a boat on a dark, windy night like this, then fought the dangerous current to get to the tunnel entrance at the river's edge. Unfortunately, saying that he snuck in through her basement could also raise questions he wasn't prepared to answer without a bit more time for tale-concocting.

Boyd could hardly have been more relieved when, just at that moment, the phone rang.

"Who could that be at this hour?" Gretchen asked.

Gretchen's attention had been distracted from Boyd for the moment at least. Meanwhile, he had the same question she did. Who would be calling now as dawn's first glimmers began to filter through the parted organdy curtains at Gretchen's windows?

"Yes, Pauline," Gretchen was saying into the receiver of the delicate white French-style telephone on her bedside table.

Pauline Basinette must be calling from the spa. Boyd doubted that she made a practice of doing that at daybreak. Something out of the ordinary must have happened for her to phone Gretchen at this hour. Watching her face told Boyd he was right about that.

She didn't suddenly assume a startled look, however—quite the opposite, in fact. Boyd had spent a lot of time observing Gretchen Wulfert lately, enough to know that she kept a close rein on her emotions, or at least on the visible manifestation of those emotions. Watching her now, he could actually see her pulling those reins as taut as she could get them.

In an instant she had banished all expression from her face, as if a frigid blast had frozen the surface. This wasn't the mask of shock she had worn at Tibbetts Point the night before. Her eyes weren't staring. They were very much alive, and it was those eyes that betrayed her. In them shone a flash of fear apparently too powerful to repress.

"I'll be right there" was all she said before hanging up and turning to Boyd.

"What's happened?" he asked.

"It's my grandfather," she told him, and her calmness belied the effort he knew she must be making to maintain such control.

He stood up from the bed, paying no attention to the reeling in his head. He put his arms around her and held her gently close. Neither of them spoke, and she didn't pull away. They stood like that for a long moment in the slowly brightening dawn. Then she eased herself out of his embrace. And, when he looked down at her, he could see that her lashes were misted with tears.

"I'll drive you," he said.

She nodded but didn't try to smile. Then she left the room.

Boyd stared at the door that closed behind her. He was aware of his own emotions tumbling more chaotically than ever. And, because of that, he was glad Gretchen couldn't see him now. He wasn't sure he could have hidden those emotions as well as she managed to hide hers.

He had just volunteered to rush Gretchen to the bedside of her aged and ailing grandfather. Part of Boyd— his heart to be exact—reached out to her in her anxiety and longed to give comfort and protection. Then there was the other part of him—the head part—that didn't want anything to happen to Frederick Wulfert for very different reasons. Boyd had questions to ask that old man, and Boyd intended to get the answers. Despite the firmness of that intention, however, he couldn't help but dread the impact those answers could have on the woman he had come to feel entirely too much fondness for.

BOYD AND GRETCHEN didn't talk much on the way to New Beginnings and hurried upstairs as soon as they got there.

"I didn't tell you the details when I called," Pauline said, meeting them at the top of the staircase. "After what I just figured out, I don't even trust the telephones."

She labored down the hallway in front of them, but instead of heading for Frederick's room, she motioned them into the pharmacy.

"I want to see my grandfather," Gretchen said, resisting the detour.

"You have to see what's in here first."

There was urgency in the way Pauline had said that. Boyd took Gretchen's arm and urged her to follow. "Let's just take a look at what Pauline has to show us."

For a moment Gretchen didn't budge. She stared up at Boyd, wanting so much to tell him how she hadn't been here for her grandfather during his earlier crises. If there was another one now, all she cared about was hurrying to his side. The compassion in Boyd's eyes told her he understood that. She was suddenly filled with emotion, as if she could turn to him, bury her head against his chest and sob her heart out. Then everything would be all right. She couldn't remember allowing herself to feel anything quite like that in a very long time.

Of course, she didn't bury her head against his chest and sob. She was still a Wulfert, after all. She simply nodded to let Boyd know that she understood the good sense of what he was saying. Then she let him lead her into the pharmacy.

"We keep your grandfather's glucose solution pre-mixed in the refrigerator," Pauline said when they joined her at the long, brushed steel counter. "Carl was very concerned about that. He said we had to make certain there was enough on hand. So we've been preparing these big bottles for weeks now.''

She gestured toward the large apothecary jar on the table. ''I went along with Carl because I thought he was so worried about his father that it was making him go a little overboard. I thought I'd humor him. I should have known he was up to no good.''

''What do you mean?'' Gretchen had been standing gratefully within the circle of Boyd's protective arm. Now she pulled away, as if she might feel stronger and more equal to whatever was coming if she were standing on her own.

''I finally figured it out this morning,'' Pauline said. ''I could kick myself for not putting two and two together before this.''

She looked truly miserable, and the face powder beneath her eyes was caked and smudging. Obviously she had been crying.

''Just tell us what happened,'' Gretchen urged more gently.

''Well, I'd noticed some cloudiness in the jars before this, but that happens sometimes. I'd just shake the jar up before filling your grandfather's IV bags. Then this morning I noticed something more than just cloudiness in the jar. Can you see these little white flakes here?''

Gretchen pressed forward. Pauline was referring to traces of small, powdery chips that had settled to the very bottom of the jar. Unless Pauline had stepped aside to let the light shine directly into the liquid, Gretchen would never have detected the sediment. Now that she did see it she felt a bit bewildered. Was this why Pauline had dragged them here at the crack of dawn? Could these tiny white specks possibly be a cause for such alarm? Pauline was getting old, after all. Maybe her judgment wasn't all that it had once been.

"Clouds are one thing, but this stuff is another," Pauline said before Gretchen's thoughts could carry her farther into skepticism. "There shouldn't be anything that solid in the solution. So I got to thinking what it could be and how there'd been that cloudiness in those jars for quite some time now. I got to thinking that maybe that cloudiness started back about the time your grandfather went unconscious, and how those little white specks could mean that something had been added to his IV solution. He was getting glucose before the coma, you know. The doctor prescribed it to build up his nutrition. He'd gotten so preoccupied with his charity work and such that he hadn't been eating right."

"What are you saying? That the doctor added something to my grandfather's glucose solution without telling you about it?" Gretchen was getting frustrated with the old woman's drawn-out way of telling whatever it was she had to say.

"I think Pauline is getting to that," Boyd said quietly.

He had stepped close to Gretchen again and put his arm back around her shoulders while the resonance of his voice washed over her. For a moment she was reminded of sitting at the very end of the marina dock as a child, watching the river flow endlessly past, and how calm it had made her feel to do that. She didn't pull away from the circle of Boyd's arm this time. She was even able to listen less impatiently as Pauline continued.

"The doctor would have had to tell me if there was something added to the IVs," she said. "I'm the one who would've mixed it in. I never got any such orders. Then, when I came in this morning to fill up your grandfather's early a.m. bag, I saw those white things and it came to me that they look like ground-up pills."

Gretchen could feel herself getting agitated again. Boyd must have felt it, too, because he stroked her shoulder gently as Pauline continued.

"That's what gave me the idea to check the drug cabinet and the pharmacy records. I figured that if anybody was taking pills out of there, it would show up because there'd be fewer pills in the cabinet than there should be. We keep very careful records of what we buy and what happens to it. Regulations say we've got to do that."

"We know that, Pauline." Boyd was the one to urge her on this time. "What did you find when you did that checking?"

"I was just getting to that." Pauline must have sensed their impatience because she did speed up her delivery a bit. "I started looking at the sedatives first. That seemed obvious, but he was smart enough not to be so obvious. He knew we keep more careful track of the narcotics than we do anything else."

"*Who* knew that?" Gretchen broke in.

"Your Uncle Carl. Who else?"

That was exactly what Gretchen had expected to hear. An icy finger of dread touched her throat and made it suddenly so tight that she had to swallow to make certain she still could.

"Are you saying there weren't any narcotics missing?" Boyd asked.

"That's right," Pauline said. "But something just about as good *was* way off the count."

Ordinarily Gretchen might have expected to hear some pride in Pauline's voice as she reported the results of her clever detective work. Instead, she sounded worried and sad.

"There's something we use for patients who have trouble digesting. It's got a sedative in it, something that's made from belladonna, but nobody would think of it first thing as a narcotic. This is the drug that's in there."

A copy of a thick pharmaceutical reference book was open on the table nearby. Pauline hobbled over to it and pointed out the name of the drug scopolamine. Gretchen scanned the text, and Boyd leaned over her shoulder to do the same.

"You're right," he said. "This stuff has a powerful sedative effect."

"That's what's in the digestive medicine," Pauline said, "and there's a whole lot of it missing from the cabinet. In fact, the capsules are all gone. I figure that's why Carl had to resort to using the tablets, and that's how come I noticed those pieces in the bottom of the jar. The capsules would have been easy to open up. Then the powder inside would dissolve in the liquid with no trouble except a little mixing, but the capsules ran out. After that, grinding up the tablets fine enough to dissolve all the way would have been a lot harder. They might look like they'd disappeared. Then, after a while, they'd settle out just like here." She pointed at the jar again.

Gretchen could hardly believe what she was hearing. Before her experiences of the past several days, she wouldn't have listened to it at all. Now she might not think there could be any truth in what Pauline was saying, but there were so many strange things going on here....

"Why would my uncle put drugs in my grandfather's intravenous solution?" Gretchen heard herself ask.

"Because he wanted to render him unconscious and make sure he didn't wake up," Boyd interjected.

Gretchen looked up at him. He seemed to be distracted and thinking about something while speaking his conclusions aloud.

"Why would Uncle Carl want that?"

"Maybe to keep your grandfather from talking about something Carl didn't want to have get out," Boyd answered slowly.

"What could my grandfather possibly know that Uncle Carl would go to such lengths to hide?"

That finger of dread inside Gretchen had grown several tentacles by now. They gripped her so hard that she felt as if she would never move again.

Pauline muttered something under her breath.

"What was that, Pauline?" Boyd asked.

"Nothing important. I was just repeating Miss Gretchen's question to myself."

But Gretchen knew that wasn't true. She had been able to make out two words from Pauline's muttering. Those words had been "Stone Cottage." Could it be that Pauline thought Gretchen's grandfather knew something about Stone Cottage, the old building at the back of the New Beginnings property? Something so important to Carl Wulfert that he would go to great lengths to keep it from getting out?

Stone Cottage had been deserted for years. What could possibly be so important about that vine-covered relic? Maybe Pauline was getting senile, after all, and imagining things. On the other hand, what she'd said about the scopolamine made a lot of sense. Still, Gretchen didn't question the old nurse further now. There would be time for investigation later, and she would do that investigating on her own. She wouldn't tell Boyd what she had just overheard. She still had her doubts about why he was rooting around in that tunnel earlier. She couldn't let herself trust him completely yet, no matter how comforting he was being right now or how safe he had made her feel for that moment he'd held her in his arms back at River House.

"I called the doctor," Pauline was saying. "He's in there with your grandfather now."

That news distracted Gretchen from thoughts of Boyd and Stone Cottage for the moment. She hurried out of the pharmacy and toward Frederick's room with Boyd in step and Pauline rumbling along behind. There was yet another question troubling Gretchen, however, and she couldn't let this one wait. She had to know the answer— or at least someone else's opinion—immediately.

She touched Boyd's arm, and he turned expectantly toward her. She had stopped halfway down the hall toward the closed door of her grandfather's room. She took a deep breath before speaking the unspeakable.

"If Uncle Carl wanted to keep my grandfather quiet about something, why didn't he just kill him?"

Boyd's voice was more gentle than ever when he answered, and his eyes brimmed with caring. "From what I just read about the effects of scopolamine," he said, "I suspect that is exactly what would have happened eventually."

Pauline had hobbled up in time to heard Boyd's statement. She didn't say anything in response. She just nodded her agreement very solemnly as Gretchen gaped from one of them to the other. She was peripherally aware of her mouth frozen open, as if the usual connection between her brain and her voice had short-circuited.

Then she was off down the hall again, running this time. Whatever her grandfather might have drilled into her about remaining calm and collected and never betraying her emotions had been abandoned. All she cared about at this moment was rushing to him and never leaving him again. She was about to grasp the doorknob and burst into his room when she felt Boyd beside her.

"I'm here" was all he said.

That was enough to halt her headlong dash and allow her to think for a moment. She had to maintain control for her grandfather's sake in case he needed her help in some way. Gretchen counted silently for a few numbers. Not until she was perfectly calm did she open the door slowly and quietly in order not to disturb anyone.

Dr. Govinda had his back to the door and didn't turn around immediately, but Gretchen knew who he was. It wasn't easy to lure physicians to the remote north country. Beryll had told Gretchen about Dr. Govinda and how fortunate they were to have a man of his talents consulting at New Beginnings. She was relieved to see him here, but that relief was short-lived.

As the doctor noticed her presence and stepped away from the bed to greet her, she saw her grandfather's face. She wouldn't have thought it possible, but he looked more ashen than ever. A sob escaped her throat, and she bit her lip hard against the torrent of sobs that threatened to follow.

Boyd was still at her side. He stepped closer and put his arm around her yet again. "How is Mr. Wulfert?" he asked the doctor, hesitating an instant before he spoke her grandfather's name. Boyd's voice was taut and strained, as if he was in the grip of emotions almost as strong as Gretchen's.

"We must withdraw him very gradually from the scopolamine," Dr. Govinda answered in an accent that echoed his Indian homeland. "Otherwise the ramifications could be quite serious."

"Will he come out of the coma?" Boyd asked.

"I expect he should eventually, but I cannot say precisely when."

"What condition do you expect he'll be in when he does wake up?"

Gretchen was grateful to Boyd for asking these questions for her. She wasn't sure she would have been able to utter them on her own.

"It is equally difficult to say what effect long-term sedation will have on any patient, especially one Mr. Wulfert's age." The doctor was obviously choosing his words with care. "There can be a number of possible results from extended exposure to this drug."

"Such as impaired mental function?" Gretchen had managed to ask that herself, though the words were barely audible. Once again she simply had to know.

"That is one possibility." The doctor's dark eyes were filled with compassion.

"What kind of impairment would be typical?" Gretchen continued, whispering a silent prayer as she spoke.

"Again it is difficult to be precise about such things. I would say that some disruption of motor function is probable. Also, with this particular drug, I might anticipate a loss of memory."

"Amnesia?" Boyd asked. He sounded genuinely concerned.

"Yes," the doctor said. "But, as I have already told you, in a case like this any prognosis would be little more than conjecture on my part."

"Thank you, Doctor," Gretchen said. She wished she could better express her gratitude for his presence but, at the moment, she was in no mental shape to try.

Pauline had lumbered into the room behind them and stood listening to what the doctor had to say. "Now I know why Carl *really* wanted to keep me on as his father's nurse." She was muttering again, as if talking to herself rather than to the rest of them.

"Why is that, Pauline?" Gretchen asked, noting that the old nurse's nose was even redder and more shiny than usual.

"Because your uncle didn't think I would be on the ball enough to figure out what he was up to." Her tone was sad and her voice quavered. Tears glistened in her eyes.

Boyd moved away from Gretchen for a moment to touch the older woman's arm. "Carl turned out to be wrong about that, didn't he?"

The tenderness in the way Boyd said that and the warmth of his smile for Pauline caught at Gretchen's heart. Even in the midst of her own sorrow, she couldn't help thinking that Boyd Emory was a kind man and that she liked him very much. In fact, what she felt for him was probably much more than liking.

"You have indeed done a splendid job of investigative work here, Nurse Basinette," Dr. Govinda added. "I am certain that the sheriff will be most interested in your findings."

Gretchen was startled to hear him say that. "We don't need to get the police involved, do we?"

"Oh, yes. I am afraid we do," the doctor said, rather emphatically for a soft-spoken man. "There has been wrongdoing here, most likely of a criminal nature. Even if the perpetrator is deceased, I have no alternative but to report the incident."

"Is it really necessary to put Miss Wulfert through this?" Boyd asked.

"It's all right, Boyd," she said.

Gretchen understood that the doctor was right, but sorely wished he wasn't. She knew what kind of talk such a story would generate in the village. Her uncle, whom so many people had hated for his mean-spirited ways, had drugged his own father into a coma and had possibly planned even worse. For the first time in her life she felt a strong surge of something her grandfather had spoken of often and with great dedication—the desire to protect and preserve the family name, but this time she knew that wouldn't be possible. She wished that Boyd's arm were still around her. She would have liked to lean against him right now for support.

"It is especially imperative that I contact the authorities in this case," the doctor was saying in his characteristic, very precise manner. "I suspect that this incident was most meticulously premeditated."

"What makes you suspect that?" Boyd asked.

"Because Frederick Wulfert's associates, including family members and senior staff, were informed that long ago he made a firm request that no autopsy be performed after his death. It is most doubtful that I would have considered expiration during a coma state extraordinary enough to justify countermanding his wishes. Thus, I would most likely never have detected this tampering with his medication. No one would have suspected it. My theory is that the culprit knew that and was consequently assured of getting away with the crime. That would suggest a very ingenious murder plot, indeed."

Gretchen began walking toward the window before he had finished speaking. She forced her feet to move, one after the other, until she reached the white rocking chair. She sank into it, unable to see a thing through the pane of glass she stared at with a stupefied gaze.

KRAFT WAITED patiently in the van for the sheriff to arrive at New Beginnings. The man would be visible, whichever direction he might approach from, because Kraft's hiding place afforded a fine view. He had selected it with that in mind. He kept the headphones on even though he calculated there wouldn't be anything significant to hear until the sheriff joined the others.

When that finally did happen, Kraft's monitoring equipment told him that the gathering was in Beryll Sackett's office. The administrator had arrived for work only a short while ago herself. She had, of course, acted as shocked as all the rest by the old nurse's discovery.

Kraft, on the other hand, hadn't been shocked at all. He had chuckled at the prospect of Carl Wulfert killing off his own father. Actually, Kraft wouldn't have thought the fat swine capable of anything that demanding. Still, he was a degenerate and an inferior and the world had been, without doubt, improved by his elimination. Kraft had long advocated the extermination of such undesirable elements.

Kraft recognized the identity of most of the voices in Beryll's office from having listened in on them for so long. Of the two unfamiliar speakers, he deduced that the deeper tones belonged to the sheriff and the singsong ones to the foreign doctor. They did most of the talking at first while the sheriff was filled in on the details. Then the sheriff asked the pivotal question. "What makes all of you so certain Carl Wulfert did this?"

"Who else would it be?" Emory asked, sounding a bit defensive. Kraft guessed Emory would be worried about any suspicion falling on Gretchen Wulfert, whom he had obviously gone sickeningly sweet over. "Carl had the perfect motive."

"What motive is that?" the sheriff asked, sounding surprisingly cagey for a yokel.

"He'd be in line to inherit the estate, I would assume," Emory said. "I thought it was your job to figure out things like that."

"I'll keep in mind that you've had a lot to put up with in the past twenty-four hours, Mr. Emory," the sheriff said. "So I'll disregard your tone of voice *this* time, but watch yourself."

"Boyd didn't mean any disrespect, Sheriff," the girl jumped in. Kraft sneered at the way those two stood up for each other. "But he is right about my Uncle Carl. He would have inherited the bulk of the Wulfert estate. My father has renounced all claim to everything."

"Why would your uncle bother to kill an old man who wasn't very healthy, anyway? How many more years could it have been until he died naturally?"

There was silence for a while after that one. Kraft sneered again. He could almost see all of them straining their inadequate little minds for an answer.

"Maybe my uncle needed money right away," Gretchen suggested finally. "Maybe he had some project he needed it for."

She was smarter than she looked, Kraft thought. She had better not get *too* close to the truth, or she'd definitely regret it.

"I'd say there's another possibility, *if* Carl is the guilty party here," the sheriff said, and Kraft cupped the headphones tighter to his ears. "Maybe he wanted to keep your grandfather quiet about something for a while. That would explain why he would put him into a coma instead of killing him."

"Maybe Carl thought he'd have a better chance of covering up the murder if he killed him slowly," Emory said, only a little more respectfully than before.

"Maybe, but I think I like *my* cover-up theory better. Do any of you know about anything Carl Wulfert might have wanted to hide?"

Once again silence followed the sheriff's question. Then he launched into a survey of other possible suspects on his list, with the old nurse right at the top. She certainly had the opportunity, and the ferret-faced administrator was quick to point out that everybody in town knew Pauline had been infatuated with old Frederick for decades and probably couldn't stand the fact that he was beyond her reach.

That sparked an argument between the two foolish women, during which Beryll Sackett's own opportunity to do the deed was eagerly pointed out by her nemesis who, unfortunately, couldn't come up with a motive. The suspect list continued, with Emory and the girl eliminated because neither of them had been in town when Frederick went into the coma.

Lester Wilson was then seriously discussed as a possibility because he supposedly was after some Wulfert property. Somebody actually suggested that Wilson could have incapacitated Frederick, then killed Carl in order to end up dealing with Gretchen, who might have been more tractable. Kraft scoffed at the thought of that pudgy weakling being capable of anything even a fraction so bold.

"Of course Carl did it, you idiots," Kraft said aloud to the empty van. The sheriff's next statement suggested that he might agree.

"If your original theory about Carl is right, that would give us a motive for his suicide. He did this terrible thing to his father and couldn't live with himself any longer."

Kraft laughed almost heartily at that. He settled back against the cracked leather seat.

Meanwhile, however, the group in Sackett's office knew more than he wanted them to, though not yet enough to get in his way. That and the earlier good news that, if Frederick did wake up, he might very well have amnesia left Kraft some time to maneuver. He would make certain he used it well.

Then again, Kraft thought, perhaps he had better not count on Frederick losing his memory. After all, Carl had claimed his father's recollection of things past was unfortunately acute. That was probably the reason Carl had put the old boy in a coma in the first place. Perhaps it was time for Kraft to finish what Carl had started but lacked the nerve to complete.

Kraft laughed aloud once more. He was definitely not deficient in nerve, or in any of the other qualities required.

Chapter Eleven

Both Boyd and Pauline had been worried about Gretchen after the sheriff left. She had been ghostly pale and near collapse and had known it. She hadn't offered much resistance when Pauline insisted on putting her to bed right there at the spa, but down on the second floor where she wouldn't be disturbed as the staff kept vigilant watch over her grandfather's condition.

As Gretchen vaguely recalled, someone had actually tucked her in. She had imagined it was Boyd, but that could have been merely the way it happened in the dreams that followed, where he figured as a prominent character. More likely Pauline did the tucking in real life, however. She was too old-fashioned to allow a man into Gretchen's room when she was sleeping, no matter how much Pauline might want them to get together.

That was, by the way, another theme that threaded in and out of Gretchen's dreams—Pauline lecturing her about healthy, handsome grandchildren and Frederick nodding his agreement. Gretchen didn't awaken from *these* dreams feeling feverish. She drifted back to consciousness in a warm, pleasant haze that stayed with her a surprisingly long time, considering the terrible circumstances under which she had gone to sleep.

Mercifully none of those circumstances came immediately to mind when she first opened her eyes to see fresh, clean clothes draped over the chair near the bed. Someone had gone to River House and selected an outfit for her to change into after having worn the same jeans and sweater for hours on end.

She examined with interest the items that had been chosen for her—a below-calf, long skirt with a slight flare, dark with a subtle pattern, and a soft sweater that picked up one of the colors in that pattern. On the floor next to the chair stood her high black boots, a perfect match for the darkness of the skirt. The gleam of the soft leather suggested that they had been buffed for her, as well.

She was surprised that Pauline would have picked out such an understatedly stylish and attractive ensemble. The nurse had never impressed Gretchen as being particularly fashion conscious. She had seen Pauline out of her starched white uniform a number of times over the years, and the woman was most likely to have on a rather disparate combination of misshapen separates. Gretchen could remember thinking that Nurse Basinette, who always looked crisp as could be in her immaculate uniform, probably didn't consider clothes counted for much off the job. Gretchen wouldn't have expected in a million years that the starched and powdery old nurse could have coordinated the pieces she had hung on this chair.

Then it occurred to Gretchen that Pauline hadn't picked out this outfit at all. Boyd had done it. He had gone to River House and let himself in through one of the windows that the housekeeper, like so many north country folks, had inevitably left unlocked. Or perhaps he had taken the key from Gretchen's shoulder bag. In most people she would have thought that presumptuous and been annoyed by it. Instead, she was grateful that he had provided what she wanted most at this moment—a hot shower and something fresh to put on afterward. And he had done so despite the fact that he had looked almost as worn out as she did during that grueling dawn gathering in her grandfather's room.

She pushed the memory of that scene from her mind for the time being. There would be more than enough opportunity for agonizing over that subject in the hours to come. Right now she was going to bask in the luxury of feeling cared for and about—as if she had been gently nestled in to a velvet cocoon hung with gossamer veils that softened all the harsh images of life, the way a gauze overlay on a camera lens softened the harsh imprint of age upon a face.

Gretchen reached out to touch the fine wool of the skirt that happened to be one of her favorites. The garment slid partly off the chair at her touch and, looking underneath it, she realized why. Whoever had left these clothes here had placed a set of satiny silk underthings beneath them. There was a delicate black bra and panties to go with it, both decorated with insets of black lace. She had bought them in a tiny shop on a quaint, narrow street in Paris. She remembered that shop smelling sweet and feminine, much like the gossamer veils in the vision she had just been experiencing. She lifted the delicate silk to her face and could still detect the scent of that special Paris place.

More than Paris, however, the softness of this silk whispered to her of Boyd Emory. He had opened the drawer where she kept these lovely things. He had chosen these particular pieces from the many folded and piled up there. He had touched their satin smoothness and breathed in their scent, just as she was doing now. He had carried them here and arranged them neatly on this chair, handling them with such care that there was never a snag or a catch possible upon the fragile fabric.

She could see him doing that, and her breath stopped in her throat as she thought of it. Even beyond that, she could sense what he had been thinking at the time, and that was more breathtaking still. He had been thinking that these gossamer garments would touch her skin and clothe her body in its most intimate places, and that he had selected them for her in a ritual not unlike that performed for a maiden being prepared to give herself to her prince upon their wedding night.

Gretchen placed the underthings back on the chair and rose from the bed, very slowly and quietly so as not to disturb the spell of the moment. She walked to the bathroom door and looked in to find what she had already half expected would be there. Her toilet articles—silverbacked hairbrush, crystal perfume atomizer, all the pretty things from her dressing table at River House—were arranged on a soft white towel on the bath stand.

She gasped softly as she realized he was all around her here, in everything she looked at and everything she touched. He had made this place lovely for her, and he had done that with a sense of her true, deep self that, until this moment, she wouldn't have believed any man could be capable of. Gretchen looked around her—at the clothing on the chair and the arrangement of the bath stand—and knew that what Boyd had done here was an act of such tenderness that she could hardly bear to take it in.

UNFORTUNATELY THE ROMANTIC aura Boyd had created for her didn't survive Gretchen's shower, where the needles of water from the stainless-steel shower head brought

reality back like an electric shock. Right now reality for
Gretchen was still fraught with too many questions and
too few answers. There had been two deaths so far, and
her grandfather could be next. She no longer accepted the
sheriff's insistence that her Uncle Carl had committed
suicide, or that Carl's attempt to silence her grandfather
wasn't somehow connected to his death.

She was also more certain than ever that she had seen
someone else on the ledge near the Tibbetts Point lighthouse last night, only an instant before Herb Dingner had
plunged into the river. Someone could have been trying
to keep him quiet, as well. Obviously it couldn't have
been Uncle Carl this time. That was the only thing she
could be *absolutely* certain of.

A wild possibility occurred to her, and she stood quite
still for a moment while it sunk into her already cluttered consciousness. What if that hadn't been Uncle Carl
who had fallen off the roof? What if his face had been
disfigured by the fall?

Shampoo stung her eyes, but she didn't wipe it away.
She was too absorbed in pondering one thought: when
nothing was what it appeared to be, anything could be
possible. Could Uncle Carl have carried his cover-up, if
indeed that was what he was up to, to the point of stag-
ing his own death? Was she living in the middle of a real-
life melodrama, or had she simply been so overloaded
with bizarre occurrences and revelations that she had
begun to think melodramatically?

Gretchen stood under the piercing spray, willing it to
clear the confusion in her mind. There was one thing she
suspected very strongly. Whatever was going on here had
to do with more than just questions about the present.
There were questions about the past involved, as well.
Both Herb Dingner and her grandfather were fascinated

by history—Herb by that of the village, Frederick by that of the Wulfert family. That fascination with the past was probably the only thing they had in common, other than having lived their entire lives in Cape Vincent. Somewhere in the preoccupation with the past could lie the explanation of why Herb was dead and her grandfather was in critical condition.

Of course, that still left Uncle Carl's death to be tied in. As far as Gretchen knew, he hadn't cared a hoot about history. Carl had been very much rooted in the present—present gratification, to be specific. Nonetheless, if his purpose for drugging Frederick had been to keep him quiet, the revelation Carl feared could very possibly have involved something from the past. Gretchen also reasoned that, whatever that past secret might be, it was probably a powerful and dangerous one. No matter how unlikable a character Carl Wulfert had been, she was sure that it would have taken a very extreme situation indeed to prompt him to put his own father into a potentially fatal coma.

Gretchen turned the hot water handle to the off position and twisted it tightly. The remaining spray chilled rapidly. She could be overestimating her uncle, but the things Pauline Basinette had told her about him made Gretchen doubt that. He had been more pathetic than monstrous. She had no illusions on one point, however: his attentiveness to her grandfather in those last weeks had probably been prompted by caution rather than concern. After all, Carl was no pharmacologist. How could he be absolutely convinced that scopolamine would work as he planned? What if his father woke up and started talking about whatever it was Carl wanted to hide? He had spent all that time at Frederick's bedside to stand guard against that happening.

That thought was even more chilling than the water. Gretchen twisted the other water control off and stepped out of the shower. She grabbed a thick white bath sheet from the towel rack and swathed herself in it. As the warmth gradually began to return to her body, she allowed herself to consider the *possibility* that her uncle had also come so often to sit by her grandfather's bedside because he felt remorse for what he had done and didn't want his father to die.

Gretchen rubbed herself down with the towel until her blood was fully circulating again. She felt less helpless now that she had a lead to follow. Early this morning in the pharmacy Pauline had said something she had obviously not meant to say, something about Stone Cottage. No one else had appeared to pay much attention to that, but it hadn't escaped Gretchen's notice.

If there was a mystery here, and if she was to have any hope of unraveling it, she would need evidence. Right now Pauline's slip of the tongue was the only clue in sight. As Gretchen hurried back into the bedroom to put on the clothes Boyd had laid out for her, she knew exactly what she must do next.

THE DAY HAD TURNED to dusk by the time Gretchen emerged from the back door of the spa's main building. She had on her long dark coat, which Boyd had brought from River House to replace the bedraggled sheepskin she'd been wearing for what felt like days. His choice had been a good one for more than just reasons of fashion. Gretchen didn't want to attract attention to this little sojourn of hers.

She had been so exhausted that she had slept through the morning and afternoon. Twilight came early this time of year in the north country, and the gathering darkness would help cover her movements while the dark coat and boots made her even less distinguishable to any watching eyes. Nonetheless, she kept close to the wall of the therapeutic wing as she made her way toward the rear of the New Beginnings property.

The overhanging veranda-style roof, meant to shield sun-sensitive patients on their summer lounge chairs, now shielded Gretchen from the third-floor windows where Pauline might glance out. Beryll's office was on the other side of the building, and she would have left for the day by now, anyway.

Gretchen stuffed her pale hair into the black beret she had found in her coat pocket. She remembered Boyd bringing it to her. How many days ago was that? She had lost track. He had discovered the beret in the yard when he was raking leaves. She also remembered how the beret had come to be there. It had been carried away by the wind when she nearly fell off the roof in the wake of discovering physical evidence of the gruesome nature of her uncle's death.

Now, as she crept along, hugging the wall and keeping to the shadows, she felt just as far out on the edge as she had been that afternoon. She couldn't escape her sense of teetering precariously. One slip would send her hurtling down into deadly danger, and she had only a narrow ledge to hang on to.

Suddenly she wished that Boyd were here with her, as he had been throughout the shocking events of the previous night. She was tempted to run back to the main building and look for him. He had said something about moving in there today. That thought soothed her. He would be nearby if she needed him. For now, she would continue on her own.

She had located a key to Stone Cottage among the as-
sortment in Carl's desk. Luckily that collection must
have been taken in hand by Beryll Sackett at some point.
Gretchen had recognized the administrator's precise
script on the identifying disks attached to each key.
Gretchen felt inside her pocket to make certain the key
was, in fact, still there as she hurried onto the fieldstone
path that led from the rear of the therapeutic wing, down
the border of the woodlot to Stone Cottage. She gripped
the key and shoved her other hand into the opposite
pocket. The one thing Boyd had overlooked in assem-
bling her wardrobe for the day was a pair of gloves.

On a summer evening this walk would have been not
only warm, but also accompanied by a chorus of what
her grandmother had always called "peepers." They
would have filled the woods and fields with their cheep-
ing song, and Gretchen would have been heartened by a
sound she had always loved. Instead, there was only the
gusting wind and the occasional shriek of a gull straying
across the road from the river. Gretchen could hardly
have felt more isolated and alone.

Stone Cottage was a rambling one-story structure with
a shingled roof that sloped down to overhanging eaves.
The construction was of fieldstone, like so many of the
other buildings in the area, hence its name. The dark
green paint on the window frames and doors was chipped
and peeling. With renovation this could have been a
lovely spot for a private office or retreat. Gretchen had
wondered more than once why her grandfather, who insisted upon such careful maintenance of all other areas
of the Wulfert property, had let this building fall into
disrepair.

Accessibility wasn't the problem. As she recalled, there
was a drive that bordered the other side of the woodlot

from River Road to the rear of Stone Cottage. Now that she thought about it, there was another road, as well, abandoned and overgrown, extending from Stone Cottage into the back country, probably to connect with one of the old, narrow-laned secondary roads that crisscrossed the area but were seldom used because the main roads were more direct.

Gretchen only knew about that road because of her berry-picking days. On long, sultry summer afternoons, back when she was growing up in Cape Vincent—especially on those days when her mother was out on the boat or sunning herself and her grandmother's silence became too much to bear—Gretchen would forage far and wide for new picking grounds. She had found some along that old road.

The discovery had been all the more exciting because her grandfather had declared this whole area off-limits for her, and Stone Cottage, as well. Too dangerous, he had said. You could get lost out there in the back country, and you could get hurt in Stone Cottage, where the floors were supposedly so rotted out you could fall straight through them. Now Gretchen wondered if the real danger might have been that she would have stumbled across some old truth her grandfather wanted kept secret.

The key turned much more easily in the lock than Gretchen had expected. Maybe someone had been here recently, or at least not as far back as she had always been led to believe. She tempered that thought with the reminder that she had to be careful about speculation. She had to have solid proof before coming to any conclusions. She had to do her best to keep her imagination in check.

The moment she stepped through the door, however, it was obvious that she wasn't imagining one thing. Her grandfather had been mistaken about the floors being rotten. They were solid as could be. Back in the old days they had built places like this to last. Gretchen chose to consider that craftsmanship ethic for a moment, rather than to dwell on the fact that she had caught her beloved grandfather in what sounded very much like a lie.

She propped the door open with a concrete block that might well have been used for that same purpose in the past. She had no flashlight tonight. She hadn't thought to bring one. The cottage windows were shuttered, and those shutters had been boarded over. The only light was from the doorway, and the dusky hour didn't provide much of that.

Her eyes gradually adjusted well enough to the gloom to make out a number of metal hospital beds at odd angles round the room. Some of them had mattresses, others only springs. There were bed stands here and there, as well, and Gretchen made out the shape of a discarded bedpan on the floor. All had been painted white, like the walls and ceiling, but appeared gray in the limited light and what she imagined must be a coating of years-old dust.

Gretchen knew that this building had been used for special cases long ago—contagious cases of terrible diseases, her grandfather had said. Suddenly she recalled him warning her away because of possible surviving infection. Her adult mind now told her that had been as much a fabrication as the supposedly rotted floors. Her grandfather had simply wanted to keep her away from here, and he had wanted that badly enough to lie to her.

She was almost certain she would find something here, but not in this deepening darkness. She was trying to de-

cide whether to return to the main building for a flashlight and then come back down here tonight or wait until
tomorrow morning and a less spooky hour to continue
her search, when the door slammed shut behind her.

Gretchen spun toward the sound in what was now total darkness. She stood absolutely still and listened. The
concrete block had been too heavy to move on its own,
and the door had been anchored firmly open. Not even
a strong gust of wind could have slammed it shut like
that. She was sure of it. Someone had pushed the block
aside and slammed the door, and that someone could be
in here with her right now.

She held her breath for a few seconds in order to hear
if someone else might be breathing in the room, as well.
She could hear nothing. One instinct told her she would
be able to tell if there was a person between her and the
door, which wasn't very far away. Another instinct told
her it was too dark to tell anything and that such intense
darkness could play tricks on the senses.

She might have called out to ask if anyone was there,
but she guessed that the sound of her own voice, echoing through these abandoned rooms, would terrify her
more than she could bear at this moment. She did have
to do something even more terrifying, however. She had
to move toward the door.

If someone was lurking in here, she might very well
encounter him—or her—along the way. That possibility
threatened to freeze her to the spot, but she knew she
couldn't let that happen. She couldn't stand here all
night, with her heart slamming in her chest, waiting for
God knows what. She would prefer walking smack into
danger over the torment of uncertainty.

Despite those bold thoughts, her first step toward the
door was more an act of desperate will than of courage.

She continued on cautiously after that, one step at a time, with her hands at waist level in front of her, ready to ward off attack should it come. She didn't reach out to grope her way through the darkness. She was too filled with dread of touching something horrifying or, worse yet, of having her arms grabbed by whoever had slammed the door.

She took small, careful steps. Her foot touched something that moved slightly, and she had to prevent herself from jumping back deeper into the darkness. Her heart slammed harder as she pushed the object with her toe. The scrape of porcelain against the gritty floor told her she had found the bedpan, and a sigh of relief exploded from her before she could stop it. She froze again, listening, but heard nothing. Now she was almost one hundred percent certain she was alone. Still, she held her breath for the few remaining steps to the wall and as she felt her way along that wall to the door.

Then another wave of terror struck her. What if whoever had slammed the door had also locked her in? For the first time she noticed against her cheek the damp chill of this long-empty place and smelled the musty deadness of the stale air, not unlike the murky tunnel she had been in the night before. If she was locked in here, she could be truly trapped. She was too far from the other buildings for her shouts to be heard through the thick old walls. She had told no one she was coming here. They would look almost everywhere else for her first. In fact, this place had been forgotten for so long that they might not look here at all.

She groped rapidly now, hand over hand, along the wall and over the door to the knob, then yanked it with such force that she nearly knocked herself over when the door jolted open. She leaped through the doorway into the night without thinking there might very well have been someone crouched outside waiting for her. All she cared about was getting out of the cottage and staying out, at least for now.

Besides, there was no one outside, or so she thought as she forced herself to turn back to the door, pull it shut and lock it. She had to keep her wits about her, and locking Stone Cottage until she could return to explore it thoroughly was the smart thing to do. She shuddered at the prospect of going inside the place again, though.

Suddenly the night seemed to be filled with the spirits of all those who had occupied the gray beds in the cottage. She wondered if some of them had died in there. That haunting thought, as much as any actual awareness of movement, prompted her to look around fast just in time to see a figure dart around the far side of the cottage and out of sight.

She had been about to conclude that she would ask Boyd to come with her the next time she came down here. Now she doubted she would do that. The person she had just seen running away—probably the same person who had slammed the door on her moments ago—had been wearing an Air Force parka. She had noticed the distinctive sheen of the material in the twilight.

Gretchen's former fear was instantly supplanted by another, equally powerful emotion—the flash of fury that usually accompanied the discovery of betrayal. Foolhardy or not, she would have taken off after him had the air not been split, at exactly that instant, by the blaring of a loud bell from the main building of the spa. Gretchen had heard that bell tested many times in her life, and there was no mistaking its sound. It was the alarm that had been installed for use only in extreme emergencies to draw any staff member within hearing distance immediately. Gretchen knew that this time the alarm wasn't ringing as part of a test. This time it was for real.

She grabbed handfuls of long coat and skirt and pulled them both above her knees, then began to run toward the main building as fast as she had run the other night by the river. The alarm was cut off just as she shoved through the back door. Still, however, she could feel the reverberations of the deafening bell all the way up the narrow back stairs.

She knew exactly where she was headed and what she had to find out there. The alarm could mean that something had happened to her grandfather. What she saw when she dashed into his room confirmed her fear. Pauline was leaning over the bed, moving more rapidly and efficiently than Gretchen had ever seen her do. Gretchen didn't intervene. Pauline was the professional here. She was the one best qualified to care for Frederick now. Gretchen understood that she couldn't interrupt that crucial process.

When Pauline finished doing whatever it was that needed to be done to the IV tube and oxygen mask, she turned to Gretchen. The old nurse was red in the face from exertion, but perhaps from something else, as well. She didn't wait to be asked what had happened.

"Someone disconnected your grandfather's oxygen and his IV," she said, her voice trembling with rage. "I gave him an injection of adrenaline, and he's stable now. But somebody tried to kill him, and I saw who it was."

She paused to catch her breath, and possibly to gain a bit of control over the anger that was so visible on her face she looked as if she might erupt from it.

"Who was it?" Gretchen asked, feeling her own fury, which was ice-cold rather than fiery hot like Pauline's.

"It was that handyman," the shocking answer came. "Boyd Emory tried to kill your grandfather."

Chapter Twelve

Boyd had driven into the village, more to counteract his restlessness than because he truly needed the few things he had picked up at Lester Wilson's store. Sometimes, when Boyd was feeling unsettled like this, he found it easier to get busy and do things than to confront the cause of his disturbance. Besides, he knew exactly why he was upset, and that there was no satisfactory solution to his dilemma.

His visit to River House that morning had simply aggravated the problem that had been growing steadily for days now. Standing in Gretchen's bedroom, which had felt so empty without her yet so full of her at the same time, had jolted the situation into stark focus for him. He had closed his eyes to shut out the sight, but that had only made it worse. He was assailed by the scent of her, that sweetness with a touch of spice he had first noticed when they were crouched together in her closet waiting for Herb Dingner.

When Boyd first met her, he had mistaken her emotional restraint for an aristocratic facade. He had changed his opinion since then. Gretchen stood up to the hard times of life, put on as brave a face as she could manage and forged forward. He had only seen her crumble twice: after what happened to Herb Dingner at Tibbetts Point and when she learned the real reason for her grandfather's coma.

Boyd had wanted to enfold her in his arms and shield her from the pain, but that wasn't possible, any more than it was possible for him to deny the pain he felt himself at being forced to witness just how dearly she loved the man Boyd had come here to destroy. Now that old man could wake up and remember nothing at all. Then all of this pain, on both sides, would have been for nothing as far as Boyd was concerned—except that it had led him to Gretchen.

This afternoon, when he brought her clothes from River House to her room at the spa, he had stood by the bed for a long time, watching her sleep. That was when he knew, beyond a doubt, that he loved her. He also knew that, once he completed this mission of his and the ugly truth about her grandfather's past was brought to light, she would never want to have anything to do with him again for as long as she lived.

Boyd had been repeating that inevitable reality to himself, as if he were rubbing a sore spot he couldn't keep his hands away from, while he drove back from the village to New Beginnings. He had just spotted the tall white house when he heard the alarm bell. He hadn't known what it was at first, but anything that loud and insistent probably meant trouble. He tromped down on the gas pedal and veered sharply onto the spa's long driveway with a splatter of gravel. As the pickup careened up the slope to the main building, the bell stopped ringing, but Boyd sensed that whatever crisis it warned of might not yet have been resolved.

He dashed up onto the wide front porch, but the door was locked. Beryll Sackett always checked that door personally before leaving for the day, and the light was out in her office. Boyd bounded down off the porch and rounded the corner of the building at a run, kicking up dried and rustling leaves as he went. He had to make certain that Gretchen was all right. She had been sleeping peacefully when he left earlier, but the way tragedy had been striking this place with regularity lately, there was no telling what might have befallen her since.

Boyd found the rear door open and raced through it, then up the stairs. Even before he reached the third floor and heard voices, he had guessed he would find them in Frederick Wulfert's room. Still, Boyd was hardly prepared for an assault by Pauline Basinette the moment he stepped through the doorway. In fact, he was surprised her rheumatic joints would allow her to move as fast as she did to get to him.

"You're the one!" she shouted as she bore down on him. "You tried to hurt Frederick."

Boyd caught her wrists and did his best to keep her considerable bulk at bay. He didn't know what she was talking about. Could she have found out the real reason he had come to Cape Vincent? Gretchen was also in the room. She looked bewildered and more than a little suspicious. In the meantime Pauline had begun to kick as well as thrash. The solid rubber sole of one of her white nurse's oxfords struck him in the shin, and he winced backward in pain.

"Help me with her, Gretchen," he called out. "I have no idea what she's talking about."

"I saw you!" Pauline shouted. "You had on this same jacket." She grabbed for his parka, and one of her wrists almost slipped from Boyd's grasp.

"Is that what you're so upset about? That someone in a jacket like mine did something to Mr. Wulfert?" Boyd was asking Gretchen as well as Pauline. "What am I supposed to have done, anyway?"

"Two things, actually," Gretchen said as she stepped forward at last and took the old nurse by the arms. "That's enough, Pauline. Let's listen to what he has to say."

Pauline kept on thrashing and kicking at him for a few more seconds, then gradually calmed herself. Gretchen told Boyd about someone in an Air Force parka shutting her into Stone Cottage and about the attempt to kill her grandfather by removing his oxygen. That attempt had also been made by someone in a blue-gray parka.

"Didn't it occur to you that other people have jackets like this one, or that somebody might have worn a jacket like mine deliberately to make me look guilty?" he asked.

"Who would do that?" Pauline asked scornfully. "Hardly anybody around here even knows you."

"Obviously somebody does," Boyd said, but he had no idea who that someone might be. Unless... He thought for a moment. Perhaps he did know who his impersonator was, after all.

GRETCHEN HAD NEVER BEEN an insomniac, but for the second night in a row she lay in her bed at River House, watching the moving shadows from the river. Of course, she had slept during the day. But she was tired out all the same. Expenditure of so much emotional energy did that to her. Still, her eyes refused to close as her mind replayed the evening over and over again on her ceiling. Consequently she slept little. Yet despite such intensive examination and reexamination of the startling events at New Beginnings, she arose in the morning as confused as ever.

She could hardly have cared less what she looked like and pulled on a pair of baggy old corduroys from a hook in her closet. With her scuffed boots and sheepskin she looked as if she was venturing off to set muskrat traps along the river. For that and a number of other reasons the last thing she wanted when she got to New Beginnings was a serious, private conference with Beryl Sackett, but the administrator insisted. Gretchen stifled a sigh and agreed as she wondered what side of Beryl's erratic personality would be on display today. The woman seemed tense as usual, rather like a coiled spring, as she assumed her perch on the edge of the same chair she had used as a shield—or was it a weapon?—against Gretchen a few days before.

"I'm afraid I have some disturbing news for you, Miss Wulfert," Beryl said. Her pale, straight-clipped fingernails tapped the black pebbly cover of the long ledger that sat atop two others just like it on her perfectly ordered desk.

"Oh, no," Gretchen groaned, unable to keep her feelings to herself this time. "Haven't we had enough disturbance around here for one week?"

"I should certainly think so, Miss Wulfert, and I wish I could spare you this added complication. However, it's a situation of some magnitude."

"In other words, if I think things have been bad up to now, I ain't seen nothin' yet."

"Well, perhaps I wouldn't phrase it quite so colorfully, but you might say something like that was true."

Gretchen hadn't expected to be that colorful herself. Maybe recent events did have her a bit out of control. Still, she was together enough to have a sense of why Beryl was coiled so tightly this morning. The administrator wasn't nervous or frightened this time. She was excited, even exhilarated.

Eager anticipation, Gretchen said to herself. Whatever bad news Beryll had to tell her, she was waiting to do so with eager anticipation.

"I've made some discoveries about the status of the Wulfert finances," Beryll said, stretching her long, thin fingers across the surface of the ledger. "I regret to report that the estate is virtually bankrupt."

Gretchen stared into Beryll's pale eyes. Whatever self-consciousness Beryll might have felt about eye contact on other occasions, there was no evidence of that now as she stared straight back. Her lips were drawn into a line. Yet Gretchen could still sense a gleeful grin lurking behind that facade. She could sense little else, however, because what Beryll had just told her was too ridiculous to comprehend.

"Did you hear what I said, Miss Wulfert?" Beryll's fingertips had crept forward to hook themselves over the edge of the ledger cover and grip it.

"I heard you, Beryll, but I'm not sure I understand."

"The situation is a very simple one, actually. The Wulfert money is all gone, in terms of property value and liquid assets alike."

"You must be mistaken," Gretchen said. There was no chance Beryll could be right. The Wulfert estate was worth a fortune or, at least, she had always assumed it was.

"Miss Wulfert." Beryll was gripping the ledger so tightly that her pale knuckles reminded Gretchen of ivory piano keys. "I was graduated summa cum laude in accounting. I'm not mistaken."

Gretchen stared at her again for a long moment. "If you're correct, exactly where could all of that money have gone?"

"I've made quite an in-depth study of that. The answer is right here in these records." She sprung loose her grip and patted the ledgers. "And there are many more such books in the safe. It seems your grandfather has managed in the past twenty years to give most of the Wulfert money away."

"How could that be? I understood the estate to be very large." Gretchen could hardly believe what she was hearing, much less take in the implications.

"That was true at one time. In fact, for generations your family was one of the wealthiest in this part of the country. Then there were the usual subdivisions of capital for inheritance and the inevitable trust funds for future heirs." She gave Gretchen a disapproving look. "Consequently the estate had diminished some by the time your grandfather's philanthropic excesses began."

"And you're trying to tell me you've discovered that my grandfather has donated the balance of the estate to charity?"

"That's precisely what he's done, but actually the situation was first discovered by your Uncle Carl. That's also obvious from these records."

"Why didn't he do something about it?" Gretchen asked, still aghast.

"He tried to recoup some of the lost capital by investing but got caught in the stock market downturn a couple of years ago. After that he barely held on while he searched for some other source of revenue. In truth, however, the estate was already too depleted to be saved by the time he took over."

"I take it Uncle Carl didn't find the revenue he was looking for."

"He apparently found one source last spring. That was how he kept New Beginnings going since then, but those funds are practically exhausted now. There have been no sizable deposits to any of the accounts for months."

"What was that last source of funds?" Maybe she could take out another loan if that was, in fact, what she should do. Gretchen was beginning to recognize the enormity of the problem she was inheriting in place of the sizable estate she had expected.

"I have no idea where your uncle got that money, Miss Wulfert. For some reason he didn't choose to note that information, which is actually a rather interesting point. Your uncle may have been slovenly in other ways, but he was extremely precise when it came to money. Yet he neglected to make even a single notation concerning the specifics of this very large amount. Doesn't that strike you as interesting?"

"Are you implying that my uncle came by that money illegally?" Gretchen was certain that was exactly what Beryll had meant.

"Miss Wulfert!" Beryll sounded truly indignant. "I've said no such thing. I simply pointed out that this discrepancy is an interesting phenomenon. I thought you would agree."

Gretchen wanted to get up and leave, and not only because of Beryll's attitude, though there was an undisguised and offensive sneer developing in her tone. More pressing than that, however, was Gretchen's desire to get away somewhere alone and figure out what was going on here and what she should do about it.

"I can't believe my grandfather could have given away everything," she said vaguely. "I know he's a generous man, but . . . Why would he have done it?"

"Perhaps he was trying to assuage his guilt."

Gretchen had been staring past Beryll at the wall. Her glance shot back to the administrator's face and its smug expression. "What would my grandfather possibly have to feel guilty about?"

Gretchen sounded very cold and hard all of a sudden, but Beryll didn't appear to be intimidated by that. "Perhaps he felt guilty for having so much money that it took him twenty years to give it all away," she answered steadily.

Gretchen could feel her anger smoldering. She consciously pushed the lid down tightly on that cauldron. "Have you gossiped about this all around town the way you do about everything else that happens here?"

"Not yet."

Gretchen clasped her hands together to keep herself from jumping up and slapping Beryll as hard as she could. "I've taken note of your disloyalty—"

"And what do you intend to do about it?" Beryll interrupted. "Are you going to fire me?"

Gretchen did stand up now, but slowly rather than abruptly. She was angry but also very sad, and the sadness seemed to be in charge at the moment. She was aware of herself moving in a languid rhythm, as if her bewilderment were an ocean she had to tread through.

"If what you say is true, and I imagine it is, then we Wulferts have no business left to fire you from."

"That's precisely the case, and it couldn't have happened to a more deserving lot in my estimation. Your grandfather with his condescending noblesse oblige and

that slimy uncle of yours and someone as cold and un-
feeling as you—''

Gretchen had turned to walk toward the door as Beryll began her tirade against the Wulferts. By the time
Gretchen turned the door handle, Beryll was ranting
about how she was getting out of this place today and
overjoyed that she wouldn't have to bring her mother
here, after all, since her mother was a wonderful woman
and shouldn't be exposed to the likes of the Wulferts.
Gretchen closed the door behind her before she could
hear more.

"I won't be leaving you in the lurch, Miss Gretchen.
You needn't worry your pretty head about that." Pauline Basinette had apparently been waiting for Gretchen
in the hallway outside Beryll's office.

"Thank you, Pauline," Gretchen said softly, trying to
collect her thoughts. "Did you overhear what Beryll said
about the spa's finances?"

"Oh, I didn't have to bend to any keyholes to hear
that. Sackett came up and told me first thing this morning, just before you got here. She couldn't wait to let me
know I'd have my walking papers soon."

"I'm sorry about that, Pauline," Gretchen began.

"I told you not to worry your pretty head, and I mean
it. I'm not going anywhere, and you don't have to pay
me, either. I told you I don't need the money. I'll just stay
on till things pick up, like I did the other time this happened. And if things don't pick up, well, we'll work
something out then."

"What do you mean by, 'the other time this happened'?" Gretchen asked. "Are you saying the spa has
been bankrupt before?"

"Pretty much so, though I don't think we ever used
that word for it. We just said the place had gone broke.

That was almost the end of the big war. People didn't have much money for places like this during those times, but then your grandfather found a way to put us back on our feet again."

"How did he do that?" Gretchen had the feeling there was something very important here to be connected up with something else, but there was too much going on in her head right now for her to figure out what either of those elements might be.

"Oh, I don't know about such things, Miss Gretchen."

Gretchen wasn't too befuddled to wonder if Pauline could be lying about that. Gretchen didn't pursue it farther, however. She'd had enough of confrontation for one morning. Besides, she knew it was going to take every ounce of strength and will she possessed just to get up the stairs to her uncle's office, close the door behind her and collapse. She barely managed a nod at Pauline before dragging herself off to do just that.

KRAFT HAD HEARD IT ALL. He had been especially amused by the consternation over Boyd Emory's Air Force parka. Of course, Emory had been exactly right on both counts when he noted to the Wulfert girl and that old battle-ax nurse that other people, many of them, in fact, wore such jackets *and* one of them could have done so specifically to incriminate him.

The nurse may or may not have accepted that logic. Kraft didn't care about her, anyway. She was an insignificant factor in this situation, a mere bumpkin not worthy of his attention. Whether she believed Emory was guilty or not was of no concern to Kraft. Her opinion, or her existence for that matter, would have no bearing on the outcome here.

Gretchen Wulfert was another story, and that was where Kraft's amusement ended. She most likely had recognized the good sense of what Emory had said and would doubt that he had either slammed the door on her at Stone Cottage or turned off the machinery that was keeping her foolish grandfather alive. She was too smart, though Kraft hated to admit it, to believe any of that about Emory—first of all, because he had no reason for such acts and, secondly, because she was obviously infatuated with him.

That meant Kraft had a problem, and he didn't like problems. Gretchen Wulfert was not only unlikely to accept Emory as the villain here; she was even less likely to let so many questions remain unanswered. Kraft had learned enough about her by just listening and putting the pieces together to have constructed a picture of a young woman who would go after the truth, even if that quest placed her in danger.

Another person might have admired that quality in her, but not Kraft. The Wulfert girl could get in his way, and Kraft didn't think kindly of anyone who got in his way. Enemies were not to be admired; they were to be destroyed.

GRETCHEN SPENT the rest of the morning in Carl's office. She heard the plop of the ledgers on the floor outside the door but didn't retrieve them until she heard Beryll march back down the hall to the stairs. Gretchen had been poring over the columns of small print numbers ever since. She didn't know a lot about bookkeeping, but she understood enough to conclude that Beryll hadn't exaggerated the situation. New Beginnings and the Wulfert family faced financial ruin. Gretchen would have to talk to the banks and an accountant to find out how close that ruin might be. Meanwhile, she needed to come up with a plan to prevent immediate foreclosure upon the many debts her uncle had incurred against the property.

She was thinking about possibilities as she drove through the village on her way from New Beginnings to River House. When she spotted Lester Wilson's store, she pulled over and stopped across the road on the curbless side of Broadway to stare at the wide display windows for several minutes without really seeing them. She knew very well what she had to do. There were few other choices open to her. She would have to let Lester buy that plot of Wulfert land he'd been after and anything else he was willing to take, as well. A lifetime of conditioning prevented her from jumping instantly to this particular unpleasant task. She could take care of that tomorrow.

Right now what she needed was a place to think, and that reminded her of her times at the end of the marina dock as a child. The marina was nearby, so she decided she would walk there. She opened the car door slowly and hauled herself out of the low-slung vehicle. Ordinarily she loved this small, sleek car that rode so close to the road, but today she was feeling more aged and less agile than usual. Any extra exertion was hardly welcome. Perhaps the falling temperature and rising wind were invading her bones. More likely the heavy events of the past few days had begun to weigh her down.

The clouds were gray-white and low in the sky, and Gretchen felt about the same. There was something else bothering her, as well. What would Boyd's reaction be to finding out she was no longer a wealthy heiress? Was her money the real reason for his interest in her? She had suspected that all along. What made that suspicion so terrible now was her recognition of how much she wanted Boyd to care about her for herself.

When she first looked up and saw his pickup headed into the marina, she thought she might be imagining it because he was so intensely on her mind. The truck was real, however. She could hear the familiar grind and cough of its engine even from this distance. This was her chance to ask him the very questions she'd been asking herself before she could talk herself into hiding her feelings and pretending that nothing could possibly cause so much as a ripple in her perfect Wulfert facade.

She started to run toward the marina. Her heavy sheepskin jacket was unbuttoned, and it flapped open as she ran against the heightening wind. Her city boots weren't meant for this kind of pace and slipped on loose gravel along the way, but she didn't care. Let the whole town see her and wag their tongues about how she had torn down the street after the handyman.

Nonetheless, even at her breakneck speed, by the time Gretchen reached the marina, Boyd had already boarded a small boat and was motoring out toward the breakwater. He would never hear her in this wind. She wasn't sure she had enough breath left to shout, anyway, as she stood on the shore, panting from her run, and watched him approach the old lightship that had been moored to the breakwater for as long as she could remember.

What could he possibly be going out there for, especially in weather like this?

She watched him pull the small boat alongside the bigger one and tie it there with some difficulty. Then he climbed aboard the lightship and disappeared into the cabin. At that moment Gretchen realized how very little she actually knew about this man to whom she had obviously given so much of her heart.

She hurried to the slip where the Wulfert launch was docked. Her grandfather kept it in the water late in the season because he loved autumn jaunts on the river. Apparently no one had thought to pull the boat out even though her grandfather wasn't in any condition for river jaunting. Gretchen was grateful for that oversight now as she untied the canvas that covered the deck and climbed aboard.

She had always loved this old boat with its mahogany hull and brass rails. There weren't many of these antique treasures left on the river, and the *Fox* had long been her grandfather's pride and joy. She felt a stab of sadness as she wondered if this boat would be lost along with the rest of the Wulfert estate. Her grandfather would rather have the *Fox* at the bottom of the river than out of the family.

Gretchen cast off the docking lines and poled the boat out of the slip with an oar. She had already decided she would take the long way around and come up on the river side of the lightship where Boyd would less likely be on the lookout for anyone to approach. Thus, she might see what he was up to before he saw her. Of course, that meant she would be in open water outside the protection of the breakwater.

The river was turbulent today. She could see that as she motored slowly toward the marina exit, but she wasn't concerned. Gretchen had grown up on boats. She had navigated this river in all of its moods, foul or fair. Her grandfather had scolded her more than once for being what he called *too* daring, like the time she had ripped the rivets out of the first hull of their ancient aluminum inboard by running it fast across the current to beat the storm at her back. Gretchen Wulfert wasn't about to be daunted by a little turbulence.

KRAFT HAD FOLLOWED Gretchen from the spa and had pulled over down the road from her when she stopped across from Wilson's grocery. He had watched with curiosity as she'd charged down the street to the marina. Kraft congratulated himself on his accurate assessment: Frederick's heir was an indiscreet young woman.

Of course, after what Kraft had heard this morning, he knew there was nothing for her to inherit. He had suspected that when that pig, Carl, had tried to put the bite on him for a second chunk of hush money. Kraft knew now why Carl had been desperate enough to threaten him. These Wulferts would stop at nothing to protect their precious family and its precious land. Kraft had learned that forty-five years ago.

Like father, like son, Kraft concluded with a self-satisfied chuckle.

Following the Wulfert girl to the marina proved yet another satisfying experience for Kraft. She was trailing Emory. In fact, she was going out onto that very choppy river after him. Kraft chuckled once again. At last the young lovers and their dalliance were playing right into his hands. She was making herself even more vulnerable than he had hoped.

Kraft drove the van to the far end of the marina property and backed it up to the pier, out of sight behind a tall cruiser that was dry-docked there. He swung open the rear door of the van so that he was facing the river. He had on the blue-gray parka he had bought a few days ago in the next town and worn since to such advantage. He took it off now. The material was too slippery for what he intended to do next.

He pulled the high-powered rifle from its hiding place and lifted it to sight along his arm. He caught the Wulfert boat in the scope and followed Gretchen's progress.

He would wait until she was out in the channel. The current would be treacherous there on a day like this.

He had been on that boat himself years ago, on the occasion of one or two of his visits here. He remembered where the engine was. One well-placed shot, and Gretchen would be set adrift. Kraft prided himself on his marksmanship. He would have no trouble making that shot. Then two more shots or so below the waterline, and she would be out of his way—forever.

Chapter Thirteen

Boyd picked up the field glasses and looked through them at River House for what he hoped would be the last time. There was nothing to see, except the thrashing of bare tree branches in the wind. Gretchen was most likely back at New Beginnings at this hour. When he left there early this morning, tensions were already in full swing, with Pauline and Beryll yelling at one another behind the closed door to the third-floor pharmacy. Boyd had made no attempt to hear what they were arguing about. During a long and lonely night that reminded him of what his life had been like before he met Gretchen, he'd decided to get out of the cloak-and-dagger business once and for all.

The business Max had sent him here for was unfinished. Boyd had unearthed only enough information to establish to his own satisfaction that what Peter Dagg had told him was true. Dagg was the man Max had sent Boyd to find a few days before Max had died and Boyd's quest had brought him to Cape Vincent.

According to Dagg, Frederick Wulfert had, in fact, been part of a scheme that unleashed monsters into the world, just as his stories had suggested. Many of those monsters were still out there, all over the country. They

might have reformed some for the sake of avoiding exposure, but they were still unscrupulous men who had
escaped unpunished for their past sins. Boyd had reason
to believe that one of the worst of those monsters was
here in the village now. He had to be the one whom Peter
Dagg, in his dying breaths, had called Kraft.

That was a code name, of course. All Dagg had known
about Kraft was that he had been the real mastermind of
the Cape Vincent operation in the late 1940s. He had
owned the Long Island estate where Dagg and others like
him had stayed for a few days before being driven north
in curtained cars along obscure back roads, headed for
what was then known as the Wulfert Sanatorium. There
all traces of the past were expunged—from their faces,
from their voices, even from their documented histories.

It had been a brilliant plan, as well as a heinous one.
No one might ever have uncovered it had Max not *happened* to attend a pharmaceutical convention in Cleve-
land, where he *happened* to be in a crowded elevator
behind American pharmaceutical magnate Peter Dagg,
and *happened* to notice the birthmark on the back of
Dagg's head.

Another happenstance had revealed that mark to Max
fifty years ago in Germany when he had been the staff
chemist summoned to administer an experimental scalp
treatment to the owner of the huge pharmaceutical com-
plex where he worked. Ordinarily, back then, the mark
was well hidden by Dagg's thick dark hair. Who would
have thought that Max would one day run into Peter
Dagg again, that being his new name rather than his
German one, when his hair had thinned and turned white
so that his scalp was visible to someone standing close
behind him?

Unfortunately Max had been impetuous or, perhaps, his natural revulsion had overwhelmed his good sense. He had confronted Dagg in person. Dagg had denied Max's accusations and had a contradictory past history, complete with dates and documents, to support it. That was when Max contacted Boyd and told him he must find proof that Peter Dagg wasn't just a wealthy American pharmaceutical magnate but a former German industrialist who had made his first fortune from a plant near Berlin where horrendous chemical experiments were performed on human subjects who also happened to be civilian prisoners of the Third Reich.

Max had run away from that place as soon as he'd figured out what was going on. Shortly afterward he had escaped from Germany and come to America, but had always reviled himself for not having the courage all those years ago to stand up to Dagg and the animals he had worked for. Boyd had pledged to Max that he would get that proof and make it stand up in court.

Unfortunately, by the time Boyd had gotten to Dagg, he was nearly dead from a supposedly self-administered overdose of his own pharmaceuticals. He had used his last gasps for a death's door confession and to avenge himself on his murderer, the man code-named Kraft, by telling the truth about him. Then Peter Dagg had died a very painful death, not unlike those he had years ago inflicted upon so many others.

When Boyd got back to Max, he, too, was dead, also supposedly by his own hand. Dagg had contacted Kraft and reported his confrontation with Max at the pharmaceutical convention. Kraft had obviously then embarked on his own style of damage control. Now Dagg and Max were both dead, and there wasn't a scrap of evidence left to support Max's implausible story.

Boyd's search for the kind of corroboration the authorities would listen to had brought him to Cape
Vincent, the place Dagg had spoken of in his dying confession. Now Boyd was certain the same events had
brought Kraft here, as well.

Who else would have trapped Gretchen in Stone Cottage last night and probably planned to do much worse
to her if it hadn't been for the alarm bell going off? Who
else would have tried to kill Frederick Wulfert last night?
Kraft had probably killed Carl Wulfert and Herb Dingner. There was no telling what he would do next.

That meant Gretchen could be in danger. Boyd had to
warn her. And, when he did, he would also have to tell
her the whole truth. Once he did that, he might very
possibly lose her. He might also have great difficulty fulfilling his promise to Max, because Gretchen would then
be able to cover up the truth, just as he had feared all
along she would.

Boyd almost wished she would do precisely that. In
fact, he had come to the lightship today to assist in that
cover-up by clearing away any sign of his recent resi-
dence here and of his surveillance station. He knew there
would be trouble ahead with his conscience, about his
obligation to the world as well as to Max. Men like Dagg
and Kraft and even Frederick Wulfert *must* be exposed.
They had been, at best, war profiteers, and at worse, war
criminals. Boyd was in a position to bring them to jus-
tice.

The struggle had already begun between his conscience and his heart when a flare arced across the bow
of the lightship.

PAULINE HAD all of the lights on in Frederick's room
even though it was still afternoon. That was partly be-

cause of the darkness of the day outside. The clouds had turned more gray than white and seemed to touch the water at the horizon. The Canadian shore was no longer visible from the third-floor windows of New Beginnings Spa.

Nonetheless, Pauline had spent many dark afternoons sitting in the gloom at the bedside of one patient or another, and she hadn't turned on the lights then. Her sainted mother had taught her that a penny saved was a penny earned, and electricity cost money. Pauline had never forgotten that, but today was different. Today she was up against darkness of another sort entirely.

She could *feel* this darkness rather than see it. She hadn't noticed it so much while there were still people around. Beryll had slammed out of the spa shortly after noon, leaving a note taped to her office door saying that her stuff was packed and should be forwarded to her in Florida. She hadn't been able to resist adding the barb that, since New Beginnings would be bankrupt within the month, they could make that shipment to her COD.

Gretchen had stayed in her uncle's office for quite some time after her angry scene with Beryll. Pauline could imagine that Gretchen might also have been gathering some things together in those hours, but not necessarily into boxes as Beryll had done. Gretchen would be trying to gather the many loose ends of what had been going on around here lately, and maybe for a lot farther back than just lately. Gretchen would be doing her best to neaten those ends up nice and orderly, the way she liked everything to be. Pauline guessed Gretchen hadn't been able to get those ends together so neat this time.

Pauline had stood at the window and watched Gretchen drive away. That was when Pauline realized she had been left alone with Frederick. Boyd hadn't been around all day, and she had no idea if or when he would be back. She had felt the darkness deepening in the room then, the dark foreboding that something was going to happen here and that it wouldn't be pleasant.

She could feel it in her bones, making them protest, even more than they usually did, with every move she made. Still, she had hobbled from table to desk to wall switch to nightstand, turning on every light until the room was flooded with so much brightness that she was surprised it didn't jolt Frederick back to consciousness from the glare through his tissue-thin eyelids.

Still, Pauline understood that she hadn't really gotten rid of the darkness. It lurked right outside the door, like black night closing in around a circle of camp fire. That night was full of wild animals. When she was a young girl and went camping with her family upriver, she had only partly believed that little fire would be enough to keep the beasts at bay. She had the same doubts today. That was why she decided she had to get Frederick, and herself, out of the spa.

She'd have to roll him onto the good gurney, the one with the wheels that didn't rattle and was easier to push, then strap him down tight. She'd wrap him in lots of blankets so that he wouldn't catch a chill in the cold wind she could see rising outside the windows. Then she would trundle him to the patient elevator. They hadn't used that elevator since summer, and it didn't always run just right. She'd been after Carl Wulfert up to the day he died about getting that elevator fixed, but, of course, he hadn't. He had never spent a nickel before he had absolutely had to. Pauline whispered a silent prayer, wondering which saint would be best to address about elevators.

After the elevator, there was the transportation to plan. In fact, she'd better take care of that first thing, even before getting the gurney. She'd get the garage keys from Beryll's office and bring out the old ambulance, which also hadn't been used in a long time. Thank heaven Beryll had gotten Boyd to start it up the other day. At least Pauline didn't have to worry about *that* being in running order. She also wasn't worried about doing the driving. She was a north country girl, born and bred, and she had been driving long before legal age, everything from tractors to salvage boats. She could manage that old ambulance anyday.

The one thing she wasn't so sure about managing so easily was time. Even when moving at her top speed, she was hardly what anybody would call fast. There was no telling how long it would take her to get Frederick out of there, and she had good reason to believe that time was of the essence. First of all, there was that creeping darkness she would have to screw up her courage to step into. She had a very strong premonition that whatever bad fortune that darkness had in store was already on its way.

More practically speaking, Mother Nature had something of her own in store. Pauline knew very well what that particular shade of gray cloud forecasted, and she didn't need any weatherman to tell her about it, either. There was a big storm brewing. This time of year that meant hard, cold rain and maybe even a blizzard. She had to get Frederick out of the spa before the storm hit.

She'd have the devil's own time wrestling that gurney in and out of the elevator, and then maneuvering Frederick into the ambulance. She felt only a little guilty for being thankful that he was so thin and wouldn't weigh much. Still, she didn't want to be fighting a storm while she was lifting him, or to be driving roads slick from new rain, or to be battling a shore gale to get him back out of the ambulance when she reached where they were going.

Pauline checked Frederick to make sure he was sleeping, then headed for the door. She hesitated only a moment before hobbling into the hallway that was so unnaturally dark for this hour of the afternoon.

GRETCHEN DIDN'T HAVE time to figure out why the boat was sinking. It simply was.

First, there had been a jolt, as if the boat had hit something. Except that she knew these waters very well, and there was nothing in this particular area of the channel to hit. The engine cut out at the same instant as the jolt. Could it have exploded? The wind was so noisy out here, and the waves slapped the hull with such force, that she had barely been able to hear the engine while it was still running. Even so, she should have heard an explosion if that was what had happened. Was that a hint of smoke she smelled or just her imagination?

The wind whipped her face as she stood up from the captain's seat and thus lost the protection of the windscreen she had barely been able to see through because of the spray. If there had been smoke, she couldn't smell it now, though the odor of gasoline seemed stronger than usual. That could be her imagination, too, of course.

Then another jolt jarred the boat, veering the prow toward the channel and knocking Gretchen forward against the dash. She grabbed the top of the windscreen to right herself just as a third jolt thrust the prow farther channelward. She sat down again and grasped the wheel, then waited for a fourth jolt to strike. For seconds that felt like hours she clung that way to the wheel, but no more jarring happened.

They must have been explosions, she thought. But what could have exploded? The engine was already out, and she could have sworn those latest jolts had been nearer the bow than the engine compartment, which jutted above the deck almost at the stern.

There was no time to figure out those answers now. Without the power of the engine the *Fox* was already drifting into the channel. In a heavy blow like this one, she could be off upstream in no time. She had to get the engine started again. She turned the ignition key and punched the starter button, but nothing happened—not so much as a splutter.

She tried again. Still nothing. The engine wasn't responding at all. In her experience a marine engine didn't usually cut out all of a sudden like that. It would flutter or chug or give some kind of warning before dying. Maybe there had been an explosion, after all.

She scrambled astern and pulled up the hatch that covered the engine compartment. It was too dark in there to see much. She dropped the hatch and scurried back to the cockpit to jerk open the cubbyhole where emergency supplies and other odds and ends were kept. She grabbed the flashlight she had prayed would be there and held her breath as she flipped the switch.

Thank heaven! It worked! Even though the beam appeared to be instantly swallowed up by the gray afternoon.

The light was more effective when shone into the dark engine compartment. The engine was smoking a little. Or was that steam off the hot metal from contact with the cold air she had let in? She did her best to flash the light around the sides of the engine. A gash on the port side suggested there had been an explosion. That probably explained the first jolt, which had felt as if it could have come from back here. She had no idea what the explanation for the other two jolts could be, since she was still certain they had come from somewhere else on board.

Suddenly all thought of what had happened to the engine, even the very scary realization that she probably couldn't start it again, was swept from her mind by something else the flashlight beam was revealing about the inside of the engine compartment. She had been so concentrated on examining the engine itself that she hadn't really registered what was going on around it.

Now she saw all too clearly. There was way too much water in there—water with a slick of oil on top of it from seepage out of the gash in the side of the engine. She flashed the light around the cramped compartment and could have sworn there was the suggestion of a flow where the water would be coming in, but she couldn't tell for sure. Nonetheless, she would have staked her life on her assessment that the hull had sprung a leak.

Her breath caught in a frightened gasp. What if her life really was at stake here?

She shoved the question from her mind before the terror of it could paralyze her, even for an instant. The *Fox* was a sturdy old vessel. She wouldn't go down in a shot, even if she was shipping water as fast as Gretchen suspected. Still, in today's rough river, she would go down faster than if it had been calm. The turbulence would see to that, forcing the water hard into the leaking area, which had probably been made by the explosion and might be a rather large opening.

One negative about the design of the *Fox* was its shallowness, with rails only a few feet above the deck. That would give her less time to stay afloat once she started filling up. Gretchen darted a glance back along the deck. There was water over the planking all right, but not enough yet so that she could tell whether it was seeping up from below deck or had accumulated from the spray.

One thing she *could* tell was that the boat was drifting farther into the channel and farther from shore. Another glance, up and down the river this time, confirmed what she had feared. She was alone out here on the water. It was late in the season for pleasure boating, anyway, and the professionals wouldn't be out in weather like this. Any help she could hope for wouldn't come from the river.

She peered at the shoreline but couldn't see a soul. This was also not the kind of weather that prompted walks along the riverbank; and, as if to make certain of that, it had begun to rain sharp, frigid needles that stung Gretchen's cheeks and smarted her eyes. She had to think of some way to attract attention, if that was possible, and she had to do it fast.

A less experienced river boater might have considered swimming for it. She was wearing her Mae West, after all. She had pulled it on first thing at the dock, just as she always did the minute she climbed aboard any small boat. Still, she knew very well that a flotation vest wouldn't be enough to save her from the treacherous current, the wild waves and the icy temperature of the water. She was a strong swimmer, but nobody was that strong. Her only hope was to attract the help she had been thinking about and try to stay afloat until it could get to her.

She lunged a bit too frantically back toward the emergency compartment, which was on the port side of the cockpit, and felt the boat list in that direction, as well. She'd have to keep her weight to starboard after this, but right now she had to see if the flares and flare gun were still among the emergency supplies as her grandfather had always insisted they be. Sure enough. They were.

Thank you, Grandpa, she whispered as she grabbed the gun and box of flares.

But where would she shoot it if there was no one out along the shore to see? Then she remembered why she had come out here on the river in the first place. Unless he had turned around and gone straight back to shore, Boyd was aboard the lightship on the other side of the breakwater. She squinted into the rain in that direction. She should be visible from the lightship at this distance. She hadn't drifted out of sight yet.

Please be there, Boyd, she pleaded into the wind as she broke open the barrel of the flare gun, shoved the shell inside and snapped the barrel closed.

She took aim and thanked her grandfather once again, this time for all of those Saturday afternoons of skeet practice at the gun club. The flare arced over the bow of the lightship exactly where she had prayed it would. The second flare was wide of the mark but would still be noticeable—*if* anybody was looking in that direction.

Please, Boyd, she pleaded again.

There were more flares, but she would wait a bit to see if he responded to these. If not, she would aim a couple of more times at the lightship, then try to signal the shore with the rest, no matter how futile it seemed to do that. Right now she had to start pumping. The bilge was old-fashioned and manual, thank heaven. She wasn't sure an electric one would have worked with the engine out.

She pulled up another hatch near the middle of the flat deck floor and grabbed the pump handle. Straight up she tugged, against resistance at first as a season's damp-induced corrosion reluctantly gave way. Gradually the action turned smoother. She heard the wet, sucking sound of water being drawn into the waste hose, like boots slogging free of swamp mud, and knew that at least some of the leakage was being expelled back into the river. She accelerated the motion—up with the sucking sound, down against resistance, over and over again—while she thanked heaven once more for the hours she had clocked on biceps machines in spas all over the world.

Gretchen straightened for a moment and mopped the rain from her face with her jacket sleeve. Despite the cold and wet she could feel herself sweating beneath her heavy clothes from the effort. She wouldn't be sweating if she went into the river. The thought made her shudder. In fact, she would have to take off this jacket if she ended up going overboard. Once waterlogged, its weight would drag against her and make the impossibility of swimming in this current even more impossible. She would have to shuck her boots as well for the same reason. Then, if the current didn't get her, the hypothermia would.

That was why going overboard would be absolutely the last resort. Unfortunately the farther she drifted from shore, the closer she came to that last-resort point. She pulled the flare gun from the pocket she had stuffed it in, reloaded and was about to take aim over the lightship, which was almost out of range now, when she saw what she desperately hoped wasn't an illusion. The small launch Boyd had taken out of the marina was rounding the end of the breakwater and heading in her direction. At this distance he might not know it was her, but he was coming, anyway.

Her face was wet with spray and rain and cold sweat. She could tell from the tightness in her throat and burning behind her eyes that there were tears running down her cheeks. At the very edge of her consciousness she was vaguely aware that she had come out here on the river because she was suspicious of Boyd. But for the moment she couldn't remember why. All she cared about was that

he was on his way to rescue her, and she had to get back
to pumping like mad to keep herself afloat until he got
here.

That was exactly what she was doing when the small
outboard chugged up at port side, bobbing against the
waves while Boyd crouched in the stern with one hand on
the tiller and the other gathering up a rope to toss aboard
the *Fox*.

"Come around to the other side!" Gretchen shouted
as she realized what he was about to do and what would
happen if he did. She accompanied her shout, which she
then repeated, with hand motions in case he couldn't hear
her in the wind.

The *Fox* was already listing perilously to port. If Boyd
tried to tie up there and haul her over the side, the added
weight could be all it would take to push the rail below
the surface of the river. Then the flow of the current
might very well suck the rest under, heaving the heavy
boat up and capsizing it. More likely than not Gretchen
would be thrown out, and the *Fox* would slam over onto
Boyd's boat, knocking him into the river or worse.

Boyd obviously wasn't a boatman, but she was. Did he
know that, and would he trust her judgment? She saw
him hesitate for just a moment, and knew he was weighing that decision. Then he dropped the rope and began
working the tiller to maneuver the small launch around
the prow of the *Fox* to starboard. Gretchen was waiting
there to grab his line and hitch it over the cleat in the kind
of loop that she could snap loose easily again once she
was aboard the smaller boat.

Suddenly Boyd was reaching for her. His movements
were more abrupt and forceful than was wise in a rocking boat on rough water. Gretchen had to counteract that
by vaulting over the side and into his arms, then drag-

ging both of them down to the floor of the launch before they could topple overboard.

Her lips brushed his cheek as they tumbled over each
other. She could smell his reassuring masculine scent
through the sweep of the wind and the pelting rain. More
than anything she wanted to nestle against his chest under that big, warm parka and let him zip her inside where
she could be safe forever.

The thought of the parka was like a shocking, sharp
edge cutting through her instant of reverie. There was
something about that parka.... A slap of wave against
the aluminum hull of the rocking boat jolted her back to
the moment. She sat up fast.

"We have to get out of here!" she shouted against the
wind that seemed to swallow her words before they were
even out of her mouth. "The *Fox* could go down any
minute and take us with her."

Boyd glanced over at the old boat. Gretchen saw the
flash of recognition in his eyes. The *Fox* was not only
listing toward port now, her stern had begun to tip backward from the weight of the engine, pulling the bow out
of the water. Gretchen's vigorous pumping had barely
managed to keep the *Fox* afloat. At this very moment she
was getting ready to sink, and she would surely do so with
the kind of force that could easily capsize Boyd's aluminum launch.

Boyd was already back at the tiller. He restarted the
motor. Then he guided them away from the *Fox* and
aimed the prow of the launch toward the breakwater.
Gretchen thought about telling him that they would have
a less bumpy ride if he ran parallel to the shore, then cut
straight left to his destination, rather than bouncing di-
agonally across the waves and current as he was doing
now. But all she really cared about was getting off the

river and out of this storm, and a straight line was definitely the shortest route to that objective. So she said
nothing.

Instead, she gripped the rails as waves thudded against
the aluminum hull, one after the other, with a jarring intensity that threatened to pitch her overboard if she didn't
hold on tight. They were almost to the breakwater when
she turned to look back at the *Fox,* just as she heeled up,
with her bow suspended skyward for a moment, then slid
steadily backward under the waves.

The urge to break down and sob her heart out flooded
over Gretchen with almost overwhelming power, and she
came close to giving in to it. She could feel the Wulfert
heritage being dragged down by the current, exactly as
the *Fox* had just been, and she understood that the family would be much more difficult to salvage. Nonetheless, she did *not* give in, of course. She was still a Wulfert,
after all, no matter how much less significant that dis-
tinction was about to become. Whatever else might be
slipping from her grasp, Gretchen was still in control of
herself.

BOYD AND GRETCHEN scrambled aboard the lightship
instead of continuing on to shore. Gretchen was shivering violently from wet and chill, and maybe from shock,
as well. Boyd knew he had to get her warm and dry as
soon as possible. He sent her into the head with two
blankets from the berth and strict instructions to strip,
dry herself down and bundle up while he stoked up the
fire in the stove that he had set earlier.

By the time she emerged the cabin was toasty warm. He
arranged her wet clothes around the stove but doubted
the waterlogged sheepskin would take less than a day to
dry. She hadn't given him her underwear. Apparently

modesty and probably some self-consciousness had prompted her to keep those on, however damp they might be.

He told himself not to dwell on that subject. Still, he couldn't keep his mind off the thought of the rough nap of the old Army blankets chafing her white skin to pinkness all over. Wisps of blond hair were drying gradually around her face from the heat of the stove and turning to a pale halo in the light of the kerosene lantern.

Boyd put his hands on her shoulders and stood for a moment, holding her at arm's length and taking in every detail of the face he knew would inhabit his dreams for a long time to come, perhaps forever. He stepped across the distance between them and felt her tremble under the blanket as he did so. A responding pulsation quivered inside himself, and he understood that neither of them was trembling because of the cold.

Then the most startling and wonderful thing happened. Gretchen reached up, put her fingers behind his neck and pulled him down to her. She had let go of the blanket to do so, and it slipped away from her body, with Boyd's eager hands assisting its fall. The touch of her skin was both cool and warm, probably from the combined effects of the river and the stove fire. Boyd preferred to think of this sensation as reflecting the contrast in herself between the cool sophisticate he'd first met in Wilson's store and the passionate women whose mouth now explored his hungrily as they moved together, still clasping each other close, toward the berth.

BOYD DIDN'T REMEMBER falling asleep, but what had happened before would live in his memory for the rest of his life. He awoke filled with the warm glow of their lovemaking and surrounded by the scent of Gretchen, but when he reached for her she wasn't there. Then he saw her.

Her clothes must have dried because she had them on again, except for the sheepskin. The cabin was still cozily warm, so she must have fed the fire while he was asleep. Yet, as he saw what she was holding in her hand and the expression on her face, Boyd was suddenly anything but comfortable.

In one hand she held his field glasses; in the other was the logbook where he had recorded his observations as he watched River House. Boyd cursed himself now for his compulsion to hang on to every detail of everything that happened to him by writing it all down. He tried to tell himself that he had been after evidence, and documentation was an important part of that process. Still, he might have been able to explain away the field glasses, but there was no way of disguising the nature of those notations.

Boyd felt the clamp of true fear upon his heart as he acquiesced to the inevitable. The time had come to tell her why he was really in Cape Vincent. Neither circumstances nor the pressure of his own emotions would permit him to hold off any longer despite the fact that Boyd understood with growing dread that Gretchen could hardly have been less ready to hear what he had to say.

Chapter Fourteen

Gretchen wasn't sure why she listened as long as she did to the infuriating things Boyd was saying. Maybe she wanted to see just how far he would go with this impossible tale. She told herself it was definitely not because there was even an echo of a ring of truth to it.

"That's enough!" she shouted finally. "You're trying to tell me that my grandfather is guilty of treason."

"I suppose that's the crime he would be charged with."

Boyd sounded strangely dejected, as if the last thing he wanted to be doing was telling her these lies. Then why was he doing it? Obviously because he believed them to be true. Still, that didn't justify his repeating such horrible accusations.

"I'll have you know that my grandfather was an anti-Nazi during World War II and even before. He got relatives of ours out of Germany in the thirties, and then helped some others come here after the war. They're still here. You can talk to them, and they'll tell you how preposterous this theory of yours is."

"And I've told you what Max and Peter Dagg said. Dagg was dying at the time. Why would he lie?"

"I don't know," Gretchen spluttered with growing anger and frustration. "Maybe they were mistaken. I've

never heard of anybody named Kraft, and if my grandfather hated Nazis as I really believe he did, why would
he take part in a scheme to give them a fresh start in
America?''

Boyd didn't respond to that right away. The pepper-
ing of rain against the cabin windows filled the long moment while she awaited his answer.

"Maybe," he said at last, sounding somber and resigned, "that's explained by the sudden upsurge in the
business after New Beginnings had done so badly during
the war years. Maybe he simply needed the money."

"I said that was enough. Now I really mean it!" She
was shouting again. "I don't want to hear one more word
of this garbage. And if you repeat one word of it to anyone else, I'll have you in court for slander."

Boyd's eyes were very sad, but his voice was calm.
"You can only convict someone of slander if you prove
that what they're saying isn't true. I don't believe you'd
be able to do that in this case."

"I don't care what you believe." Gretchen was far
from calm. "Now, you can either come back to shore
right this minute, or I'll take the boat and strand you
here."

It occurred to her that this wasn't a gracious thing to
say to someone who had saved her life a couple of hours
ago, but she was too furious and confused and heartsick
to stop herself. She wanted more than anything to sit
down and cry, but she wasn't about to do that in front of
Boyd Emory. She had to get away from him as fast as she
could. She grabbed her sheepskin jacket from the chair
back where he had hung it to dry in front of the stove.

"Let me give you my jacket," he said, taking hold of
the sheepskin. "This thing is still soaking wet."

She snatched her coat from his grasp. "I don't want you to give me anything."

Gretchen could see in his eyes that he understood how much she meant what she was saying. She chose to ignore the small voice inside her that wondered if that understanding was truly accurate.

KRAFT KNEW that even in this burg they would label the cause of this fire as arson right off from the smell and the inevitable traces of the gasoline he was using, but he didn't care. The time had passed for subtlety. He had seen the Wulfert boat floundering toward midchannel and had known he had to get out of there in case someone else noticed, as well. Even if they did, the chances of anybody getting to her, all that way out from shore in a rising storm, were nil.

Someday they might salvage the boat, of course, which was something of an antique and valuable to people who cared about such things. Then they would find the three blast holes in the hull, one corresponding to the hole that stopped the engine. They would figure out what had happened, but not who had done it.

If they had to pin it on someone, the favorite suspect would probably be that drifter Emory. The wrath of the spurned lover had driven him to the ultimate revenge. Then he had come here to New Beginnings and torched the entire place, from the main house to Stone Cottage, before moving on to do the same to River House.

These provincial villagers would be very happy to lay the guilt at the feet of the outsider, the smooth-talking world traveler who didn't fit in with these yokels, anyway. Their own Lester Wilson had a much better motive—greed. Maybe he could pick up the scorched land cheap, he would be thinking. Of course, if he had overheard what Kraft had done this morning, Lester would know the Wulfert fortune was kaput, and this land would be selling for a song.

Which piqued Kraft's love of a killing—in financial terms, that is. As an old friend of the family, his interest in the property wouldn't seem unusual. The place did have development potential, and real estate had been a very lucrative interest of his at various times in his business history. Besides, he could exploit the alleged sentiment, and the locals would eat it up. The irony of that appealed to him: the grieving friend buys his old confrere's land to carry on in his memory—after having made certain that old friend *was* nothing more than a memory.

This conflagration would be the end of Frederick at last. Kraft had noted the light in the third-floor window of the tower wing and the nurse's bulky form in the rocker there. The way he was engineering this fire, the flames would catch and flash so fast up the stairwells and along the hallways that there would be absolutely no chance of escape, especially for an unconscious old man and his overweight, arthritic nurse.

Kraft smiled as he tossed the last of several gasoline cans aside. The rest were in the van, saved for River House. There would be a great light in the sky tonight. He would get it started, and this wind would make certain it spread fast and furiously, devouring this property and the other and Carl's evidence in the bargain, wherever it might be.

They would never connect him with any of it. He had hardly been noticed during his stay here. He had blended in too well to attract much attention. If and when he returned, as the new land baron this time, no one would see any resemblance between his dapper, distinguished self and this unkempt, innocuous one.

The only loose end was Emory. He seemed to be a smart fellow, smart enough to guess there was something fishy going on here. Kraft, however, calculated Emory's motivation also to be greed. He was after the wealthy heiress for her money. Now she was gone, and there was no money left. If, by some miracle, Emory escaped a murder and arson charge, he would be gone, as well, off to more promising climes, wherever the international set was sunning at the moment and pickings were good for a man like him.

Kraft pulled a box of wooden matches from the pocket of the blue-gray parka that would be the only thing anyone remembered should they happen to see him near the scene. He would have his moment of triumph in more ways than one tonight. Besides wiping out the last trace of the Wulfert legacy that had meant so much to that sniveling fool Frederick, Kraft would create a fire storm—two fire storms, in fact—to remind these Yankees of the ones they had created in 1945 in his beloved Hamburg.

Kraft grimaced at the thought of how they had destroyed his fatherland and the greatest leader this vile century had ever known. Now those who still followed that leader's example had to content themselves with small victories. But no matter. Kraft had done everything in his power to champion the ideal back then, and he would do nothing less now.

With a flourish and a click of his heels he struck the first match.

GRETCHEN RECOGNIZED the exhaustion of depression aching in what felt like every muscle of her body as she turned off the road onto the driveway of River House. The wet jacket she was wearing added to her discomfort. Even with the car heater on full blast she could feel the dampness seeping into her bones, a fit companion to her general gloom.

Might as well feel as lousy on the outside as I do on the inside, she thought.

At least the wind was less ferocious here, robbed of some of its intensity by the close-together trees on both sides of the narrow drive. Gretchen was relieved to be able to loosen the fierce grip she'd had on the steering wheel ever since leaving the marina to fight her way through the blustering storm toward home. She was grateful for even that hint of relief after what had been the most unrelentingly disastrous day of her entire life. All she wanted now was to get inside the house, shed these damp clothes and crawl under the comforter in her own bed in her own room.

For however long it still *is* my room, she reminded herself.

She sighed and went on to tell herself that there was no point in thinking about the family's imminent financial ruin now. She felt bad enough about the present, and maybe even the past. She didn't need to be tormenting herself with the future, as well.

The sky above the trees had already turned dark, but Gretchen didn't think it could be that late yet. The storm must have hurried the darkness, though she couldn't really be certain of the time. She had left her watch on board the lightship. The memory of that, and of Boyd, sent a sharp pang piercing like a stiletto through her gloom and straight to her heart.

She winced and bit her lip so hard that she might have broken the skin, but at least she kept back the tears. She could barely see through the rain-streaked windshield as it was. There would be time for tears later, and she imagined she would shed quite a few once she was inside out of this storm.

She was at the spot where she always parked her car when she noticed the tire tracks leading forward from there along the side of the house. They weren't the kind of deep marks that would have been made in a warmer time of year when the ground was soft, but they were unmistakable nonetheless. Someone had driven a vehicle, maybe a truck judging from the width of the wheel base, toward the riverbank side of the house, straddling the stone walk and plowing through the dried-up flower bed on its way.

"What now?" Gretchen grumbled as she pushed the car door open against the wind and climbed out.

She followed the tracks along the stone path, bent over to lessen the impact of the gale, which was stronger here where the surrounding trees were thinner. The howl of the wind was high-pitched and deafening. The gusts packed tremendous power and came one after the other, while the rain pelted her and she wished she had the beret that she suspected was somewhere at the bottom of the Saint Lawrence.

Rounding the corner of the house to the riverbank side and bent over as she was, Gretchen didn't see the ambulance at first. When she did, she straightened suddenly despite the blasts of wind that threatened to topple her at any moment. She recognized the old white panel-sided vehicle with red crosses on the doors from her childhood days, though she hadn't seen it in years. Someone had driven it in here and backed it up to the French doors of the morning room.

Gretchen couldn't imagine who would have done that or why. Maybe in a calmer moment, away from the racket of the wind and storm, rested up from the rigors and heartbreak of the past several hours, she might have been able to put some pieces together here and come up with a logical, nonthreatening explanation. Right now all she could think of was the skulking form she had seen the other night lurking in the woods not far from this very spot, and the door swinging shut at Stone Cottage to trap her in musty darkness. There had been too many strange and menacing occurrences around here lately for her to assume there was no danger now.

She remembered the firewood she'd cut and stacked at the side of the house and crept around there, crouching low and out of sight from the windows. She selected a sturdy piece of timber, long enough to give her some reach and range of swing and narrow enough in circumference to get a good grip on. She hefted the timber to accustom herself to its weight before clutching it in front of her and backtracking to the French doors.

She stayed low in the shadow of the ambulance and peered into the morning room. She couldn't see a thing. Whoever had gone inside hadn't turned off the lights, and Gretchen couldn't see any light reflected from the rooms beyond, either. Only somebody up to no good would be creeping around in the dark, she reasoned. Unless the power had gone out in the storm.

Gretchen thought back for a moment. The yard light had been on when she parked the car. There had been no power failure. If someone was inside the house now, that someone didn't want to be seen. To Gretchen's present turn of mind that meant this uninvited guest had nefarious motives of some kind. She crouched lower still, gripping her makeshift weapon at the ready and crept toward the doors.

She felt under the edge of the patio mat for the key that only the family had ever known was there, but it was gone. Could someone have removed it before tonight? Maybe Uncle Carl? He had always been paranoid about burglars finding that key and sneaking in. Gretchen was about to try the door handle, in case the intruder might have left it unlocked, when the door moved so suddenly that she nearly fell through the opening.

She probably should have scrambled out of there at that instant. Instead, she looked up to see who had opened the double doors and found herself staring straight into the barrel of a shotgun.

"Come one step closer and I'll blast your worthless hide to kingdom come."

Gretchen toppled back against the rear door of the ambulance, both from shock and relief. The voice was raspy-deep and changed by the fear and tension of the moment, but it was still recognizable.

"Pauline, it's me," Gretchen cried into the wind. "What are you doing here? And what are you doing with that gun?"

Gretchen was eager to hear both answers, almost as eager as she was glad that both a companion and a weapon were close at hand.

BOYD WAS IN THE SHED at the marina, waiting for the storm to subside, when he heard the village fire siren blaring over the clamor of the wind and rain. He had planned to go to the lightship and clear out his things as soon as the gale calmed down some. He didn't have any clear plan after that. He knew he had to get Gretchen to listen to him somehow. His entire future depended on that, and hers, as well. Whatever had happened in the past couldn't possibly be important enough to sacrifice the rest of their lives together. He was contemplating how much of the past wasn't really past because of its consequences in the present when he heard the alarm.

There were no windows on the shore side of the shed, so Boyd went outside into the storm. He pulled his parka hood up and shielded his eyes so that he could see. The glow in the sky looked like fire reflected in low-hanging clouds, and it was coming from the direction of New Beginnings Spa. Boyd was at his truck and vaulting into the driver's seat before the possibility that he could be mistaken even occurred to him.

GRETCHEN HEARD the siren, but she didn't pay much attention. She was too busy worrying about whether Pauline had endangered Frederick's already precarious condition even further by transporting him here from the spa.

"I think it may have done him some good," Pauline said as she inspected her charge. "I'm pretty sure I saw him move a little on his own when I was taking him out of the ambulance. Then, just a couple of minutes before you got here, I could have sworn he sighed."

"Why do you have him here in the dark?"

Pauline had set up all of the accoutrements of a hospital room, including IV pole and medicine tray, though Frederick was still on a collapsible gurney with restraining rails. There were no lights in the room, and the old nurse scrambled fast, considering her usual gait, to stop Gretchen when she went to turn one on.

"I figure we'd be sitting ducks in here with the lights on," Pauline said.

Gretchen thought about asking who they would be sitting ducks for, but didn't. She would have felt like a hypocrite, sneering at Pauline's fears. Gretchen wasn't particularly at ease herself at the moment.

Nonetheless, Pauline had set the shotgun down behind the writing desk, and both of them appeared to have forgotten it was there as they relaxed a bit, simply because each was no longer alone with the other on hand. The man in the Air Force parka had slipped through the French doors before either Pauline or Gretchen could make a move against him. Pauline screamed at the sight of him, and Gretchen just stared as he flipped on a table lamp and kept his rifle pointed.

"Kraft? Is that you?"

The voice asking that question was little more than a whisper, but it struck Gretchen with more of a shock than the appearance of the stranger with the rifle had done.

"Grandpa?" she said. "Are you awake?"

The emaciated old man on the gurney didn't appear to have heard her. He squinted at the man with the rifle and lifted a trembling finger to point at him, as well.

"Go back," the old man rasped. "Go back where you came from." That was all he could manage before falling back on the pillow.

"Where are you going?" The man Frederick had called Kraft poked the rifle barrel at Pauline as she started toward the gurney.

"I'm going to take care of Mr. Wulfert," she said. "And you'll have to shoot me to stop me."

Kraft's laugh was mocking and self-satisfied. "You're too late for taking care of my old friend Frederick or any one else, my dear," he said with counterfeit charm. "It was clever of you to make me think you and the old boy were still in the tower room. Did you use the old trick of pillows in the chair made to look like a person? Miss Wulfert is a clever one, too. She managed to get off that boat somehow even after I put three holes in the hull.''

Neither Pauline nor Gretchen responded.

"Well, it doesn't really matter what either of you did,'' Kraft went on. ''In just a few minutes now you'll all be beyond salvation, however clever you might be. Carl Wulfert also thought he was clever, and that oaf Dingner, as well. Look what happened to them.''

"You murdered them, didn't you?'' Pauline sounded as contemptuous as Kraft.

"Only Dingner, and all that took was a little push. Hardly a challenge. As for Carl, he robbed me of the opportunity to give him a push, as well, as I definitely planned to do once I'd gotten him to talk. He tried to blackmail me, after all. I paid him off last spring, but that was only to keep him quiet until I formulated my plan. He deserved to be murdered, actually. Too bad he panicked and slid off the roof on his own. I would much rather have killed him myself.''

Gretchen, meanwhile, had already made the agonizing connection between the name her grandfather had called out to this man who said they were old friends and the shameful story Boyd had tried to tell her aboard the lightship. Gretchen no longer doubted that story. She should have been overjoyed that her grandfather had revived from his coma. Instead, all she could think about was that he had written fables about monsters because he was one.

"What are you doing?'' Pauline shouted at Kraft, who was walking along the wall and pouring something out of a can.

"I'm going to warm up this chilly evening for you," he said as he pulled a box of wooden matches from his pocket.

"You're not going to burn this place up with us in it." Pauline took a step toward Kraft.

"If you make another move, I'll shoot your precious Frederick where he lies." To back up his words Kraft pointed the gun barrel toward the old man on the gurney, who appeared to have slipped back into unconsciousness.

The smell of gasoline jolted Gretchen into the awareness that she had to distract Kraft, if only for a moment. Pauline, however, apparently had plans of her own.

The sound that rose from the old woman's ample bosom was low-pitched at first, like the warning growl of a cornered beast. That pitch heightened, along with the volume, as she lunged forward. She had something in her hand, but she had spun it hard and straight at Kraft's knees before Gretchen recognized it as a bedpan. Kraft stumbled over folds in the faded Oriental carpet and nearly fell backward as the gun went off with a thundering blast.

The bullet spark caught the gasoline. Flames shot immediately to life and sped in a chain reaction across the doorway and around the outside wall in both directions. Kraft must have encircled the house with a trail of gasoline before coming inside. In seconds the exit through the French doors would be a wall of fire.

Before that could happen Kraft leaped across the flames and was gone. Then the wall of fire shot up higher than the windows. There would be no escaping for anyone else through the French doors now. Also, the gas tank of the ambulance was in the rear of the vehicle, which had been backed up to the doors. When the fire hit the tank, there would be an explosion that would take this entire end of the house with it.

Pauline had already released the wheel locks on the gurney and was tugging it over the threshold into the parlor. Gretchen ran to the other end of the gurney and pushed it to the center of the room in a single burst of strength. She looked around for the best way to proceed and immediately recognized their dilemma.

Flames surged upward outside the windows, and the dining room beyond the parlor was ablaze. Through the other doorway she could see the bookcases in her grandfather's library being eaten, one shelf after the other, by fire.

"There's no way out, miss!" Pauline shouted over the crackling flames. Her voice was choked from smoke.

Gretchen was already tugging the gurney toward the side stairs that led to the second floor. She wadded blankets around her grandfather to make a sling as Pauline bustled up to help, though the nurse couldn't have known what Gretchen had in mind and she wasn't about to waste precious breath explaining.

"Keep low" was all she said, reminding herself to get below the smoke as they slung her grandfather off the gurney and began dragging him toward the single, slender hope of escape that remained.

BY THE TIME BOYD got to the spa everything was on fire, from the main building back along the therapy wing to Stone Cottage. Only a fire that had been deliberately set, with flash points in several locations, could be as widespread as this one.

Kraft had been here. Boyd was certain of it.

If there had been anyone inside, they wouldn't be coming out again. Kraft hadn't meant to leave any survivors. The significance of that realization hit Boyd with an intensity akin to that of the ball of flame now roiling up the tower wall and along its turret roof. The fire trucks were pulling into the driveway of New Beginnings as Boyd spun his pickup back onto the highway.

He roared down Broadway at a speed he wouldn't have thought the old truck capable of, then rocketed out of the village in the other direction. He thought better of taking the driveway down to River House. He jumped out of the truck to run through the woods instead. He was almost to the house when flames flashed up from the morning room and spread with lightning swiftness along the sides of the house.

He saw the silhouette of a man running along the path, then flinging something through the back door, where more flames exploded in response. Boyd guessed the man was Kraft, but he wasn't about to go after him now. He could already hear the sheriff's siren screeching out of the village in this direction, probably after Boyd because they'd seen him fleeing the spa fire. They would pick up Kraft as he left the River House grounds. Right now all Boyd cared about was Gretchen. He was as close as he could get to the searing heat of the fire when he saw her through the tongues of flame that licked up the windows. She and Pauline were staggering into the stairwell, dragging a long white bundle between them.

Boyd took off for the riverbank, slipping on the frozen ground and squinting against the cold sleet that was replacing the rain. He scrambled and crawled, grabbing at vines and roots that tore his hands, to pull himself along the bank above the churning river. If he fell in, there would be the current to fight before he could make his way back. He knew he mustn't risk that delay and forced himself to work his way more cautiously toward his destination.

Boyd crashed through the overgrowth at the river end of the tunnel into River House and smelled the smoke immediately. He dashed forward with his arms pawing the darkness ahead and to the sides to prevent a collision with the walls. The smoke grew more dense with every step he took. What if Gretchen had been overcome already? What if she had fallen unconscious on the stairs and the flames had overtaken her?

Then he heard the glorious, choking sounds of life from the other end of the tunnel. He plunged and stumbled toward those sounds while tears from more than just the smoke streamed down his cheeks.

GRETCHEN GULPED in great mouthfuls of chill air that seared her scorched throat. For a moment back there, when they first entered the tunnel, she had thought it was all over. Pauline could barely crawl any longer. Grandpa, who had seemed so light when they began carrying him, had turned to a stone-weight burden that Gretchen then had to shoulder alone. At exactly that tortured moment she had heard Boyd call her name. An instant later she was calling back to him, her smoke-strangled words hardly audible even to herself.

Now they were on the riverbank where they had stopped to rest and breathe. Her grandfather's head was cradled in her lap when he took hold of her arm in a grip so weak that she could barely feel it. The night was dark, but she could just make out his face and see that his eyes had fluttered open. She understood that he was very near death, but there was something she had to know.

"Why, Grandpa?" she asked, forcing her scorched throat to speak. "Why did you help Kraft and his friends?"

"Family," he whispered. "They had Wulferts over there in Germany, and they said they would kill them if I didn't go along." He gripped her arm a breath tighter before continuing. "It wasn't for the money. I didn't care about that. I gave it all away. But not until after your grandmother found out what I had done. She would have guessed something was wrong if I had started before."

Gretchen could see his eyes shining in the darkness and understood that they must be full of tears. "We don't have to talk anymore about that now, Grandpa," she said.

"That's right. No more now," Pauline repeated gently. She was crouched down and easing Frederick from Gretchen's lap.

"Let them be together," Boyd whispered close to her ear as she tried for a moment to hold on to her grandfather. "She's taken care of him for so long. Don't deny her caring for him this one last time."

Boyd's arms were around her the instant she relinquished her grandfather as she knew she must. She leaned against Boyd's chest and felt his strength holding her up and his body shielding her from the wind. She huddled against him and stayed very still for a while.

Somehow she knew she would be in his arms for as long as she lived; and, whatever his life might be, she would make herself part of it. She had come to Cape Vincent in search of a place to settle down and belong. She had found that place in the heart of the man she loved. Whether they stayed put or traveled the world around, with Boyd, Gretchen would be forever at home.

As their lips met, their cheeks were touched by the pure white flakes of the first new snow.

PENNY JORDAN

Sins and infidelities...
Dreams and obsessions...
Shattering secrets
unfold in...

THE HIDDEN YEARS

SAGE — stunning, sensual and vibrant, she spent a lifetime distancing herself from a past too painful to confront... the mother who seemed to hold her at bay, the father who resented her and the heartache of unfulfilled love. To the world, Sage was independent and invulnerable— but it was a mask she cultivated to hide a desperation she herself couldn't quite understand... until an unforeseen turn of events drew her into the discovery of the hidden years, finally allowing Sage to open her heart to a passion denied for so long.

The Hidden Years—a compelling novel of truth and passion that will unlock the heart and soul of every woman.

AVAILABLE IN OCTOBER!
Watch for your opportunity to complete your Penny Jordan set.
POWER PLAY and SILVER will also be available in October.

MILLION DOLLAR JACKPOT
SWEEPSTAKES RULES & REGULATIONS
NO PURCHASE NECESSARY TO ENTER OR RECEIVE A PRIZE

1 Alternate means of entry: Print your name and address on a 3" ×5" piece of plain paper and send to the appropriate address below.

In the U.S.	**In Canada**
MILLION DOLLAR JACKPOT	MILLION DOLLAR JACKPOT
P.O. Box 1867	P.O. Box 609
3010 Walden Avenue	Fort Erie, Ontario
Buffalo, NY 14269-1867	L2A 5X3

2. To enter the Sweepstakes and join the Reader Service, check off the "YES" box on your Sweepstakes Entry Form and return. If you do not wish to join the Reader Service but wish to enter the Sweepstakes only, check off the "NO" box on your Sweepstakes Entry Form. To qualify for the Extra Bonus prize, scratch off the silver on your Lucky Keys. If the registration numbers match, you are eligible for the Extra Bonus Prize offering. Incomplete entries are ineligible. Torstar Corp. and its affiliates are not responsible for mutilated or unreadable entries or inadvertent printing errors. Mechanically reproduced entries are null and void.

3. Whether you take advantage of this offer or not, on or about April 30, 1992, at the offices of D.L. Blair, Inc., Blair, NE, your sweepstakes numbers will be compared against the list of winning numbers generated at random by the computer. However, prizes will only be awarded to individuals who have entered the Sweepstakes. In the event that all prizes are not claimed, a random drawing will be held from all qualified entries received from March 30, 1990 to March 31, 1992, to award all unclaimed prizes. All cash prizes (Grand to Sixth) will be mailed to winners and are payable by check in U.S. funds. Seventh Prize will be shipped to winners via third-class mail. These prizes are in addition to any free, surprise or mystery gifts that might be offered. Versions of this Sweepstakes with different prizes of approximate equal value may appear at retail outlets or in other mailings by Torstar Corp. and its affiliates.

4. PRIZES: (1) *Grand Prize $1,000,000.00 Annuity; (1) First Prize $25,000.00; (1) Second Prize $10,000.00; (5) Third Prize $5,000.00; (10) Fourth Prize $1,000.00; (100) Fifth Prize $250.00; (2,500) Sixth Prize $10.00; (6,000) **Seventh Prize $12.95 ARV.

   *This presentation offers a Grand Prize of a $1,000,000.00 annuity. Winner will receive $33,333.33 a year for 30 years without interest totalling $1,000,000.00.

   **Seventh Prize: A fully illustrated hardcover book, published by Torstar Corp. Approximate Retail Value of the book is $12.95.

   Entrants may cancel the Reader Service at any time without cost or obligation (see details in Center Insert Card).

5. Extra Bonus! This presentation offers an Extra Bonus Prize valued at $33,000.00 to be awarded in a random drawing from all qualified entries received by March 31, 1992. No purchase necessary to enter or receive a prize. To qualify, see instructions in Center Insert Card. Winner will have the choice of any of the merchandise offered or a $33,000.00 check payable in U.S. funds. All other published rules and regulations apply.

6. This Sweepstakes is being conducted under the supervision of D.L. Blair, Inc. By entering the Sweepstakes, each entrant accepts and agrees to be bound by these rules and the decisions of the judges, which shall be final and binding. Odds of winning the random drawing are dependent upon the number of entries received. Taxes, if any, are the sole responsibility of the winners. Prizes are nontransferable. All entries must be received at the address on the detachable Business Reply Card and must be postmarked no later than 12:00 MIDNIGHT on March 31, 1992. The drawing for all unclaimed Sweepstakes prizes and for the Extra Bonus Prize will take place on May 30, 1992, at 12:00 NOON at the offices of D.L. Blair, Inc., Blair, NE.

7. This offer is open to residents of the U.S., United Kingdom, France and Canada, 18 years or older, except employees and immediate family members of Torstar Corp., its affiliates, subsidiaries and all other agencies, entities and persons connected with the use, marketing or conduct of this Sweepstakes. All Federal, State, Provincial, Municipal and local laws apply. Void wherever prohibited or restricted by law. Any litigation within the Province of Quebec respecting the conduct and awarding of a prize in this publicity contest must be submitted to the Régie des Loteries et Courses du Québec.

8. Winners will be notified by mail and may be required to execute an affidavit of eligibility and release, which must be returned within 14 days after notification or an alternate winner may be selected. Canadian winners will be required to correctly answer an arithmetical, skill-testing question administered by mail, which must be returned within a limited time. Winners consent to the use of their name, photograph and/or likeness for advertising and publicity in conjunction with this and similar promotions without additional compensation.

9. For a list of our major prize winners, send a stamped, self-addressed envelope to: MILLION DOLLAR WINNERS LIST, P.O. Box 4510, Blair, NE 68009. Winners Lists will be supplied after the May 30, 1992 drawing date.

Offer limited to one per household.

LTY-H891

HARLEQUIN®
OFFICIAL SWEEPSTAKES
RULES

NO PURCHASE NECESSARY

1. To enter, complete an Official Entry Form or 3"× 5" index card by hand-printing, in plain block letters, your complete name, address, phone number and age, and mailing it to: Harlequin Fashion A Whole New You Sweepstakes, P.O. Box 9056, Buffalo, NY 14269-9056.

   No responsibility is assumed for lost, late or misdirected mail. Entries must be sent separately with first class postage affixed, and be received no later than December 31, 1991 for eligibility.

2. Winners will be selected by D.L. Blair, Inc., an independent judging organization whose decisions are final, in random drawings to be held on January 30, 1992 in Blair, NE at 10:00 a.m. from among all eligible entries received.

3. The prizes to be awarded and their approximate retail values are as follows: Grand Prize — A brand-new Mercury Sable LS plus a trip for two (2) to Paris, including round-trip air transportation, six (6) nights hotel accommodation, a $1,400 meal/spending money stipend and $2,000 cash toward a new fashion wardrobe (approximate value: $28,000) or $15,000 cash; two (2) Second Prizes — A trip to Paris, including round-trip air transportation, six (6) nights hotel accommodation, a $1,400 meal/spending money stipend and $2,000 cash toward a new fashion wardrobe (approximate value: $11,000) or $5,000 cash; three (3) Third Prizes — $2,000 cash toward a new fashion wardrobe. All prizes are valued in U.S. currency. Travel award air transportation is from the commercial airport nearest winner's home. Travel is subject to space and accommodation availability, and must be completed by June 30, 1993. Sweepstakes offer is open to residents of the U.S. and Canada who are 21 years of age or older as of December 31, 1991, except residents of Puerto Rico, employees and immediate family members of Torstar Corp., its affiliates, subsidiaries, and all agencies, entities and persons connected with the use, marketing, or conduct of this sweepstakes. All federal, state, provincial, municipal and local laws apply. Offer void wherever prohibited by law. Taxes and/or duties, applicable registration and licensing fees, are the sole responsibility of the winners. Any litigation within the province of Quebec respecting the conduct and awarding of a prize may be submitted to the Régie des loteries et courses du Québec. All prizes will be awarded; winners will be notified by mail. No substitution of prizes is permitted.

4. Potential winners must sign and return any required Affidavit of Eligibility/Release of Liability within 30 days of notification. In the event of noncompliance within this time period, the prize may be awarded to an alternate winner. Any prize or prize notification returned as undeliverable may result in the awarding of that prize to an alternate winner. By acceptance of their prize, winners consent to use of their names, photographs or their likenesses for purposes of advertising, trade and promotion on behalf of Torstar Corp. without further compensation. Canadian winners must correctly answer a time-limited arithmetical question in order to be awarded a prize.

5. For a list of winners (available after 3/31/92), send a separate stamped, self-addressed envelope to: Harlequin Fashion A Whole New You Sweepstakes, P.O. Box 4694, Blair, NE 68009.

PREMIUM OFFER TERMS

To receive your gift, complete the Offer Certificate according to directions. Be certain to enclose the required number of "Fashion A Whole New You" proofs of product purchase (which are found on the last page of every specially marked "Fashion A Whole New You" Harlequin or Silhouette romance novel). Requests must be received no later than December 31, 1991. Limit: four (4) gifts per name, family, group, organization or address. Items depicted are for illustrative purposes only and may not be exactly as shown. Please allow 6 to 8 weeks for receipt of order. Offer good while quantities of gifts last. In the event an ordered gift is no longer available, you will receive a free, previously unpublished Harlequin or Silhouette book for every proof of purchase you have submitted with your request, plus a refund of the postage and handling charge you have included. Offer good in the U.S. and Canada only.

HOFW-SWPR

HARLEQUIN® OFFICIAL SWEEPSTAKES ENTRY FORM

4-FWHIS-2

Complete and return this Entry Form immediately – the more entries you submit, the better your chances of winning!

- Entries must be received by **December 31, 1991.**
- A Random draw will take place on **January 30, 1992.**
- No purchase necessary.

Yes, I want to win a FASHION A WHOLE NEW YOU Classic and Romantic prize from Harlequin:

Name _____ Telephone _____ Age _____

Address _____

City _____ State _____ Zip _____

Return Entries to: **Harlequin FASHION A WHOLE NEW YOU,**
P.O. Box 9056, Buffalo, NY 14269-9056   © 1991 Harlequin Enterprises Limited

PREMIUM OFFER

To receive your free gift, send us the required number of proofs-of-purchase from any specially marked FASHION A WHOLE NEW YOU Harlequin or Silhouette Book with the Offer Certificate properly completed, plus a check or money order (do not send cash) to cover postage and handling payable to Harlequin FASHION A WHOLE NEW YOU Offer. We will send you the specified gift.

OFFER CERTIFICATE

Item	A. ROMANTIC COLLECTOR'S DOLL (Suggested Retail Price $60.00)	B. CLASSIC PICTURE FRAME (Suggested Retail Price $25.00)
# of proofs-of-purchase	18	12
Postage and Handling	$3.50	$2.95
Check one	☐	☐

Name _____

Address _____

City _____ State _____ Zip _____

Mail this certificate, designated number of proofs-of-purchase and check or money order for postage and handling to: **Harlequin FASHION A WHOLE NEW YOU Gift Offer,** P.O. Box 9057, Buffalo, NY 14269-9057. Requests must be received by December 31, 1991.

ONE PROOF-OF-PURCHASE

4-FWHIP-2

To collect your fabulous free gift you must include the necessary number of proofs-of-purchase with a properly completed Offer Certificate.

© 1991 Harlequin Enterprises Limited

See previous page for details.